THE TREASURE OF LOVE

Book of Love, Book Thirteen

Meara Platt

ARE YOU SIGNED UP FOR DRAGONBLADE'S BLOG?

You'll get the latest news and information on exclusive giveaways, exclusive excerpts, coming releases, sales, free books, cover reveals and more.

Check out our complete list of authors, too!

No spam, no junk. That's a promise!

Sign Up Here

www.dragonbladepublishing.com

Dearest Reader;

Thank you for your support of a small press. At Dragonblade Publishing, we strive to bring you the highest quality Historical Romance from some of the best authors in the business. Without your support, there is no 'us', so we sincerely hope you adore these stories and find some new favorite authors along the way.

Happy Reading!

CEO, Dragonblade Publishing

Additional Dragonblade books by Author Meara Platt

The Book of Love Series
The Look of Love
The Touch of Love
The Taste of Love
The Song of Love
The Scent of Love
The Kiss of Love
The Chance of Love
The Gift of Love
The Heart of Love
The Hope of Love (novella)
The Promise of Love
The Wonder of Love
The Journey of Love
The Dream of Love (novella)
The Treasure of Love
The Dance of Love

Dark Gardens Series
Garden of Shadows
Garden of Light
Garden of Dragons
Garden of Destiny
Garden of Angels

The Farthingale Series
If You Wished For Me (A Novella)

CHAPTER ONE

London, England
August 1821

DONAL BRAYDEN'S HEART pounded as he stared at the bespectacled Miss Luciana Lessing reading *that* book in the Duke of Edgeware's library, her hands delicately holding its faded red cover, and her big, green eyes fixed on the pages, while that agile brain of hers absorbed the secrets to winning a man's heart.

She was reading *The Book of Love.*

His book, now that his brother's wife had seen fit to shove it at him as though he were some sort of pathetic, desperate loner who needed instruction on finding love. He needed no instruction. He had only to toss a glance, and a bevy of willing women would respond.

Of course, not Lucy Lessing.

She was not one of those women.

She was the sort who hid in a library, while one of the most important society balls of the season was going on just beyond the door. The sort who took pleasure escaping into the dusty pages of a tome on crop fertilizers or ancient Roman history or some other excruciatingly boring topic that seemed to fascinate no one else but her.

The girl was truly odd.

In a delicious way, but that did not bear mentioning.

Startled, she looked up and quickly shut the book. "Good

evening, Mr. Brayden. Did you want the library? I shall leave you to it."

"No, Miss Lessing. I want you."

No. No. No. That had not come out right.

Her eyes widened. "You want me? For what possible reason?"

Bloody hell.

"I mean to say, I am taking you into my custody."

She gazed at him as though he were the stupidest man alive. "You are arresting me for reading a book?"

"It is my book. You may do with it what you like." Donal crossed to the window to peer out of it before returning his gaze to her. "And no, you are not under arrest. I am to guard you."

She shook her head and gave a light laugh. "Whatever for?"

Was she purposely being dense? She knew he was an agent of the Crown, one of the best. It wasn't so long ago he had been with her at the Earl of Monkton's estate, protecting the earl and his wife, who happened to be Lucy's sister. Of course, he had been protecting Lucy as well. All of them were in danger from the earl's crazed brother.

Fortunately, that wicked lord was now dead.

But Lucy was facing another threat, one far more serious, because someone was specifically targeting her and wanted her dead.

She resisted his attempts to protect her, even as the Duke of Edgeware himself joined them and handed him forged papers and funds that would hold them for quite some time while on the run. "You'll need these."

Not only was she resisting, but blithely greeting his brother and his brother's wife as they stood at the library door, having come to assist him.

His brother, Lorcan, was also an agent of the Crown. Both he and his wife, Cammy, had joined him in searching through Edgeware's grand house for Lucy.

Finally, at the urging of all four of them, the danger of her situation began to sink in.

"All right." She took *The Book of Love* as she rose and came around Edgeware's desk. "This comes with us."

Donal didn't care. He just wanted them gone before things got nasty.

He breathed a sigh of relief as he hurried her out, unnoticed, through one of the rarely used servants' passageways.

"It is awfully dark in here."

"Hush, Lucy." He took her hand because the passage was not well lit, and the stairs they had to descend were narrow. He kept hold of her hand because he did not want her to fall, and continued to hold it while he led her away from Edgeware's elegant townhouse that was ablaze in light from the elegant, scented tapers in the chandeliers and wall sconces, and the torches burning at measured intervals in the garden, which had been turned into a fairy kingdom.

Typical of Lucy to be hiding in the library while there was music and dancing and a feast set out for all amid the magical splendor.

They kept to the shadows and cut through the mews behind the duke's home, coming out on another elegant street where he had a conveyance waiting. "There's my carriage," he said softly.

"Mr. Brayden…" Lucy leaned against him as she spoke so that her cheek brushed his shoulder. "How can you see anything? It is dark as pitch out here."

He squelched the jolt of heat that tore through him at her casual touch. Perhaps it was the delightful scent of her skin that set him off, sweet as wild honeysuckle in a misty meadow. "I am trained for this."

"Can one be trained to see in the dark?"

"One can be trained for anything." Why was she asking him these irritating questions?

And why was his body still aroused by her?

It did not bear consideration.

She was an assignment, nothing more.

Bespectacled bluestockings were not his type at all.

He breathed a sigh of relief as Fielding, another of the Duke of Wooton's trusted agents, sat perched in the driver's seat and waved them forward.

"Get in. Quickly, Lucy." He opened the carriage door and placed his hands around her waist to lift her in.

Blast.

His body was doing it again, responding inexplicably to her nearness.

Bespectacled. Bluestocking. Boring.

Bespectacled. Bluestocking. Boring.

And burning…no, not burning…he was not burning for her.

This was not possible.

He let go of her abruptly.

She fell to the carriage floor, and *The Book of Love* spilled out of her hands.

"Stay down," he cautioned since she was better off not being seen with him. He set the book aside on the seat bench opposite his, then put his hand atop her head to keep her from bobbing up.

She slapped it away. "You might have just told me to stay down. You did not have to drop me like a sack of grain. I thought agents were supposed to have finesse."

The carriage took off as soon as he shut the door.

"Ack—tell that idiot to slow down, or he'll kill us all. And what better way to draw attention than to race hellbent through the streets of London? Honestly, are all agents of the Crown utter dolts?"

"Will you try to be a little more appreciative of our efforts? We need to get you out of town fast. Forgive us if you are feeling a few bumps to your elegant derriere."

She tried to sit up, but he nudged her down again. "I mean it, Lucy. This is not a game."

Yet he did feel bad about the way he had treated her, rudely tossing her to the carriage floor. He ought to have been gentler. Nor did it feel right to leave her crouched down there while he was comfortably seated on the bench.

He moved off it and knelt beside her.

But he was a big man, as were all the men in his family, and instead of keeping her company, he had inadvertently squeezed her into a corner.

"Oh, thank you. That is ever so helpful," she said, her voice dripping with sarcasm.

"Lucy, be quiet."

She gasped. "Why ever should I listen to—"

He pushed her down and removed his pistol from the lip of his boot just as shots rang out, and their carriage came to an abrupt halt.

Damn it.

Why had Fielding stopped?

Lucy trembled as she pressed against him like a barnacle to the hull of a ship. "Mr. Brayden, are we supposed to be—"

"No," he barked, shoving her down again as the carriage door flew open and someone pointed a pistol at him.

Donal shot the man.

Then grabbed the man's unspent pistol and shot the one who came right after him.

Two down.

How many more were out there? And what of Fielding? He wasn't firing back. There was only one possible reason…he was dead.

The window behind him shattered, raining glass down on Lucy.

She screamed.

He cursed, shoved aside the bodies blocking the door, and hauled her out just as something fiery came sailing through the broken window and immediately set the seats aflame.

They were out of the carriage now and entirely exposed.

But he realized the burst of flame must have temporarily blinded their attackers.

He lifted Lucy over his shoulder and ran as fast as his legs would carry him into the darkness of nearby Hyde Park. He was breathing hard, his lungs about to explode, but he dared not stop. It would not take whoever had tossed that torch very long to realize his fellow conspirators were dead, and he and Lucy had escaped.

Something jabbed into his back as he ran. "What the hell are you poking into me?"

"Your book."

Blessed saints!

Lucy had grabbed *The Book of Love* and was clutching it for all she was worth.

This was so like her.

Never mind about her own survival.

Her first thought was on saving her reading material.

Truly, what an odd girl.

"Stay quiet, Lucy."

"All right," she whispered back.

The grass and earth muffled all footsteps, so Donal could not tell if they were being followed. He ducked behind a row of bushes, still keeping hold of Lucy tossed over his shoulder. She had on dancing slippers and an ugly gown. She could not run in either of those, so he was not about to set her down until he felt they were safe, and no one was following them.

They remained silent for several minutes, Lucy obviously scared out of her wits and no longer tossing him cutting remarks.

He would have been pleased...should have been pleased. But her shapely derriere was at his face, and his lips would be against one nicely rounded cheek if he dared turn his head even a smidgeon to the right.

So, he looked to his left, which was the direction from which they had fled. Anyone coming after them would appear from there. He heard distant cries of alarm as a crowd began to gather around the burning carriage and saw the amber glow of their torched conveyance against the night sky.

Fielding.

He wanted to get word to the Duke of Wooton and report

his death, but how could he manage it without putting Lucy in jeopardy? She was his priority. He hoped agents of the Crown were at the carriage now and would report his death and their escape to Wooton.

Assuming Fielding was dead.

He hadn't seen the man fall.

Was it possible he had survived but been too badly injured to shoot the assailants? Or, could the man be involved in... He would consider Fielding later.

After several minutes, he determined it was safe and set Lucy down. He took another moment to reload his pistol. "Lucy, are you hurt?"

She did not respond.

He realized she was quietly sobbing.

He wrapped his arms around her, ignoring the poke of that damn book she would not release. "It's all right," he said as she rested her head against his chest. "I'll keep you safe."

"I'm so sorry. I was sure it was all a jest."

He ran his hands gently over her body to make certain she had not been cut by any falling shards of glass or otherwise injured. But she seemed to be all right, if one overlooked she was scared out of her wits.

"My brother has an apartment in Bloomsbury. It is empty right now. We'll make our way there and figure out what to do next. I think someone on the inside is informing this unknown enemy of our plans. They are too close on our heels, seeming to know our next steps before we even take them. It stands to reason they know where I am expected to hide you."

"Then what are we going to do?"

"Go elsewhere, of course."

She eased out of his embrace and rubbed her arm across her face to crudely brush away her tears. "My sister will be worried to death."

"Lorcan and Edgeware will assure her we are not dead." He stared at Lucy, realizing she had lost her spectacles. There was nothing he could do about it now. She looked slender and vulnerable and utterly beautiful under the glow of moonlight.

He did not know why he thought so.

Her hair, which was never fashionably styled in the first place, had lost a few pins, and other pins were dangling on stray wisps. Her silk gown was completely out of fashion and deserved to be destroyed. He had never seen a more unflattering creation.

And yet, he could not get over thinking she was beautiful.

Well, no hideous flounces or frills were going to hide the sleek line of her body or…Lord, help him…the shapely fullness of her breasts. Why was he noticing this now? "Can you walk, Lucy?"

She sniffled. "Yes."

"Good. Let's make our way out of the park before we encounter more trouble." His concern was not only for those assailants but for the assortment of rogues one would generally find up to no good once darkness fell. Rogues were primarily out to steal purses, but they were also toughened by life on the streets and would not hesitate to stick a knife in their victim's ribs if one dared put up a fight. "I'll grab us a hansom cab to take us close to Lorcan's apartment."

"Mr. Brayden, thank you."

"Call me Donal, will you?"

"I'd rather not."

He was surprised. They'd spent time together at the Earl of Monkton's estate and now this. "Why? Because you think you do not know me well enough? We are certainly going to spend an awful lot of time together, Lucy. You will probably know me better than my own family does by the end of this assignment."

She said nothing, just held the book tightly to her chest.

"Lucy, look at me." He kept his manner gentle since he did not want to further overset her. But it rankled him that she was keeping to formality. "Do you not like me? I know I have not been much of a gentleman this evening, but a gentleman would not have been able to keep you alive."

"I know. It isn't that."

"Then what is it?" He placed his hand on her cheek and ran his thumb over it to wipe away a stray tear. She did not resist his touch and seemed to be calmed by it. So he traced the outline of her lips, his thumb running lightly over the beautiful curve of her mouth.

She did not resist that either.

Blessed saints.

What was he doing?

Lucy was an assignment, nothing more. "Here comes a hack. Let's get moving."

"Yes, of course."

He put his arm around her to lead her out of the shadows, his gaze no longer on her but their surroundings. The moon was bright enough that he could pick up the glint of a knife amid the foliage. The wind was strong enough to allow him to pick up the scent of strangers close by, for most who were here at this hour were unwashed or drunk or both.

"Bloomsbury," he told the driver once he and Lucy had jumped inside.

"You're not going to shove me down again, are you?" she asked as the carriage clattered away from the park.

"Not this time," he said with a grin, peering out the window to the distant crowd still gathered around the other carriage that remained on fire.

That it still burned was troubling to him.

Did their assailants know the secret of Greek fire?

It was particularly dangerous because once ignited, it could not be doused.

"Mr. Brayden, you are nibbling your lip."

"Just planning our next move, Lucy." He had the driver drop them not far from Lorcan's apartment and watched him pull away before sneaking her into his brother's place, which was on the second floor of a rambling townhouse that had been broken up into several apartments. He released a breath once they were safely upstairs.

He led her inside. "Wait right there."

He crossed to the window and drew the drapes tightly shut, then went to the table and lit the lantern that stood on it.

He turned to Lucy. "All right, come in. Take a seat."

She watched in silence as he pumped water into a basin for her to use and searched around for drying cloths. "Are you hungry?"

"No." She looked around the small apartment.

"Not much, is it?" His brother's place consisted of two rooms, one of which served as the parlor, dining room, and kitchen. The other was his bedchamber.

His own place was little better.

As agents of the Crown, they spent almost no time at home. They only needed a place to lay their head between assignments. Of course, he could afford better. Far better. So could his brother. But why bother?

"This place is perfect. Right now, it is heaven." She set her book on the table…his book, but she really had the superior claim to it since he had no intention of reading it, while she had held onto the blasted thing through shootings and flames. "Is it safe to leave the lantern on, Mr. Brayden?"

"For the moment. The drapes are snugly drawn, so the apartment should appear dark, especially when surrounded by all the bustle and torchlight in the streets."

She came to stand beside him. "It is awfully noisy out there."

He grinned. "It is called merriment, Lucy. This is a student's haven, and they like to stay up late drinking. I know you enjoy the quiet of a library, but crowds are good for us, especially drunken crowds. We'll slip right through unnoticed. I just need about an hour to arrange our getaway."

She nodded. "All right. But I want you to know that I understand merriment. In fact, I am a very merry person."

"I am sure you are." He wanted to burst out laughing, but it would be rude, and there was something endearing about Lucy and her library ways. "Are you certain you are not hungry? There is a tavern downstairs that is still open, and Lorcan vows the food is delicious. I'll bring up some light fare for us, enough to hold us through the morning. We'll be on the run by then. Make yourself comfortable. I won't be gone long."

Her eyes rounded in alarm. "You're leaving me?"

"Only for a little while. No longer than an hour, I promise. No one knows you are here, Lucy. Just keep away from the windows and do not draw the drapes aside. I'll be back as soon as I can."

She looked frightened, but there was nothing he could do about it at the moment. He dared not take her with him while he made new arrangements to get them out of London.

He opened the door and quietly slipped out, heading straight to a neighborly ostler who could be relied upon to keep his mouth shut. He found the man just about to close up for the evening. "I need a carriage and two good horses, Mr. Runyon. How fast can you have them ready for me?" He paid him and gave him a little extra to encourage his prompt service.

"Thank ye, Mr. Brayden. Ye'll have yer horses and carriage within twenty minutes."

Donal then stopped at a nearby tavern and purchased a jug of cider, a shepherd's pie for him and Lucy to share tonight, and some hot cross buns to hold them into midday tomorrow. "Lucy, I..."

His mouth gaped open as he returned to the apartment. "What in blazes are you doing?"

He had told her to make herself comfortable, but he hadn't meant for her to take off her gown. Or shake her hair loose. Who knew her hair was so lush or that it would fall in a spectacularly riotous auburn tumble over her shoulders?

She wore only her chemise, and it hid nothing of her body as she stood illuminated in lantern light. The sleeves of her chemise were off her shoulders as she dabbed at a few scratches on her skin.

She gasped and fumbled for her gown. "I...I...did not expect you back so quickly."

He dropped his packages on the table and strode to her side.

Her eyes were wide and breaths shallow. "I'm not decent! Turn away, Mr. Brayden."

He watched her as she began to flutter like a hummingbird, dropping the gown several times and almost ripping it as she tried to put her foot through the opening and missed. She lost her balance and fell against his chest.

He closed his arms around her. "Stop, Lucy. Do not work yourself into a state. I am a professional. You are my assignment. Calm down. You have a few cuts that need tending. Here, let me help you." Was that his voice? Thick and gritty?

Was she buying that line about his being a professional and she only an assignment?

Blessed saints.

How had he not noticed her exquisite body before this? "You need help, and we don't have much time. This is no time to be priggish. Stop fluttering. You are safe with me. I am not going to kiss you."

"Who said anything about kisses, Mr. Brayden?" Her big, green eyes just sucked him in.

"Didn't you?" He took the damp cloth from her hands and began to clean the few scratches he found.

"No."

He swept her hair aside to examine her neck and back. His fingers grazed the necklace she wore, a simple chain with a charm on it that he could not make out because it plunged between the exquisite valley of her...

This was when he knew he was in deep, deep trouble.

Not only did he want to kiss her, desperately kiss that beautifully shaped mouth of hers, he wanted to plunge right into the tempting valley where that charm lay hidden.

No! That would violate his code of honor, morally and professionally.

The sound of laughter from a nearby tavern reached his ears, growing louder and louder as others joined in what had to be a hilarious jest.

He glanced at the red leather tome perched silently on the table.

He knew.

Blessed saints, he knew.

The jest was on him.

Lucy touched his arm, and fire shot through him. "Mr. Brayden, you look green. Are you all right?"

CHAPTER TWO

L UCY HAD JUST asked him if he was all right.
Donal knew he wasn't.

He was used to keeping firm control over his missions, maintaining a detached clarity that allowed him to coldly calculate options and determine what choices to make or not make to enhance the chances of survival for the person he was guarding and for himself.

However, Lucy was not a *person*.

Lucy was a hidden gem.

"Mr. Brayden? Oh, dear. Are you going to be ill?"

"No, Lucy. But I will tell you one thing. If you dare call me Mr. Brayden again, I will…I will kiss you into December, and if need be, into January and March as well."

"What about February?"

He stared at her dazedly. "What?"

"You skipped February. I was merely curious about why you would omit—"

"The point is, I'm going to kiss you every time you call me Mr. Brayden. So what's it to be?"

"You are serious?" She gasped. "Is this your way of punishing me?"

It was more of a punishment for himself, for one taste of Lucy would leave him aching. Of this, he had no doubt. "My name is Donal. Use it. Why are you still fluttering?"

"Mr. B–" She looked up at him, the big, green pools of her eyes drawing him in and about to drown him. "I mean…Donal. How can I be calm when those crazed assailants are still out there trying to kill me, and you are in here threatening to kiss me? Don't you think it is better if we maintain a professional relationship? Intimacy is not a good idea."

Hell of a bad idea.

"This is why I think you should call me Miss Lessing, and I should call you Mr. Brayden. We dare not get too friendly. Please do not misunderstand me. Under other circumstances, I would be delighted to be your friend. I do find you most likeable. However, we will be thrown together for a time and…if we start to care for each other too much, in a companionable way, nothing more…you may lose the clarity of thought necessary to keep us out of danger."

He crossed his arms over his chest.

Clarity of thought?

The Duke of Wooton had confided in him that Lucy was his daughter. Was there any doubt this was true? Listening to her speak was like listening to the duke himself, a man who most in society referred to as the Duke of Ice for his ability to reason with a brutal coldness. Only, Lucy was not cold.

She was warm and sweet and clever.

"If we grow too casual in our friendship, we may take risks for each other that are unwarranted," she continued, licking her perfectly shaped lips and pressing forward in the face of his silence. "Do you understand my point, Mr. Br…Donal?"

"Not in the least. Why should it matter if I call you Lucy and you call me Donal?"

She cleared her throat and began to explain again, unnecessarily, of course. Had he not been worried about this exact thing? Growing too close and taking foolish chances because the thought of Lucy hurt was already throwing his body in a hot roil. "You see, um…Donal. You are obviously handsome and well, protective. And, well…I have no idea what you think of me.

Probably a boring spinster."

"Lucy," he said with a depth of feeling that surprised even himself, "you are a delight. I never considered you boring."

"Oh. Thank you. I had no idea." She pursed her very kissable lips. "You are quite charming yourself. Not that you think of me as charming. But the thing is…if not for you, I would have died tonight. And I am very grateful for that. You saved my life, and I doubt there is another agent in all of England who could have managed it. So, I need you to remain who you are and as you always have been, a man fixed on his duty. I need to be a number…a mere calculation…until we understand what is going on."

She shook her head and continued. "Why on earth would anyone want to kill me?"

"I know the answer to that question, Lucy." He raked a hand through his hair. "And I will tell you once we are safely out of London. But not now and not here."

He studied the ugly gown she had not yet managed to don. She was holding it protectively against her chest. He had walked in on her undressed had completely rattled her and sent her into a panic. So how would she respond upon learning she was the duke's secret daughter?

He could not risk having her fall into a frenzy while they were still here. She had to remain calm and give thought to what she was doing. What if she began to shout at him? Or wail and moan? Or run off?

Being noticed would seal her death warrant.

"I promise I will tell you all I know once we are safely away." He strode into Lorcan's bedchamber and crossed to his wardrobe, hoping his brother had not completely emptied it out now that he and Cammy had purchased a new townhouse to start their lives as a married couple.

He was familiar with this small apartment and did not need more than the dim glow of the lantern light from the other room to see his way around. With luck, he might find one of Cammy's gowns tucked in among his brother's clothes. It was not so farfetched. Lorcan took his own service as an agent for the Crown quite seriously and would have left clothes and supplies for himself and his wife in various hiding spots, on the chance they had to make a fast escape.

This sort of planning was instinctive to any agent of the Crown, although there would be less need for such precautions now that Lorcan was married. Wooton would give his brother less dangerous assignments. It was a policy that worked, the bachelors in the group receiving the most dangerous assignments, while the married men took on the lesser tasks.

Of course, any task could turn dangerous in the blink of an eye.

He breathed a sigh of relief upon peering into the wardrobe and finding several gowns. "Lucy, come in here and try this one on."

He held up a dark green muslin as she hesitantly stepped to the doorway.

"I think it will fit you." She and Cammy were similar in height and build.

Another advantage of having her take the gown was that Lorcan would immediately know they had made it safely out of London. He hoped his brother would come by soon and notice some of his wife's clothing was missing.

"Here. I'll turn my back while you put it on, and then I will help you lace it. Unfortunately, your dancing slippers will have to serve you for now. I don't see any walking boots for Cammy in here. Her feet are small, anyway. I'm not sure they would have fit yours."

She emitted a strangled gasp. "I do not have big feet."

"No... I wasn't suggesting..." He knew better than to pursue the topic since it would only make matters worse.

But he had not meant it as an insult.

Her feet were fine.

Only they were bigger than Cammy's, which logically meant

she would need slightly bigger shoes. "Give me that gown you are still holding in a death grip, and take this one. You'll find it much more comfortable than that silk monstrosity…"

Bloody hell.

Was this what he was reduced to? An oaf who could not get his foot out of his mouth for love or money?

"You hate my gown, too? You called it ugly before. And now it is a monstrosity?"

Because it was. Whoever designed it for the girl ought to be shot.

He cleared his throat. "It does not do your beauty justice. What fool chose it for you?"

"I did," she said quietly and with obvious pain in her voice.

He rolled his eyes and groaned.

Bloody hell again.

"Sorry, Lucy. But a body like yours does not need all these frills, bows, or other adornments. Those merely detract from your beauty. And that color does not suit your complexion."

"Are you saying it makes me look sallow?" She grabbed the dark green gown from his hands and tossed him back the hideous ballgown that was creamy ivory silk, but the tones were too yellow for her skin.

He made the mistake of politely suggesting as much.

Her eyes were now blazing. "I had no idea you had such a flair for color and design. If ever you retire from your profession as a cold-blooded, heartless, and cruel agent, you could open up a modiste shop to serve the Upper Crust. I am sure with your connections, you could acquire a prestigious royal charter for yourself—designer to the queen. Why, you would be all the rage in London. Especially if you put on a French accent and call yourself Monsieur Donal."

He sighed. "Lucy…"

"Oh, and I am ever so grateful to you for pointing out all my mistakes. It is what every young woman hopes to hear when she bothers to look her best for the most important ball of the

Season."

"Seriously? You were trying to look your best?" He turned to her in amazement and flicked her hands away from her bosom when she tried to keep him from adjusting her neckline. "I cannot believe we are having this conversation."

"Nor can I, Mr. Brayden…Donal…and don't you dare kiss me. I would much rather you never speak to me again. How long must we be thrown together?"

"We could be on the run for months." He turned her away from him in order to tie her lacings and hide the fact that she had him in turmoil again. "So you had better get used to my frank talk and stop taking offense at everything I say. I am not trying to insult you. In truth, I don't know the first thing about colors or patterns. But I do know a beautiful woman when I see one, and I also know what looks good on her. Obviously, you have no awareness of your body. You haven't a clue how breathtaking you are."

He now turned her to face him.

Even in the dim light, she looked magnificent.

She also looked utterly bewildered.

"Let's get one thing straight," he said, placing his hands on her softly rounded shoulders and trying very hard not to caress them. "You are probably the prettiest woman of my acquaintance, and your feet are perfect. If I pass a comment, it is about what you choose to put over your glorious body to hide it. This is all I am going to say about your looks. We have to get out of here now. More important, you have to listen to everything I say and immediately obey me. A moment's delay to ask a question could be the difference between life and death."

She continued to regard him as though he were speaking in tongues.

"Lucy, do you understand?"

She nodded. "Yes, life and death. But can you try to be a little less arrogant? Not quite so condescending?"

"Is this what you think of me?"

"What does it matter? Give me a moment to pin up my hair. It will be noticed if I leave it down." She paused to stare at him. "You may as well comment on this unruly tumble before we take another step. You have opinions about every aspect of my person, don't you?"

Would Wooton toss him out of the agency if he throttled his daughter?

"Your hair is lovely." He drew her into the other room and grabbed the pins resting in a pile atop the table. "It will be faster if I do it up for you. I've done this many times before."

"I see. Is this a service provided to your paramours after you bed them? What fortunate women," she said dryly, patting her hair and reluctantly acknowledging a job well done as he quickly finished the task. "And here I am discovering yet another of your talents. You could also have a career as a lady's maid if you ever decide to retire from your present occupation."

"Be quiet, Lucy. There is only one woman I have ever done this for...and now there is you."

She turned to face him. "Oh, is this supposed to make me feel special now?"

"You are a nuisance, aren't you?" He shook his head. "I used to do this for my mother when she was ill and dying. She was in a lot of pain, so my brothers and I did whatever we could to make her comfortable. I'd seat her by her bedroom window to look out upon the garden she loved so much. She would smile as I gently ran a brush through her thinning strands. Then I would pin it up for her and wrap her prettiest shawl around her fragile shoulders. It was a small thing, but she took great pleasure from it."

Lucy was gaping at him with tears glistening in her eyes. "That is the most beautiful thing I have ever heard. So help me...if this is a lie, I shall hit you over the head with the biggest stick I can find and not stop hitting you until that thick head of yours splits wide open."

"It is not a lie. And I would appreciate your holding off on the urge to hit me until this assignment is over."

She surprised him by placing her hand flat against his chest, at the spot just over his heart. "I will not hit you. Truly, I...I wish someone cared for me like that. My parents, well, it was obvious they worshiped Eliza, and I was the afterthought. It was Eliza who had special moments with them, Eliza who lightened their hearts. But she is that wonderful sort of girl, and we have always been close."

She turned away and sank onto the wooden chair beside the table, then buried her face in her hands. "You called my gown ugly and wondered how anyone could choose it. I chose it, and do you want to know why?"

He knelt beside her and put his arm around her shoulders. "Tell me, Lucy."

"Because it is how I feel inside. This is how my parents always made me feel, sallow and uninviting. Oh, they were dutiful. I never lacked for clothes or comforts. But a mother's touch? A father's look of pride? No, those were all for Eliza." She patted *The Book of Love* as it sat silently atop the table. "When I saw this book, I knew I had to read it. I've spent my entire life struggling to be loved. How do you make people care for you? How does one find love?"

He groaned. "Blessed saints."

She gave a mirthless laugh. "I cannot even find my spectacles. They fell while we were being attacked. I suppose it doesn't matter. I can manage without them. They are just another thing I used to put up walls around me because one gets tired of being rejected. It is easier to disappear behind them and avoid the hurt entirely."

He held her in his arms a moment longer because he did not have the heart to pull away just yet. Finally, he did and cupped a finger under her chin to draw her gaze to his. "I hope that blasted book holds all the answers for you. But I promise you, Lucy. You are not at fault. Dry your eyes. You and I will have plenty of time to talk about this while we hide out."

Since she did not have a handkerchief on her, he took care of the task by lightly rubbing his thumbs across her soft cheeks. "We had better go," he said in a husky murmur. "Grab the book. I'll take the food. Are you very hungry? Can you hold off for a couple of hours more?"

She nodded.

It did not take them long to get to the ostler and their waiting carriage.

Donal helped Lucy in, this time taking care not to shove her into it as he had done the last time. In his own defense, he had been caught unaware by the power of a touch, especially touching this girl. "Stay down. I'm sorry, Lucy. But I cannot risk your being seen. It has to look as though I am driving an empty carriage."

"What about you? Those assailants will easily spot you."

"Not in my disguise. Well, it isn't much. Just a hat to pull down over my brow and a big overcoat that I will stuff with straw to give the appearance of a big man with an even larger belly."

She cast him a gentle smile. "All right. I hope you know what you are doing."

She settled on the floor of the carriage, making herself as comfortable as possible by drawing her legs close and tucking her knees under her chin.

He quickly stuffed straw into a burlap sack, climbed up into the driver's seat and tucked the sack under his coachman's overcoat. He then tucked the hat atop his head.

With a flick of the reins, they were off and making their way through the crowded streets of London. Despite the lateness of the hour, the streets were still bustling with activity. This served to their advantage, knowing the carriage would be lost among the others clattering along the roadway.

As soon as they reached the outskirts of town, Donal spurred the horses, so they were trotting at a fast clip despite it being nightfall. Since they were still close to London, these roads were emblazoned with torchlight, and he meant to take advantage of the illumination they provided. He slowed the horses only once the torches no longer lit the road at close intervals, and the ground remained dark for long patches.

He had driven them south, giving the impression to anyone watching they were headed to a hideaway in that direction. The top agents of the Crown knew of several houses along the southern route where they could safely take shelter.

Of course, nothing was safe now.

But it could not hurt to give the impression their destination was Tunbridge Wells. After ensuring they would be remembered arriving there, he would quietly hire a man to drive the carriage on to Dover, while he and Lucy rode horses west to Weymouth.

His grandfather had owned a manor in that seaside village, one which he and his brothers recently inherited upon his death. It was perched atop a hill, overlooking the town and the English Channel. *La Manche*, the French called it. All these small, coastal towns had filled with military activity during the Napoleonic Wars but were much quieter now that the threat had passed.

He and Lucy could hide out there for at least a week before anyone caught up to them. Hopefully, the place was habitable. He remembered it as well maintained but would have to take her elsewhere if it was now vermin-infested or the roof about to fall atop them.

One problem at a time.

When the roadway turned completely dark, he slowed the horses to a walk and drew them up behind a copse of trees to sufficiently hide them while they grabbed a moment's rest. Since the sky was clear and surprisingly unobstructed by clouds, they would be able to continue by moonlight.

With care, of course.

He was not about to risk damaging their horses.

He hopped down from his perch and opened the coach door. "Lucy, how are you faring? I'm sorry if the ride was bumpy."

She groaned to her feet. "Nothing to apologize for. I am fine, just a little stiff. And very hungry. Do you think we might have a quick bite now?"

"Yes. Careful. Can you see to make your way down?"

"No, it is too dark. Will you help me?"

"Of course." He took her hand to guide her. He had the eyes of a night predator, or so he had been told. But it was a necessity when so much of his work involved prowling around under cover of darkness. "I am famished, and the aroma of that shepherd's pie is making my stomach growl."

He did not bother to mention what her delicious scent was doing to him.

Yet another thing that did not bear mentioning.

He still did not understand what it was about Lucy that put his body into spasms. She was not even trying to seduce him, nor did she understand what the art of seduction was.

Perhaps this was her appeal.

The women he consorted with were too experienced.

There was no charm to their encounters.

All it took was a bold exchange of glances, a knowing nod, and then a quiet alcove where they could go at it like ferrets.

There was no wonder in their mutual discovery.

He shook out of the thought. "I did not think to purchase a candle. We might have dined by candlelight."

"A nice thought, but would it not give our position away?"

"Yes, Lucy. It likely would. We are not far enough out of London to let down our guard."

"I don't mind. I've never eaten in total darkness before. I wonder if the food tastes different when you cannot see it?"

He led her to a fallen log not far from their carriage, un-wrapped the meat pie, and handed her one of the forks the tavern's cook had thoughtfully packed along with their food.

"Well, here goes. This will be a new experience for me," she said and almost stuck his hand with her fork while hunting for a slice in the dark. "It is odd not to be able to see what one is putting into one's mouth. Oh, I just bit down on something long and hard."

He coughed.

"A carrot, I think."

Blessed saints, he was going to embarrass himself if he did not get himself under control. "It is just food. That's all. Savor the flavor of it on your lips."

She laughed. "I am starved. I plan to gobble it down."

"Don't, Lucy. This is one of life's little pleasures. Take your time. Enjoy the warmth of it in your mouth. Taste the spices on your tongue."

"All right. Are you sure about this? I never thought of food in this way before."

This girl had a lot to learn about the sensual arts. It hurt his soul to think she considered herself inferior goods. The light in her heart had been squashed by the Lessings and their indifference. He had no doubt they'd provided a good roof over her head and all the material niceties. Wooton would have deposited sufficient funds in their account for this. Knowing the man, he would also have made certain it was not squandered elsewhere and been quick to punish the so-called parents if they had stinted on her in any way.

But how could he force them to provide affection to a child who was not theirs when they did not feel it? Although how could anyone not adore her? She must have been a sweet little thing.

"The moon is full tonight, Lucy. Have your eyes adjusted yet? Can you see the food any clearer?"

"Not really. I'm not doing a very good job of savoring it either. I'm sorry, but I was hungry and could not help swallowing it down fast."

"Well, I suppose it does not matter. Here, take a sip of the cider, and let's finish up. There's a stream nearby. I cannot unhitch the horses, but I'll need to lead them closer to the water so they can drink. We'll move on once they have slaked their thirst."

"May I sit on the driver's bench with you? Or must I stay in hiding in the carriage?"

"I would rather you stayed hidden these next few days. It is important to the ruse."

"All right. I suppose I shall have to wait to ask questions about what is going on. I should have taken the opportunity as we ate, but I was too hungry, and now we will be on the road again."

"I would not have told you now anyway. We are still too close to London, and we need to concentrate on getting you safely hidden first." He packed up the remains of their meal, secured the cork on the bottle of cider, and carefully stowed it in the carriage.

He took her hand in one of his, using the excuse that he did not want her tripping in the dark while she walked beside him. He then took the reins in his other hand and guided the horses closer to the stream.

It was odd how every sensation felt heightened when one could not see beyond one's nose.

Her hand felt nice in his.

He liked the closeness of their bodies.

He had not felt this way about any other woman before.

Yes, he'd taken his pleasures with the opposite sex. Finding a willing woman was never his problem. But those acts provided physical gratification and nothing more, an exercise to satisfy his carnal urges and those of the bed partner who happened to be writhing under him.

But Lucy?

She was no man's dalliance.

She was the sort he would hold in his arms throughout the night. She was the sort he would kiss and caress after the coupling. Hers was the face he would remember when closing his eyes to sleep and wish to see when he opened his eyes in the morning.

He shook out of these ridiculous thoughts.

But it was hard not to think of her and how beautiful she looked by moonlight.

"Up you go," he said, lifting her into the carriage and cautioning her to remain either seated on the floor or stretched out flat on the seat bench so no one would see her as their carriage passed by.

"I still don't understand the reason, but I will do as you ask. I could do with a little sleep anyway. Um, is that all right? Or do you need me to stay awake?"

"Grab your rest while you can. We'll have little of it until we reach our hiding spot." He watched as she settled across the bench and curled herself into a little ball.

"Donal," she said as he was about to close the door, "what about you? Do you not need a few hours of sleep?"

"I'll manage. We are trained for this sort of thing."

"For sleep deprivation? Does it not affect your wits?"

"Let's hope not, for both our sakes." He shut the door and climbed up onto his driver's perch. He had removed his coachman hat and the big cloak and straw-stuffed padding, when first stopping in this copse.

He now donned them again and drew one of his pistols onto the seat beside him.

The roadway was quiet for the moment, but he dared not let down his guard. In addition to Wooton's assailants, there were rogues who would not think twice about stopping him at pistol point to steal purses off each passenger.

This was another reason he wanted the carriage to appear empty. No one was going to stop a poor driver when it was the rich passengers these thieves were after.

The inky night sky was turning to the gray light of dawn by the time they rumbled into Tunbridge Wells. He drew the horses up in front of the Royal House Inn, one of the finest coaching inns between here and Dover that happened to be run by a former Crown agent who could be relied on to help him out.

He hopped down off his perch and took a quick look around to make certain no one was watching while he opened the carriage door and lightly shook Lucy awake. She was still stretched out across the seat and had *The Book of Love* tucked under her arm as though afraid she might lose it if she had to leap out of carriage in a hurry.

She stirred awake the moment she heard the door open and was about to sit up when she heard his whispered warning. "Stay down, for now, Lucy. I need to be certain the inn is safe before I bring you inside. The ostler should be out in a moment. He and I will bring the carriage into the mews, and then he will unhitch the horses and take them to their stalls. Stay quiet, and he won't realize you are in here. I'll return for you soon."

"Donal, wait," she said, her eyes widening as she realized he was about to abandon her.

Well, he wasn't really. "What is it?"

"What if the inn is not safe?"

This was entirely the point of leaving her in hiding, and he quickly told her so. However, she did not look in the least assured.

"How long before I should begin to worry?"

CHAPTER THREE

"LUCY, IF I do not return for you within ten minutes, you are to keep calm and find yourself the best hiding spot you can."

She shook off her haze of sleep, frankly surprised she had managed to close her eyes at all while the carriage bumped and bounced along the road, not to mention while assassins were still chasing them. Fear of dying a horrible and violent death had a way of draining a person and leaving them exhausted, she supposed.

Had those villains lost their trail?

She hoped so, but who could be certain of anything?

Donal pursed his lips and grunted.

It was obvious he was considering the possibility of being caught in a trap the moment he entered the inn. "The innkeeper can be trusted. Look to him to help you if I am taken down."

"No...Donal..."

He cast her a tired smile and took her hand, running his thumb lightly over the top of it to calm her. "I will be careful. I always am. But if I am hurt or killed, you must keep running."

He handed her some pound notes from the envelope the Duke of Edgeware had provided, and then gave her the direction of a cottage in Weymouth. "Tuck those away securely on your person once I leave."

Since his gaze fell to her chest, it was obvious he meant for her to hide them in her bodice. She drew her necklace out and quickly tucked the money away. "How am I to get to Weymouth?"

"The innkeeper's name is Samuel West. He used to work for the Crown and still helps us out from time to time. He will figure out a way to get you safely there. Trust him and no one else here."

He released her hand, stared at her necklace a moment, and then shut the carriage door.

She scooted onto the floor and held herself flat while Donal spoke to the ostler who was just arriving. Then she felt the carriage jolt to a start as it was moved to a building at the rear of the inn.

She held her breath and listened to the conversation between Donal and the ostler while their team was unhitched. "Never ye worry, Mr. Brayden. I'll feed and water these fine horses. They'll be well cared for in my stable. Ye just let me know when ye want them hitched again."

"Thank you, Mel."

"Beggin' yer pardon, but what are ye doing here dressed up as a coachman?"

"I just dropped off someone of importance a couple of towns back. Now all I need is a few hours rest, and I'm off for my next assignment."

"I see. Heading back to London then?"

She heard Donal give the man a cheerful pat on the back. "You know the rules, Mel. I've already told you more than I ought. Just have the team readied when I ask for them."

Lucy waited until all was silent before creeping out of the carriage. Since Donal had mentioned to the ostler that this was an empty carriage, she had no doubt the man would be back to snoop around. There was something in his tone she simply did not trust.

Was she imagining it, or was there something false in Mel's joviality?

Perhaps it was nothing, but he was quite snoopy and asked too many questions of Donal. This was supposed to be a safe retreat, and those here ought to have been discreet.

She patted her chest to make certain the funds were safely tucked away and then gathered the food and book in her arms. Before descending the carriage, she looked around to be sure there were no traces of her presence left behind. Confident she had thought of everything, she scampered to the ladder and climbed to the loft.

It occurred to her the ladder could be drawn up.

She tugged the surprisingly heavy thing up as quietly as possible in the hope no one would consider looking for her here.

Perhaps it was silly to assume anyone would be fooled, but for a certainty, no one would be fooled if that ladder stayed down. One's eye would naturally be drawn to it, and the next natural step would be to climb to the loft and have a look around.

She dared not compliment herself on her cleverness but hoped Donal would approve. After making herself comfortable behind several bales of hay, she remained as still as she could and listened for the sound of footsteps.

The minutes passed.

Without a pocket watch at hand, she had no idea how much time had gone by. It felt much longer than ten minutes without a sign of Donal.

She began to worry.

Dear heaven, what would she do if he were injured?

She could not leave him behind.

First of all, she had no experience as a Crown agent. How would she fend for herself in the wild? Well, Tunbridge Wells was not quite the savage wilderness, but one wrong move, one misplaced word, would get her killed.

All the more frustrating, she did not know who was after her or why anyone would want her dead.

Taking a quiet breath, she closed her eyes and considered her options.

What was she good at doing?

Well, she was rather good at going about unnoticed. She often crept into libraries to get away from the crush of guests at those stultifying *ton* parties she attended. Not that she attended many. But no one ever paid attention to her at the few she did because she was no heiress, and her father was no one of consequence.

That her sister had married the Earl of Monkton, a love match no less, was an unexpected feather in the Lessing cap. She had thought it would bring her more notice, but her parents had done nothing to put her forward. In truth, it often felt as though they were taking extraordinary measures to keep her off the marriage mart.

They accepted the minimum of invitations and those only at her sister's urging.

Lucy supposed her parents meant to keep her at home in order to tend to them in their old age. Someone had to do it, so why not her? No one else seemed to want her anyway. She was resigned to her fate and quite content to live out her adventures through her books.

Hence her penchant for stealing into libraries at those elegant parties. She had even caught couples in a romantic tryst a time or two, but they never noticed her. Apparently, passion and desire left one shortsighted and heedless.

She would not know about such things.

Nor was she likely to survive long enough to experience so much as a first kiss.

It was a terrible shame.

Perhaps Donal would consider taking on the chore. But what if the thought repulsed him? Perhaps she ought to delicately talk around the subject, get a better sense of his opinion of her. Perhaps test out something less bold first.

"Lucy, what in blazes are you doing up there?"

She poked her head out from behind a bale of hay and gasped his name in relief. "Donal! Thank goodness." She lowered the ladder as silently as possible. "What took you so long? And how did you know I was up here?"

"It is my business to notice everything. The ladder was down when I left you." He steadied it and motioned for her to climb down quickly. "My heart stopped when I opened the carriage door and found you gone."

"Really? You worried about me? Well, I suppose I am your responsibility for now." She had their sack of food and the book in her arms as she tried to make her way down each rung.

"What are you holding? Toss those things down to free your hands, or you're going to—"

She lost her footing and was seized in panic as she began to tumble down. This is what he was trying to tell her, obviously warning her to free her hands to maintain a steadier grip.

She toppled into his solid arms.

Oh, sweet heaven.

She had no idea his arms were so splendidly muscled.

Well, she did know.

But had no idea how incredibly nice it would feel to actually be carried in them.

"Bollocks, that book stuck me in the ribs. Why didn't you let go of it?"

He still held her, shifting her in his embrace so that its red leather spine was no longer poking him.

Those magnificent muscles.

"What?"

Goodness, his arms were hard as granite stone.

He arched an eyebrow. "You should have let go of that book."

She frowned and shook her head emphatically. "I am never letting go of it."

"Lucy, it is just a book."

"No, it isn't." He must think her a ninny, but she did not care. "It holds the secrets to love."

"Come with me," he said with a sigh and gently set her down.

"I am taking you in through the kitchen. We haven't much time. The scullery maids will be stirring soon. Sam has a secret room. That's where we will hide out for the next few hours. I need to sleep. We both could do with more food."

"Then what?"

"I am not certain yet. I will figure it out later." He took her hand, protectively enveloping it in his while he led her inside the inn with all due caution.

A big man with bushy, dark eyebrows she assumed to be Samuel West met them at the door. In polite company, introductions would have been made. Instead, the man gave her a curt nod, then turned away and immediately began to guide them through a maze of hallways.

Lucy was not offended by the innkeeper's abrupt behavior since this was the nature of their secret work.

The less these agents said to each other, the better.

In truth, she would have considered this clandestine Crown business quite thrilling if not for the fact that her life was at stake. Having people shoot at you and then try to burn you alive tended to take the fun out of any adventure.

She tried to concentrate on where they were going, but there were so many twists, turns, and endless hallways, she quickly lost her bearings. She was usually very good at directions, but the night had been an unusual one, and she was not quite recovered yet. Also, the inn had not looked very big from the outside, but there were more rooms than expected and lots of hidden nooks and doorways to confuse her.

Samuel lumbered down a set of stairs that led to what appeared to be the inn's larder.

Donal was still holding her hand as they followed him down the dark, narrow stairs into this obviously well-supplied storeroom.

She glanced around, noting the stock of weapons along with linens, pots, jars of plum jam, eggs, meat, potatoes. One could survive here for a year if the place were ever under siege.

They reached a stone wall.

"What now?" she asked in a whisper.

It turned out to be a secret doorway.

"Fascinating," Lucy said, making certain to keep her voice low. "I never would have guessed this was anything other than a wall. The door is very well hidden."

Donal gave her hand a squeeze to warn her to be quiet.

"Sorry," she silently mouthed.

He cast her another warning look but did not appear to be very angry. He continued to hold her hand quite gently and was adamant about keeping her close.

He had a protective way of looking at her that made her insides melt.

Was it any surprise?

He'd had this effect on her ever since their first meeting at the Earl of Monkton's estate. She had walked into the earl's study, and suddenly, there he was. Big and glorious. His body forged of hardest stone and those deep gray eyes of his missing nothing.

He'd taken full command and completely dominated the elegant room.

She had later met his brothers. These Brayden men were similar in looks, all of them having those penetrating gray eyes and dark hair, as well as big, muscled bodies. Shayne and Lorcan were nice-looking, too. But Donal was easily the handsomest of the brothers. There was something quite wonderful in the way he'd protected the earl and her sister when the earl's crazed brother had come after them.

He had also taken the time to worry about her, seeming always to have his eyes on her and know exactly where she was at all times.

Oh, those eyes.

They were heartbreaker eyes, steamy and filled with promise.

How could any woman resist him?

"Lucy, you can put the book down now."

"What?" She quickly shook out of her thoughts and realized

the innkeeper had left them alone in this rather cramped, hidden room. It had a tiny bed that could only sleep one. A rickety chair. An equally rickety table with a lantern, basin, and ewer upon it. The lantern had been lit, so she was able to see quite well around this dank space that resembled a dungeon more than a bedchamber.

She peeked into the ewer and saw it was filled with water. "Is it fresh?"

"Yes," Donal said with a yawn. "As for food, I'm afraid we only have the leftover pie and some buns to tide us over for now."

"The cider as well."

"Sam will bring us more when he can." He nodded and yawned again. "Lucy, I am dead on my feet. I need to sleep."

"Of course. Take as long as you need. I managed almost a full night's rest while you were driving the carriage. I shall be fine right here. Do not worry about me. I have the book and light enough to read by."

For some reason, her comment brought an endearing smile to his lips. "Wake me if you need anything. Most important, do not leave this room without me."

"All right. But what is the point of all this secrecy? The ostler knows you are here. Anyone will see our carriage, although I suppose they won't know it is ours unless the ostler mentions it. And I suppose he only saw you. I heard what you told him, that you had dropped me off and then stopped here to rest up for your next assignment. But those villains know I am with you. So, we are not really fooling anyone with–"

"Lucy, please. I know hiding in here is not much, but it is enough to hold us for now."

"I did not mean to suggest it was bad. You have kept me alive so far, and I am exceedingly grateful. It's just that—"

"Turn off that brain of yours, will you? For the moment, all anyone knows is that I am here alone. This inn is what we call a 'safe' place, where agents can come and go in secret and not be given away. The only one who knows you are here with me is Samuel. He will not talk. I have worked out our next steps with him, which I shall tell you later. Right now, I am going to sleep."

Having said that, he stretched out on the bed, which was too small for his height. His booted feet dangled off the edge, but this did not seem to bother him at all, and he was lightly snoring within a minute.

Lucy wanted to reach over and stroke his hair…touch his face.

She loved the masculine angles of it, the firm chin and the day's growth of beard, now casting its grizzled shadow upon his jaw. He had high cheekbones and a broad mouth. His eyes were deep-set and dangerous in their appeal.

Of course, they were closed now.

But they were still divine.

She sighed and opened the book, eager to learn as much as she could about love. Would it provide an explanation of more than love between a man and a woman? Although that would also be quite helpful.

But what had puzzled her all of her life was familial love, that which existed between a parent and child. Her parents had doted on Eliza.

Why had they never felt the same about her?

CHAPTER FOUR

L UCY CLEARED HER throat and began to read from the beginning of the book. The first chapter was familiar because she had started it while hiding in the Duke of Edgeware's library during his ball.

But she had not gotten very far before Donal burst in and insisted they leave.

Besides, these paragraphs on men having two brains were quite fascinating and merited further review. Did she dare ask Donal about his low brain—assuming such a thing existed—when he woke up?

However, this was not topmost in her mind. Her first questions to ask him would be about who was trying to kill her and why in heaven's name these unknown villains were desperate enough to shoot them and set fire to their carriage to accomplish it?

This had to be a matter of mistaken identity or a mistaken belief she had overheard something sensitive, possibly rebellion plans against the Crown. If only these plotters would listen to reason, she would assure them she had overheard nothing. Of course, they would likely kill her and Donal, anyway, since now they had given themselves away as rebels.

She shook her head and returned her attention to the book, which explained the differences between men and women and the way they approached love.

First difference, men had two brains.

Two male brains.

A low, unthinking one that worked on pure instinct for survival and breeding purposes. Once this brain was awakened, it was like setting off a lightning storm within a man's loins. But would a highly trained agent of the Crown such as Donal respond in this frenzied way to the mere sight of an attractive woman?

Would he ever consider *her* attractive in this way?

The author said a man looked first at a woman's bosom, and if he found it pleasing, he would then look at the rest of her. Donal had said some nice things about her appearance but more to calm her down than to declare any feelings for her.

He had also called her gown ugly and considered her a boring bluestocking.

"At this low-brain level, thousands of women might appeal to him," she murmured, reading on. This unknown author was describing a male's instinctive response to every woman with whom he would like to mate.

She snorted while trying to swallow her laughter.

Thousands? Seriously?

Would that not exhaust him? Or keep him too busy for anything else?

How would Donal respond if he caught her undressed and got a good look at her breasts? In truth, he had already caught her wearing nothing but her chemise after returning earlier than expected to his brother's apartment with the pie and cider.

He had appeared surprised.

Appalled.

Aghast.

This hardly qualified as unbridled lust.

She had not been watching him closely to measure his response because of her blind panic while trying to dress and had almost ripped her elegant silk gown in the attempt.

Well, next time he caught her scantily dressed, she would be prepared. She would watch him closely for any signs of lustful desire.

Assuming there would ever be a next time.

And if there was, how was she to know what these feelings of stirred passion looked like?

Clues would be helpful.

She could not ask Donal since she meant to test his responses.

Hopefully, there would be some helpful hints in this book.

"Oh, you are going to be so angry with me," she whispered, studying him as he slept.

Would she ever have the power to break his iron control?

It was quite unfair that he should be so handsome. He was smart, too. Why could he not have been graced with one such quality and not the other? Brains or good looks. But to have both? How was a woman to resist him?

Even in sleep, he devastated her senses.

All the more reason, she should stop gawking at him and read on.

Sighing, she tore her gaze away from the smooth rise and fall of his chest and turned to the next page, which discussed the male protective instincts.

This was also fascinating.

The low brain was about lust.

The high brain was about love.

Well, she liked to think of it as love, although the author described it more as survival of that male's bloodline. The passages discussed the importance of his moving on from the primordial urge to mate with just anyone. Breeding children off as many healthy women as possible did not assure their survival. What mattered most was the male's need to choose one female and protect her and the children they had together.

Without that protection, who was to keep the wolves from eating them?

Of course, the reference to wolves referred to any form of danger to be faced by a woman at her most vulnerable. So, the man had to stop seducing every woman at hand and find the one true mate of his heart. She was the one with whom he would have children and the one he needed to concentrate his efforts to defend.

Warmth curled in Lucy's belly.

She had never thought of herself in the role of wife and mother. In truth, she had mostly considered herself an outcast. But with a man like Donal? "Don't be a fool."

He would never want her.

Yes, he was currently protecting her from the wolves trying to eat her. But this was an assignment for him, not a matter of choosing his mate.

She moved on to the next chapter because this one was distressing her. She was not bothered so much by the discussion of the male's spawning behaviors but by the fact that no man was ever likely to behave this way over her.

"The senses," she said in a whisper, holding back a sniffle. "Look, touch, taste, hearing, and scent."

These chapters were easy.

Donal was a living, breathing example of pleasant sensations. He would ravish any young woman's senses with his manly, good looks and his warm, gentle touch. Toss in the deep, sultry timbre of his voice that she found so calming and reassuring. Add the ridiculously appealing scent of him, an intoxicating mix of island spices and male heat.

There you had the recipe for any woman's dream man.

But she did not understand how to apply the sense of taste. How did one taste a person? "With a lick? With a bite?"

"Lucy, what in blazes is that book teaching you?"

She gasped and slammed it shut. "I thought you were asleep."

He sat up and stretched his marvelously honed arms and broad shoulders. "No, a good twenty or thirty minutes usually does it for me. What were you muttering about to yourself?"

"Nothing."

He gave a low, hearty laugh. "I might believe you if your cheeks were not so bright pink. You, Miss Lessing, are furiously blushing."

She groaned. "It is a trick of the light, I assure you."

"You are also a terrible liar."

She glanced at the book that now lay shut atop the table and began to fidget in her chair. "If you must know, I was reading the chapters on the five senses. But I cannot understand how one person tastes another short of eating them like cannibals."

"*Blessed saints.* I'm sorry I asked."

"I understand how one tastes food and finds some more pleasing to one's palate than others. I am also aware that some foods have properties that…" She cleared her throat. "That enhance…um, certain pleasures. But how does one apply this to love? And I am not speaking of merely the act of…dear heaven…the act of coupling. People do not smell like food unless one considers a drunken sot reeking of ale or someone's breath after eating a raw onion."

He was regarding her so oddly.

Nor was he adding anything helpful to the conversation, so she continued. "Who would ever want to get near someone like that? But even concerning more appealing scents. I mean, one does not look at a person and think, oh yes, he smells like a hearty oxtail soup or like raisins. Or, she smells like a cinnamon bun or a strawberry. Well, maybe one does think such things because the fragrance of fruit can be quite delightful. Oranges, strawberries. Cherries. And I adore roasted chestnuts in the winter. I'm not sure they are considered fruit. I suppose they are not. But my point is, well…"

She forgot entirely the point of what she was saying as he cast her a wickedly endearing half-smile that stirred awake the butterflies in her stomach and set them fluttering. "Do you understand this, Donal? Will you explain it to me?"

He rose and came to her side. "I understand it, but I will not explain it to you."

She stared at him in surprise. "Why not?"

He placed his hands on either side of her seat back, trapping her between his divinely muscled arms. "Because it is dangerous."

"Dangerous?" She wanted to tell him to move away because she could not think clearly when he was so close. But she could not seem to form the desire to have him move even an inch back. "Are you jesting? If so, I do not find your remark funny at all. Getting shot at is dangerous. Trying to understand how one enjoys the taste of a person can hardly be put in the same category. Fruit and cakes do not shoot at you or toss fire at you."

"No, but putting your lips to another's skin and savoring them can get you into a lot of trouble."

She licked her lips. "Savoring them? Yes, you spoke of this regarding food when we stopped outside of London last night. How does one savor?"

He sighed.

She felt the warmth of his breath against her cheek. "Donal, would you show me how it is done?"

"No!"

One would think she had pushed him into a bed of spiked nettles. His eyes widened, and he jerked his hands off either side of her chair, hastily backing a step away.

"What have I said that is so outrageous? Consider it an act of science and nothing more. I know you do not like me in this way. You need not worry that I will think something more than scientific discovery is taking place. I am well aware you regard me as an assignment only. And am I not the one who first suggested we maintain a professional distance? You are the one who insists on the intimacy of using our given names. I would have been happy to call you Mr. Brayden. And I will not turn into a fluttering goose simply because you—"

"Enough, Lucy."

Did his groan have to sound so agonized?

"But my point is—"

"I understand your point. What you don't understand is the impact it will have on you."

"Honestly, Donal. I feel as though we are talking in circles. Is this not precisely the reason for our discussion? How will I ever find out if I don't experience it? I would not ask this of anyone else. I am asking you because I trust you."

"The answer is still no." He sank back onto the tiny bed, stretched out on it once more and tossed his arm over his eyes as though to obliterate the repulsive thought of ever savoring her.

She sat silently for a long moment, not breathing while struggling to hold back her tears. If only she were stronger, she could pretend his rejection did not hurt.

Why should it hurt so much?

After all, this is what she had endured all her life up to now. For as long as she could remember, it was Eliza who was hugged and admired while she was ignored.

Now, Donal was doing the same to her.

How had her life sunk so low?

Nobody wanted her except for those evil villains who wanted to kill her.

What had she ever done to anybody to deserve this fate?

She rested her arms on the rickety table and then buried her head in them, just wanting to hide from the world for a moment until she could regain her composure. But she found herself crying instead.

Silent tears.

She had become very good at those.

Perhaps she wasn't so silent because Donal was suddenly kneeling by her side and drawing her into his arms. "Lucy, I was not refusing you because I did not like you."

"Please, spare me the lame explanations. If you wish to be helpful, then just tell me what it is about me that is so odious to everyone? For the life of me, I cannot figure it out. Just be honest. I don't need politeness. I have been politely ignored for my entire existence by those who should love me. No matter what I do to be helpful, no matter how nice and dutiful I try to be, they remain cold and unmoved. Nothing I ever did touched their hearts."

"You are speaking of the Lessings?"

She nodded, her head now buried against his chest because she refused to lift it to look up at him. "Yes. I thought the hurt would ease as I got older, but it did not. If not for Eliza, I would be going through life as a ghost. No one seeing me. No one caring. I do not understand why, and now I am going to an early grave, never knowing. That is the most frustrating thing of all."

"You are not going to die. I am with you and will protect you."

"Why? If my own parents do not care about me, then why should anyone else? What is so important about me that the Duke of Wooton himself should assign you to guard me? Donal, you must tell me. It is time I was told something. Does everyone believe I have stumbled upon some important secret? I assure you, I have not."

She tried to draw out of his arms, but he would not let her. "I cannot tell you, yet, why I am guarding you. I promise I will once we get to Weymouth. You are too overset, and I dare not risk upsetting you further." He sighed heavily. "Stop crying, Lucy. Let me dry your tears."

"You needn't fuss over me. I will put myself back together on my own. I suppose the strain of being on the run has turned me into a watering pot. I am never like this. Quite the opposite, I have become rather good at burying my hurt."

He remained close by her side all the while it took her to regain her composure. In truth, having him beside her, his expression so obviously one of concern…as though he actually cared about her, only made things worse.

But she was finally herself once again. "You do not need to remain by my side. I am fine now."

He did not budge, simply remained frowning. It was not a frown of anger because he seemed thoughtful rather than incensed. Perhaps he was trying to think of something nice to say to make her feel better. That he had to try so hard to think of the right words was dismaying in itself. He would have her crying again if he did not say something to her soon.

Anything.

"Tip your head to the side," he said with a soft groan.

Well, that was a nonsensical statement if she ever heard one. "Why?"

"Do you want me to savor you or not?"

Her mouth gaped open, and her eyes widened in surprise. "I thought you did not want to."

"I don't."

"I see, you are doing this out of pity for me."

"I am not doing this out of pity."

"Well, I do not need your pity."

He caressed her cheek. "It has nothing to do with pity."

"Why are you accepting to do it then? Because I am perfectly fine managing on my own...well, obviously I am not fine. Just...I will hit you over the head with this chair if you dare feel sorry for me or dare to laugh at me. Promise me you won't laugh."

"I give you my word of honor. Do you want me to do this or not?"

She tilted her head and closed her eyes.

He lowered his lips to her neck.

Sweet blessed mercy.

There were other ways to die by fire than having flaming explosives tossed at you. The mere touch of Donal's lips to her skin was enough to set her alight like a burning torch. Were she not in his arms, she would have tumbled out of her chair.

Or merely turned to ashes in this chair.

No wonder those trysting couples had never noticed her hiding out in *ton* libraries. Who could notice anything while their bodies were ablaze?

He suckled the pulse at the base of her neck. "Um, oh my."

She gasped as his tongue licked up her neck. "You have obviously done this before. It must take practice to be so good...oh...as I was saying...to be so..."

"Good?"

"Yes."

He began to suckle her earlobe.

"Oh, my heavens. That is very good, too. Donal—"

"Lucy, stop talking. Savoring is about feeling. No comments necessary."

"I understand, but my body is very hot. Incendiary actually, and I—"

He abruptly drew away. "Don't tell me that."

"Forgive me. I thought you would want to know how I was responding." She followed his movements as he drew away and began to pace across the small room. "But I will keep my findings to myself since you do not care."

"Who says I don't care?" He raked a hand through his hair and turned to her with a look she could not understand.

She rose but was afraid to draw near for the feral look in his eyes. "I phrased it badly. You've done this before and obviously knew what my response would be. I only meant to confirm your…savoring me…was successful. Will you be angry if I thank you?"

There was still a wild look in his eyes as he shook his head and smiled. "I am not angry, and you do not need to thank me. Blessed saints, Lucy. Do you understand now why this sensation of taste is dangerous?"

She nodded. "I half understand it."

He shook his head. "Half? I thought I was quite thorough."

"You were."

"Then what are you missing?"

"What would happen if I were to lick you?"

CHAPTER FIVE

W AS LUCY SERIOUS?
Did she really not know that his body would catch
fire if she touched her lips to him, ran her tongue along his skin?

He would have her naked within ten seconds and be making
love to her like a frenzied animal. But she had no idea what he
was thinking, and he meant to keep it that way. "Turn off that
brain of yours, will you? This is all the savoring either of us is
going to get. What we have to do is eat, rest, and be prepared to
get out of here as soon as Sam tells us all is in readiness. But there
is one other thing I ought to teach you."

"About the elements of love?"

Gad, she was running rampant over his heart with her sweet,
earnest look. "No, Lucy. About survival."

"Oh. What is it you want me to know?"

"There will be times when we are apart and cannot simply
call out to find each other. This is why we ought to use bird calls.
Can you whistle?"

"Not well at all."

"Can you make the sound of a bird?"

"What sort of bird?"

"Any bird."

"Should it not be one common to this area?"

Her questions should infuriate him, but this was Lucy, and he
adored the way her mind worked. "You are the only person in

England who would notice."

"I'm sure there are others who would. Bird watchers, for example. Well, perhaps not those vile assailants. Will you show me how it is done?"

He put his hands to his mouth and emitted a trilling call.

"That is very good. What sort of bird is that?"

He arched an eyebrow. "Does it matter? I hardly think the men chasing us are the sort to care."

"I enjoy birdwatching."

"That is utterly fascinating but of absolutely no relevance at the moment. The point is to have you recognize the call as mine and be able to respond in like fashion so that I can find you if the need ever arises."

"All right, I will give it a try." She puffed out her cheeks and rolled her tongue to try to imitate the sound. *Birrr. Cheep, Cheep.*

"Lucy, that is terrible. Take another breath and try to use the air between your cheeks. Now cup your hands to your mouth." He wrapped her hands in his and tried to place them, so they created an echo effect against her lips.

She looked up at him with her big, green eyes and her cheeks adorably puffed.

She made that same, pathetic *cheep, cheep* sound that did not sound like a bird at all.

"Donal, that one is too hard for me. Do you know another?"

He nodded, for he knew them all. "Try this one, the call of a warbler."

She botched it.

"All right. Here's the call of a thrush."

Equally dismal.

"A wren."

No.

"Try the pipit."

No again.

"The finch."

She tried to mimic it to no avail.

"Try the tit."

"The what?"

"The...never mind. It is a common variety of bird. I was not referring to your..." He cleared his throat. "Here, try the owl." He made hooting sounds.

"Hoot. Hoot."

"Better, but not quite. You cannot sound like a person imitating a bird. You have to be the bird."

She sighed. "I think I can do better mimicking a duck or a goose."

"All right. Give it a try."

She quacked.

"Try the goose."

She honked.

He bit the side of his cheek to keep from laughing.

He wanted to kiss her, he surely did. "That one is best. Be the goose."

"And what will you be?"

"The thrush." He made the call of a male thrush. "When you hear it, respond with your honk. I will find you. Do not come out of your hiding spot."

She practiced her goose honk several times more but stopped when he started laughing again.

"Is it that awful, Donal?" She appeared dismayed.

"No. It is perfect. But do not practice it out in the wild, or you will have every randy gander in the south of England flocking to your call."

She rolled her eyes and honked at him again.

He responded with his own thrush call.

They both started laughing.

Lord, her mirthful trill sounded sweet.

Several hours passed before Sam returned.

Donal was starting to worry, but he dared not show it, or else Lucy would be alarmed. He needed to keep her calm and both of them thinking clearly. What he also needed to do was forget the sinfully delicious way her skin felt against his lips.

Or how tempting she'd looked while trying to make those bird calls.

One would think big eyes and puffed-out cheeks would look quite unattractive. But on her, it was all he could do to refrain from kissing her.

Of course, he would not do it.

Not even a day had passed since Edgeware's ball and the attempt on Lucy's life. He had already broken every important rule of an agent of the Crown; the first and most obvious being do not think with your heart.

How was he to avoid it where Lucy was involved?

Everything about her charmed him.

Her ugly ballgown.

Her bookish nature.

Her ridiculous bird calls.

Her vulnerable heart.

"I know plans are a little more scrambled than you like," Sam told him after apologizing for his late return and explaining the arrangements he had made for them. "You will have to don your disguise as coachman and drive your carriage south. My son will be waiting for you by Lord Cranbrook's orchard. He'll be hiding in the copse by the bend in the stream where it runs past the orchard. Stop the carriage. Head to the copse as though you intend to take a piss."

He turned to Lucy. "Begging your pardon."

She cast Sam an earnest smile. "No offense taken. Please, do go on."

"Donal, hand your coat, hat, and the straw stuffing to my son, who will then drive off with the carriage to Dover. I have tethered two horses by the bridge near the old mill. That spot is safe enough. No one goes there now that the mill has been abandoned."

"And what of me?" Lucy asked.

"You are to put these on." He handed her a white mobcap

and apron. "Do you know how to hang up the wash to dry?"

She blushed lightly. "Yes, I've done it often enough. But at this hour? Isn't the wash usually put up in the morning?"

"It will not draw attention. This is a busy inn, and we often put out a second load of washing in the summertime when the sun is out until all hours."

Donal frowned. "Lucy, you have done this maid's chore? The Lessings allowed it?"

"They did not force me to do any menial work, but the maids and Cook were very nice to me and would allow me to chat with them while they worked. Especially when my parents were not around. We would fall into easy conversation, and they could not refuse me if I insisted on helping them out. I tried to be discreet about it because I did not want them to get into trouble."

He noted the pained expression in Lucy's eyes and wanted to kick himself for his stupidity. Of course, this ignored girl with a big, sweet heart would be desperate for any crumb of affection. He expected the Lessing servants felt quite sorry for her. "Never mind. It works in our favor. Here, let me help you with that cap."

"This is a ruse to get you out of the inn itself," Sam explained. "However, you will actually have to do the work."

"I don't mind."

He nodded. "Once the wet sheets are up to hide you, then you are to run into the woods behind the inn and make your way west to the bridge by the old mill. I will point you in the right direction. You cannot miss it. Hide there until Donal comes for you."

Donal finished tucking her curls under the cap and gripped her lightly by the shoulders. "If I am not to you by nightfall, take one of those horses and ride as fast as you can to where I told you."

"What if you are hurt? How can I leave you?"

"That is entirely the point. If those villains somehow catch up to me, then I want you nowhere near me. You need to save yourself, Lucy. All our efforts are pointless if they catch you. I want your promise on this. Say it."

Her voice shook, and he knew he had upset her, but this was no game and keeping her alive was all that mattered. "Say it, Lucy."

"I promise." She looked ready to cry.

He kissed her lightly on the cheek. "I'll see you soon."

She put a hand to her cheek, softly touching the spot where he had kissed her.

Lord, he had to stop making these small mistakes.

The ostler was waiting for him with the carriage at the ready. "The horses have been fed and tended. They're good to go for hours," he said as Donal lumbered toward him in his coachman's disguise.

"Thank you, Mel. Just be sure you keep quiet about my ever being here and where I'm headed."

"Never saw ye," he said with a ribald laugh.

Donal knew he had to get word to Wooton about this man. Not to say he had betrayed anyone…yet. But there was something in his manner that put Donal off. Mel used to be a reliable worker who minded his own business and received good wages for it. But there was a predatory look in his eyes now, something that warned this man could be bought. What had changed in him?

He wasn't going to worry about it now.

In fact, using Mel to provide those assailants false information worked in his favor.

Donal drove the carriage southward through the town, maintaining a steady clip until he reached the orchard. There was the copse, just as Sam had told him. He drew on the reins and brought the horses to a stop.

He climbed down and made his way to the cluster of trees growing beside the stream The warm breeze rustled through the leaves. The water was little more than a gentle flow at this point in its meandering course through the quiet countryside.

Donal had kept a pistol hidden within his sleeve and now

slipped it into his hand. He trusted Sam and knew his lad could also be trusted. But it did not hurt to stay cautious. "Mr. Brayden," young Dickon said in an urgent whisper. "Over here."

The lad was no more than sixteen years old but already as tall as Donal and equally broad in build. He quickly looked around to make certain this was not a trap. Once satisfied, he took off his disguise and helped Dickon put on the oversized cloak, properly securing the stuffing at the belly, and then helped the lad fix his hat so that none of his blonde hair showed.

Donal's hair was dark, almost the color of coal.

A hint of yellow peeking out, and the assailants would immediately know they had been duped. "Be very careful, Dickon. Do not remove that hat for any reason until you reach Dover. But before you remove it, find yourself a crowded tavern. Let yourself be seen but do not do anything to bring more than casual notice to yourself. Afterward, find a quiet spot where you can take off your disguise and hide it well, then make your way home. Do you need any funds?"

"No, Mr. Brayden. My da's taken care of that for me. Good luck to ye."

"And to you." He patted the lad on the back, waited several minutes to make certain he had not been followed, and then made his way to the old mill bridge. Having to keep to the woods slowed him down, as did his inability to shorten his route by cutting through town.

There was no help for it since he could not risk being seen.

The sun was beginning to sink on the horizon by the time he reached the bridge. There was an oppressive stillness to the hot, summer air, as was usual at this time of the day. The horses were not in sight, although he doubted they would have been left out in the open. Likely they were left loosely tethered in the shaded woods beside the stream.

However, he was less concerned about them than of finding Lucy.

Had she made it here safely?

Found the horses?

He put his hands to his lips and made the call of a thrush.

He heard nothing and tried the distinctive trill again. "Lucy," he whispered, "come on. Where are you?"

After what seemed an eternity but could not have been more than the count of five, he heard the responsive honk of a goose. His heart eased as he quietly slipped through the brush toward the sound and came upon the horses first.

Lucy could not be far away.

He made his bird call again.

She honked again.

He knew exactly where she was. "Smart girl," he muttered to himself, heading for the slight dip in the hill and the rocks beside it.

He ought to have called to her, but he preferred to make certain it was her and not a trap.

The fallen leaves muffled his footstep, and he easily made his way behind her. She was crouched beside a rock, trying to peek over it to find him. He wanted to laugh out loud...or just wrap her in his embrace because he recognized the distinctive, red leather tome at her feet, which she had carefully propped against the rock.

Lucy was so desperate to find love, to understand why and how people bonded to each other, that she would not risk losing *The Book of Love*.

It was endearing, and at the same time heartbreaking, that she should feel the need to keep it with her at every step.

This girl deserved to be loved wholly and unconditionally.

He came up behind her, pulled her into his arms, and placed his hand over her mouth to prevent her from crying out. "Lucy, it's me. Sorry if I scared you. I had to be sure no one was holding you at the point of a pistol."

She calmed immediately and threw her arms around him when he released her. "What took you so long?"

"I had to walk back here while keeping off the main roads.

Are you all right?"

She nodded. "I passed the time reading, but I was too worried about you to concentrate on the passages. I have no idea what I read."

"You'll have plenty of time once we reach Weymouth. Grab your book, and let's go. We have to ride as far from here as we can before nightfall. The paths are too dark to safely travel once the sun sets. I'll also need to find us a safe place to camp out."

"All right, but I'm afraid I will slow you down. I am not an accomplished rider. However, I can ride. Just not very well."

He nodded. "Do your best, Lucy. I think we'll both breathe easier once we are away from here."

He held her hand to lead her to the horses, then suddenly stopped and motioned for her to keep quiet.

She nodded and cast him an uncertain look as he led her back behind the rocks. Someone was coming their way. More than one rider, he realized as the approaching hoofbeats grew louder. He eased the pistol out of the lip of his boot.

Lucy knelt beside him, holding her breath.

He put a finger to his mouth, motioned for her to stay put, and then crept closer to the bridge to catch a glimpse of these riders.

Somehow, he was not surprised to see Mel, the ostler. But who were these other two he was meeting? One was a woman who appeared to be about forty years of age, and the other, a gentleman who was slightly older.

Both were finely garbed.

What were they doing with the likes of Mel?

"I told ye, he didn't have the girl with him," Mel said, sounding quite testy. "Brayden took the carriage about two hours ago and drove south to Dover. I inspected it, and she wasn't in there. Now I want my money. I gave ye the information."

"You gave us nothing," the woman said, obviously enraged.

The man beside her tried to calm her down. "Andrea, we know they are on their way to Dover. He must have her.

Wooton put this Brayden fellow to guard her. The man would not pass her off to someone else. So, she must be in the carriage. A secret compartment, perhaps? We must catch up to them."

"Not before ye give me what ye owe me," Mel groused.

"Very well," the woman said, "here is what you deserve."

She drew out a pistol and shot Mel.

"Andrea!" The man beside her became panicked. "What have you done?" He quickly dismounted to check on Mel's wounds. "You've killed him, you fool. Now everyone will be after us."

"They won't ever know we were here. They'll blame it on this Brayden fellow. Come on, let's ride for Dover."

"What about that man?"

She shrugged. "His friends will find him eventually."

They gave Mel not another thought as they rode off together southward.

Donal waited until they were out of sight, then put his ear to the ground and listened until he was no longer able to hear the echo of pounding hooves.

He then returned to Lucy, who was huddled behind the rocks, her arms around herself and her eyes wide.

How much had she seen? "Lucy, are you all right?"

She nodded.

"Come on, let's go."

He took her hand to lead the way to their horses. One was a gentle, dapple gray mare and the other a deep-chested gelding.

Lucy looked up at him as he was about to lift her onto the mare. "Donal, who is Andrea?"

"I have no idea. I was hoping you might know."

She shook her head. "Never heard the name before."

"Here, let me tuck the book into this travel pouch, and then we ought to ride hard away from here."

"What about the ostler?"

He shook his head. "Sam will find him soon enough. I'm sorry, Lucy. He's dead, and we cannot take the time for him."

She looked pained but made no protest.

"I knew there was something off about Mel," he said, keeping an eye on her to make certain she would not start falling apart as they passed his lifeless body. "I was going to write to Wooton to warn him about the man. No point in it now."

Lucy emitted a ragged breath. "Samuel told me this gray is called Rose Petal, and the roan you are riding is Fancy. Oh, Donal. It feels so cruel to just leave him there."

He did not know what to say, so he just urged them on. They needed to put as much distance as possible between them and Samuel's inn before the sun went down.

They spoke no more and rode off.

Lucy turned out to be a fairly good rider and grew more comfortable with her gray as the time wore on. The pretty mare was gentle and grew accustomed to Lucy fairly quickly.

He was pleased.

They would make good time to Weymouth at this pace.

As the sun went down, Donal knew they had to find shelter. Fortunately, Sam had packed food and more cider to last them for the night and into tomorrow. Finding provisions was one less problem to worry about. "Lucy, we will have to camp out tonight. We are still too close to Tunbridge Wells to risk stopping at an inn."

She nodded. "I can survive it."

He cast her a tender smile. "If we do not tarry in the morning, we should reach Brighton by tomorrow evening. I'll find us lodgings. It should not be too difficult to find a quiet inn on the outskirts. However, I cannot leave you unguarded."

"What do you mean?"

He cleared his throat. "I'll have to register us as husband and wife and request only one room."

He waited for the protest, but she merely nodded again. "Sharing a room with you seems wisest. Until we know who these villains are and why they want me, I would much prefer to have you within arm's reach."

"Thank you, Lucy. It is exactly how I feel. You are my responsibility, and I am not going to let anything bad happen to you. Just so you are aware, it'll take more than a day to reach my grandfather's estate in Weymouth. More like three or four, depending on the weather."

"I understand. This means we'll have to share a room each night."

"Yes. My plan is to stop in the busier towns along the way. The more people around and the more inns to accommodate them, the less likely we are to be noticed and remembered."

"What happens when we reach Weymouth?"

"Hopefully, my grandfather's house is in decent condition. My brother Shayne has been appointed executor of his estate. But that only happened recently, and with all that went on in Taunton with the Earl of Monkton's brother and his nasty group of friends, I doubt Shayne has had much time to attend to the Weymouth house. Grandfather had grown a bit eccentric in his waning years, so I'm not sure in what condition we'll find it now."

"We shall manage," she assured, pursing her lips in thought.

"I think Shayne kept the caretaker and his wife on after our grandfather's death. Vandals would have grabbed everything of value down to the hearthstones and panes of glass if they thought it was abandoned."

"Then we won't be alone in the house? Do you think they can be trusted?"

He nodded. "Yes, the Gentry family won't give us away. They'll be discreet and run errands for us since we will not be able to go into town ourselves for fear of being seen."

They had slowed their horses to a walk as they spoke, for they were also quietly making their way through a wooded glade in search of a decent place to settle for the night. He knew what he was looking for—a flat patch of grass not far from a running stream and isolated from any town.

He was also looking for trees with sturdy leaves to provide a canopy for them on the chance it rained. "Let's stop here, Lucy."

"All right. You must be quite spent. I don't think you've gotten more than an hour's rest since yesterday."

"I am a little tired," he admitted. "But let's eat first while there is a sliver of daylight left. I dare not risk lighting a campfire."

"I'll set out the meal while you tend to the horses," she suggested. "Does that sound like a workable plan?"

"Yes." He helped her down, and both of them quickly attended to their chores. He liked being around Lucy, liked her helpful, no-nonsense manner. Not that she was prim or priggish or rigid. No, she was a soft, little thing and seemed to take pleasure in helping out.

Most of the people he had been charged to guard were peers of the realm and not used to lifting a finger for themselves. It was a pleasure guarding Lucy. In truth, he wished he could do everything for her. She deserved to be spoiled.

Once he had settled the horses for the night, making certain they'd been fed and given sufficient water to drink, he sat beside her. "What do we have here?" he remarked, eyeing the savory pie and apples she had set out.

"It is a mince pie. Would you care for some cider?"

He nodded.

"We also have sweet dumplings, but I thought we should save those for tomorrow morning."

"Sounds like a good plan." He smiled in approval.

She cast him a bright smile in return.

They ate in silence since they needed to eat fast and clean up before the sun completely faded. He did not know what animals were about—probably no big, ferocious ones. Still, he did not want their campsite to be overrun by squirrels, birds, and other small creatures feasting on their crumbs.

When they had cleared away the food, he sought to make pallets for them since Sam had not packed any blankets. Even though August was a warm month and today had been quite hot, the temperature would cool overnight. By morning, they would be shrouded in mist. He was used to it but expected it would chill

Lucy to the bone. "You had better use my jacket as a makeshift blanket."

She took it from his hands, frowning. "What about you? Won't you be cold?"

"No. I'll manage. But I want you to sleep by my side. I need to keep you close. The better to protect you. I will not do anything untoward. You are my responsibility, and I take my duties quite seriously."

"I understand. You need not worry about offending me. I shall not flutter about and worry about being compromised. I would rather spend each night beside you than be dead and not have to worry about anything any longer."

The thought of lying beside her each night seemed rather splendid. Of course, his mind immediately went to baser thoughts because Lucy was beautiful, and he wanted to devour her, even though she did not know it.

Blessed saints.

He was one of the Crown's best agents.

Smart. Strong. Disciplined. Able to endure all manner of hardships.

Was all his training enough to resist this lovely girl?

CHAPTER SIX

DONAL DID NOT have long to dwell on lustful thoughts before he fell fast asleep. To his dismay, he had slept deeper and more soundly than he ought to have done while on guard duty. This is what came of trying to stay alert on one hour's rest over the span of two days.

This is also what came of struggling with feelings he should not be having. It had nothing to do with that stupid book Cammy had thrust at him, and Lucy was now poring over because she wanted to know how it felt to be loved.

Perhaps once this assignment was over, he would stop behaving like a ridiculously protective ape about her, stop thinking of her as beautiful, and stop thinking of her at all.

It was not as though he would be abandoning her to a cruel fate. Once the danger had passed, the Duke of Wooton would recognize her as his daughter, and she would become a much sought-after prize among the *ton*.

Indeed, she was likely to forget about him long before he ever forgot her.

In truth, he did not think he would ever forget her.

The first streaks of light came over the horizon to signal the oncoming dawn. He turned to study Lucy, barely making out the soft curves of her body amid the mist, despite her nearness.

Those gray tendrils enveloped both of them but would burn away as soon as the sun rose high enough in the sky to heat the cool ground.

Lucy had inched to his side sometime in the night and was nestled in a curled ball against him. His jacket was tucked around her so that only her face peeked out above the collar. She *snorfled* in mild protest when he eased away to take care of his morning necessities. However, she did not wake and quickly fell quiet again.

He washed up in the stream, then saw to the horses.

After tending to them, he saddled both and left them to graze along the grassy bank.

The mist, much thinner now, still lingered on the ground, hovering over their campsite and more thickly over the water. This helped hide their campsite from anyone passing by. "Lucy," he said, coming to her side and gently shaking her shoulder to wake her. "Time to go."

She turned to him with a sleepy smile, but after a moment, remembered where they were and why they were on the run. "Oh, of course." She scampered to her feet too quickly and stumbled as she got herself twisted in his jacket.

"Easy!" He caught her in his arms to steady her and held onto her several moments longer than necessary because her body was soft and warm. He did not seem able to resist this tempting girl. "We'll leave whenever you are ready. But do you mind if we eat while riding? It should not be too difficult to munch on an apple or eat a dumpling while in the saddle, and I am eager for us to be on our way."

She nodded. "Whatever you think best. Just let me tend to myself. I'll be quick about it."

"Take your time. With the mist still on the ground, I don't need you tripping and falling. I've saddled the horses. We'll leave whenever you are ready."

She finished quickly, having only her hair left to be brushed and properly pinned up. "Let me help you with that," he said, coming to her side.

Her eyes crinkled with mirth. "Ah, my lady's maid. Thank

you. You do a far better job than I ever will."

As she angled her head to give him better access to the stray wisps, his gaze settled on her slender neck and the light chain around it...and the way it fell between her breasts. He ached to run his lips and tongue over her delicate skin, trace a path toward that sweet reward.

Lord, he was going to have to jump in the stream again to cool himself down if he did not stop thinking of her in this way. "Done. Let's go."

He helped her onto the saddle, stifling a groan because the sensation of her lithe, warm body beneath his palms shot flames through him. "Do you want a dumpling or an apple?"

"I'll take an apple. Oh, dear. Your voice sounds a little...gritty. I hope you are not coming down with—"

"I am perfectly fine. Throat's a little dry. That is all." He took a dumpling for himself, mounted Fancy, and led them westward through the glade. The rest of the day passed uneventfully. However, he remained ever watchful and led them off the path a time or two to avoid other riders.

It was nearing dark by the time they reached the quaint market town of Arundel with its towering castle to mark the seat of the powerful Duke of Norfolk. Although the town was not directly on the coast, it was close enough to the water to catch the scent of brine in the air. By the banners flying, he could tell the duke was not presently in residence.

Too bad.

He knew the man and could have imposed on him to give them shelter for the night. But without him present, Donal dared not appear at his door with Lucy. In truth, there was no need. There were plenty of quaint inns along the coastline where one could discreetly spend the night.

They continued southward to a seaside town not far from Arundel. "I know you are tired, Lucy. But we won't be riding much longer now."

As darkness fell, he followed the torchlights and found an inn of good reputation with a fine kitchen. It overlooked the English Channel, which took them a little out of the way but was safer than staying in town where he might be recognized from his past assignments in protecting the Duke of Norfolk.

He signed them in under a false name, paid for their best room, and ordered their meals brought up to them. The bed linens were clean and the bed large enough to accommodate both of them, but that was not going to happen. "You'll have the bed, Lucy. I will set up a pallet for myself by the hearth, but not until we've finished our supper and the maid has cleared away our plates."

She nodded as she lit the lone lamp, then smiled in satisfaction at the soft glow of amber light illuminating the room. "I would suggest you needn't set up a pallet at all. We could easily share the bed. Um, I don't mean it in any way other than…well, I suppose it is not a good idea. What I mean to say is that it is more important for you to get a good night's sleep and be at your best to protect me. I should be the one to take the pallet by the hearth."

"We'll figure it out later," he said as the maid came in with their food.

"Mr. Markby, did ye have no bags with ye?" the girl asked, using the false name he'd given and realizing they had come in with nothing but the clothes on their backs and a small travel pouch.

"As I told the innkeeper, our carriage broke down several miles back. We can manage for one night without a change of clothes since we are only going as far as Plymouth. It is our home." He winked at the girl. "I shall happily help my wife shed her clothes if she finds them cumbersome."

The girl tittered and scurried away.

Lucy's cheeks were pink. "Honestly, Donal. Now she will think we are…"

He tucked a finger under her chin and grinned. "She will think we are randy newlyweds who ought to be left to themselves. Just be warned, the reason I always succeed in my assignments is that I use whatever tools are at hand. If we have to be caught in a kiss to look convincing, be ready for it and play the part of an infatuated young bride."

"You would kiss me?"

He nodded. "If the situation called for it."

Her eyes widened. "Um…that could be a problem. You see, I have never been kissed before. Is there something I ought to know? Something that would give my inexperience away?"

His body tensed.

Of course, how could he forget this girl had been touched by no one ever? "No secret. Should the need arise, just put your arms around my neck and let me do all the work. Let's eat. I'm starved."

"Me, too."

The room had a small table and two chairs.

Lucy appeared a little bit dazed as she sank into hers. Perhaps it was fatigue catching up to her or his stupid comment about possibly having to kiss her.

And now that he'd raised the possibility, he could think of nothing else.

Lord, why could he not get these thoughts about her out of his mind?

They ate in silence, not merely because the quail in a honey glaze served with leeks and potatoes was excellent, but because he spent the time silently chiding himself, while Lucy obviously spent the time wondering how a kiss would feel.

Did she have to be so obvious in her expression?

Finally, she broke the silence. "Is there anything you can tell me about these assassins and why they are on my trail?"

"No, Lucy. Not yet. Just be patient, and I will tell you everything I know once we are in Weymouth. Truly, it is complicated information and not something I can blithely reveal to you, especially because you are clever and thoughtful. If you were a peahen, I might have been persuaded. But you are not."

"Then these secrets you are holding back are things that will hurt me?"

He set down his fork and took a sip of the ale the maid had brought up for him. Lucy had preferred cider. "It may be hurtful. The honest answer is, I simply do not know how you will take the news. It could come as a relief to you. It may answer a lot of questions for you and will certainly raise several more."

She swallowed a bite of her quail. "Donal, you've told me nothing."

"I am not trying to be difficult, believe me. I will be much happier once we can talk openly about your situation."

They finished their meal in silence.

When they were done, Donal put their plates outside their door and then latched it shut.

Lucy poured some water from the ewer into the basin, grabbed the soap, and began to wash up before retiring to bed. "I suppose I must sleep another night in my gown. Well, Cammy's gown. It isn't even mine."

"You'll be more comfortable with it off. Can you not sleep in just your shift? I'll help you with the laces but otherwise will keep my back turned. Indeed, it is a good idea. I am not the only one who needs a good night's sleep. You need to be just as refreshed and alert. You'll be tossing and turning uncomfortably all night if that gown stays on you."

She cast him a cynical stare.

"Fine, it was just a suggestion. You are my assignment. I am a professional. Nothing untoward will happen." How many times had he assured her of this already?

If only he could believe it himself.

But Lucy would never trust him again if he stepped out of line. Keeping her safe was all that mattered.

"All right," she said in a whisper and turned so that he could assist her with the laces. "But promise you will keep your back turned while I wash up and slip into bed."

"I will. I promise." He tried not to breathe her in while he undid her ties. Despite the hours of hard riding, she still carried the scent of honey and nectar-sweet dew. He also tried not to notice as she took the pins out of her hair and shook out the long, tumbling mane.

"Hand me the gown," he said, reaching his arm out while he was turned away. "I will hang it up for you."

The distracting chore took not even a minute.

He folded his arms across his chest and tried not to listen to the sound of water falling upon her skin as she resumed washing up. Everything had a distinctive sound. The sucking *whoosh* as she lowered her washing cloth into the basin. The dripping *whoosh* as she wrung out the excess water. The whisper of a *whoosh* as she lathered the cloth with a lavender-scented soap and slid it along her arms…her neck…her bosom.

Lord help him, he could tell every spot on her body that she washed…and she was washing her entire body.

The scent of lavender now filled the room along with the sweet, female scent of her. When had his senses ever been so finely attuned to a woman? He was as aroused as a rutting boar, his nose picking up the scent of a desirable female with whom he wished to mate. "Are you almost done, Lucy?"

He hoped he had not sounded harsh.

She was doing nothing wrong.

He was the one who needed to keep his mouth shut and chase the wanton thoughts out of his head.

"I'm done. Just give me a moment, and I will hop into bed. Oh…but I still think you ought to be the one to sleep here. We'll switch when you are finished washing up."

"Stay there, Lucy. I am not taking the bed. I am—"

She giggled. "I know. You are a professional. I am your assignment."

He shook his head and emitted a low rumble of laughter. "But I will take a pillow and the counterpane if you can spare it."

"Yes, of course."

"Close your eyes while I undress."

"All right. They are closed. How much are you taking off?"

"Everything."

She squealed and buried her head under her pillow.

He emitted another soft laugh.

A clean washing cloth had been set out for him, so he used it and the lavender soap to wash the day's layer of dust off him. He also washed his hair since it was easy enough to do with the plentiful water.

The night was warm, and there was a soft breeze off the water, so he kept the window open and moved Lucy's gown next to his shirt, hanging both up beside the window to freshen them out. He had removed all his clothes while washing up but now donned his trousers. He would sleep in them, for he could not risk jumping up naked off his pallet if something startled them awake.

He needed Lucy to be ready to run or duck down or hide, not stand there gawking at his dangling, male parts.

The moon was full and silvery, partially obscured by thin streaks of clouds. The sky was mostly clear, not shrouded in fog yet, and he could see a blanket of shimmering stars invade the blackness of the night.

Lucy sat up in bed. "It is beautiful, is it not? Do you mind if I come to your side to look out the window? Just for a little while. I have never been to the sea before."

"All right. Come here." He hadn't meant to open his arms to her and doubted she had meant to step into them. But there they were, suddenly in a position they dared not be.

He turned her so that her back was to his chest, and she looked outward to the water. She rested her head against his shoulder. "Listen to the waves, Donal. Is it not the most soothing sound you have ever heard?"

"Yes, it is."

She closed her eyes and inhaled. "This is what *The Book of Love* meant when discussing the five senses. I don't mean in a romantic sense because…" She turned slightly to glance up at him, smiling impishly. "Not in a romantic sense because you are a professional, and I am merely your assignment. But one's senses come alive at a moment like this. Can you smell the lavender of our soap and the way it mingles with the salt air? And the soft, calming rhythm of the waves?"

She sighed and continued. "I've never seen a moon so big and silvery before."

"It is quite impressive."

"Yes, very." She remained in his arms as they stood by the window and studied the stars. He had not meant to wrap his arms around her but had no intention of drawing them away yet. Perhaps another minute or two. Then he would suggest she return to bed.

She mentioned it first. "I had better turn in. How early a start do you wish to get?"

"Right after sunrise. All right?"

She nodded along with a yawn. "Good night, Donal."

"Sweet dreams, Lucy."

He checked his pistols and kept them within close reach.

"Donal?"

"Yes, Lucy," he replied, watching her climb into bed and slide her delicious body between the sheets.

"You've been meticulous in setting out your weapons. Do you think those villains will find us tonight?"

"Doubtful."

"Then I shall sleep like a lamb knowing I have you to protect me."

He was glad she found comfort in his presence. But he was not as comfortable as he would have liked. While staring out over the sea, he'd noticed a flashing light, a signal of some sort coming from a vessel on the water, quickly followed by the flash of a responsive signal from the inn.

He doubted it was the villains having found them.

Most likely, it was smugglers.

Still, he did not like that there would be this sort of activity going on tonight.

What was being smuggled?

And had any of them noticed him and Lucy watching?

CHAPTER SEVEN

AFTER LUCY FELL asleep, Donal put a chair against the door and balanced the ewer atop it knowing it would smash to the floor if anyone attempted to enter their chamber. But come morning, it still remained where he had placed it, precariously perched upon the chair.

He breathed a sigh of relief as he quietly rose and gathered his pillow and counterpane to place those items back atop the bed. He then moved the ewer off the chair, returned it to the tabletop, and placed the chair back in its place by the table.

Lucy was still asleep, her lovely form outlined beneath the sheet. She seemed so at peace, like a kitten curled in a ball while lost in a deep slumber. This appeared to be the way she liked to sleep, tucked in and curled up. It felt odd for him to know this and yet somehow right that he should.

Once dressed, he returned to her side and gently shook her awake. "Lucy, the sun is up. It's time for us to go."

"All right. Give me a moment." She yawned, still unable to open her eyes. "It feels like we just fell asleep."

"I know. Unfortunately, we have another long ride ahead of us."

She nodded and sleepily sat up.

The sheet slipped down around her waist to reveal the warm pink of her skin. The fabric of her shift was not quite sheer but thin enough to reveal more than he ought to see. He moved away before he was tempted to slip it off her and do some more savoring of her body.

He crossed the room to grab her gown and strode back to hand it to her. "I'll lace you up when you're ready."

The shift had ridden up to her thighs, and he saw a good length of her shapely legs as she tossed aside the sheet and stood. "Thank you. But can you give me a moment of privacy?"

He nodded. "I'll be standing right outside the room."

While by their door, he took a moment to peer downstairs to see if anyone was stirring yet. He heard muffled voices from the inn's common room, but it sounded as though the inn's staff was talking among themselves. He heard the mention of the fake name he'd given the innkeeper and immediately tensed.

"Do ye think he saw anything?" he heard the innkeeper say.

A young woman answered, and he recognized her voice as that of the maid who had attended them last night. "Maybe, but I don't think he will report us."

"How can ye be sure about it, Maisie?"

"Because I don't think they are married, at least not to each other. A man doesn't burn with longing like that for his own wife."

Blessed saints.

Had he been that obvious?

"I think he's stolen her away, whether just for the night or they plan to run away together, I don't know. But he'll have a lot of explaining to do if he dares report us because we'll tell on him and the pretty lady he's brought here."

"Well, I'm going to watch them closely," the innkeeper said. "They don't leave here alive unless I'm convinced ye're right."

"Don't be stupid," another woman said, now joining the conversation. She sounded older and was perhaps the innkeeper's wife. "We'll be caught for certain if they turn up dead. I think Maisie's right. They've come here to hide from her family and ain't going to tell nobody anything. Besides, we pay the local patrol well enough to look the other way. Even if they report us, who's going to do anything about it? Certainly not Captain Brockhurst."

Donal wanted to make his way downstairs and listen to more of their conversation now that they had moved away, and he could no longer hear them. But there did not appear to be any guests down yet, and they would suspect him for certain if he was found roaming on his own at this hour.

The sun was up, but it was barely sunrise.

It would not be too long before the inn's other guests began to stir, especially if they had a distance to travel. Only then would he dare head downstairs with Lucy. Even though he did not like to be seen more than necessary, in this instance, they would be safest in a crowd.

Lucy opened the door to let him back in a few moments later. She had donned her shoes and done up her hair, leaving only the gown to be laced. "Donal, you are pursing your lips and frowning. Is something wrong?"

"I'm not sure." He turned her slightly to get a better angle on the lacings. "Nothing to do with your assailants. But I think the innkeeper is involved in smuggling. He or one of his men might have seen us at the window last night, and now he is worried we are going to report them."

"But we didn't see anything. We were looking at the moon."

"We were also looking at the water."

She studied his face and inhaled sharply. "You did see something, didn't you?"

He nodded. "I was not going to tell you, but I think I had better since we may be about to walk into something unintended."

She paled. "How are we to get out of it?"

He took her hand in his. "We may have to stage a scene."

"What do you mean?"

"The way out of this potential coil is to wait for the maid, Maisie, to come up here and listen in at our door, which we are going to keep slightly ajar while preparing to leave."

She nodded. "Then what?"

"You are going to whisper something about having to get back to your family before they find out about us. At some point, you can also mention your father does not approve of me. But do not throw in too much information at once, or they'll sense it is rehearsed."

"All right. I will do my best. What if she starts to ask specific questions? Who is my father? Where do I live? How did you sneak me out from under his nose? How will you get me back home before he notices I am missing? What if I am caught in a lie?"

He caressed her cheek. "Lucy, stay calm. I think we are better off letting our actions speak for us."

"What do you mean?"

"It may also become necessary for me to kiss you. In truth, I think this is the easiest solution since you are not a trained agent, nor are you used to talking your way out of a tense situation. Just let me kiss you and do all the talking."

She nodded again, this time hesitantly. "There is one flaw in your plan."

"What is that?"

"As you know, no one has ever kissed me before. What should I expect? And what should I do? They'll catch onto us if I appear to be a novice, won't they?"

He was not surprised by her remark.

Perhaps he should have done something about it last night because everything about her did scream she was a girl untouched.

His heart turned soft as he took her into his arms. "You have a point."

He was trying to keep himself collected, but the thought of kissing Lucy affected him more than he liked to admit. Even though he was experienced, there was something about this little bluestocking that made him want to make the moment their lips touched perfect for her. "I am going to kiss you once, so you know what it feels like and are prepared for what happens when I do."

"What is supposed to happen?"

"If I do it right, your insides will melt a little. I don't mean actually turn hot and melt. Perhaps it will be more of a fluttering feeling, like butterflies in your stomach. It happens when a woman likes the man she is with. I will kiss you ardently if the situation calls for it. Keep in mind that I am a professional and—"

"I am merely an assignment. I know. It is just pretend. Quick, Donal. I hear footsteps clomping up the stairs. But please make it special. I've always hoped my first kiss would be something to carry in my heart forever."

Blessed saints.

"I will, Lucy. Close your eyes and put your arms around my neck."

He waited for the footsteps to pause at their slightly open door, then lowered his mouth to hers. "I love you," he said, just loud enough for Maisie to hear.

Then his lips descended on Lucy's, and he allowed feelings to pour out of him that he had never released before or ever felt the inclination to release with any other woman of his acquaintance.

But with Lucy…everything felt different.

He felt buffeted upon storm waves as yearning, ache, and a wild, possessive hunger poured out of him, whirled around him, and pounded him with unrelenting force.

Still, he kept his wits about him because Lucy's safety was at stake.

His mouth closed over hers with enough pressure to prevent her from talking because he dared not let her say anything to give them away. His arms closed around her body like iron bands and held her to him as though he was desperate never to let her out of his embrace.

Lucy was trembling by the time he released her. "Hush, sweetheart. Don't cry. We'll see each other again soon, I promise. But you cannot let anyone know we were here together. It is our secret to keep."

She nodded, easily playing along. "I won't breathe a word to anyone. Father will take me away from you if he ever finds out."

"Next time we meet, it will be to run off with you to Gretna Green and truly make you my wife."

She looked up at him with wonder in her eyes. "I'll be ready. I promise."

"Come on, love. I had better sneak you back before anyone in your household grows suspicious. Remember, not a word to anyone about where we have been. We'd better hurry."

He held Lucy's hand and motioned for her to be silent as he listened for Maisie's footsteps scurrying back downstairs.

He waited a minute and then nodded. "Let's go. She will have told the innkeeper what she overheard by now."

Lucy appeared shaken as he led her downstairs. She stood silently beside him, huddled close as he asked the innkeeper to have their horses brought around. He said nothing to ease her apparent distress because it added legitimacy to their ruse.

He would talk to her once they were on the road and apologize for that kiss.

He'd devoured her, and she was unprepared for it.

In truth, neither was he.

They rode off without incident, neither of them speaking until their horses needed to be rested. By this time, they were several hours away from the inn and were nearing Portsmouth. They stopped at a busy tavern on the outskirts of that coastal town. Once they were settled at a private corner table, he turned to her. "Lucy, I am sorry if the kiss was…too much."

She shook her head. "No apology necessary. You had to do it to keep us out of trouble. It was a nice kiss, Donal. I appreciate that you tried to make it special because it was my first."

They ate quietly for the rest of the meal and were on their way again before noontime.

The entire day passed without either of them speaking further of their kiss. Donal did not know whether to say something more to Lucy because he knew she had been affected by it. He did not like her thinking it was merely a necessary deception in the line of his duty. Yet, to have her know she meant something more to him was dangerous.

First of all, he wasn't sure what his feelings were for her exactly.

Second, as she had pointed out from the start, caring for each other would interfere with his cold and calculated thinking and could get them both killed.

Perhaps he should not have added the "I love you" before his lips descended on hers. In truth, he hadn't meant to, but it had just slipped out.

Anyway, it was a good touch and necessary to their ruse.

That's all it could have been.

That's all it should have been.

He went about his business as usual on this last night before they reached his grandfather's property in Weymouth. He found them a respectable coaching inn outside of Portsmouth, ordered their meals brought to their room, made his pallet by the hearth, and avoided mentioning anything other than details of tomorrow's journey.

Fortunately, Lucy spent much of the night reading that book she seemed to find so fascinating. One would think she was studying for exams at Oxford the way she pored over the pages and would occasionally flip back to a passage and then forward again.

Every once in a while, she would look over at him, her brow furrowed in thought, but she never said anything to him. He chose not to start a conversation either. They were a day outside of Weymouth, and he would soon be telling her about the Duke of Wooton and her connection to him, one of England's most powerful men.

He did not know how much convincing she would require.

More important, how would she take the news that her entire existence to this point had been a sham?

Her parents were not really her parents.

Eliza, the sister she loved, was not really her sister.

How could she not be crushed by the revelation?

Nor did he wish to add more upheaval in her life by talking about the kiss that should have been just a fake moment of intimacy between them but had felt shockingly good and far too real for his liking. Try as he might, he could not dismiss it as a mere necessity or forget how exquisitely good she had felt against his lips.

No, she did not need to have that burden piled on her shoulders.

Better to dismiss the kiss as an act in the line of duty.

But she had stirred his heart.

Well, she had stirred something in him.

He was not going to propose marriage or declare his undying love when he could not possibly have strong feelings for her. She was Lucy. She was his assignment. That he liked her brains and body counted for nothing.

That he liked everything about her surely could not be significant.

"Donal, is something wrong?"

Her soft voice sent a ripple of pleasure through him. "No. What makes you think there is something wrong?"

"You are tossing and turning like a pup who cannot seem to curl into a comfortable sleeping position."

Had he been doing that? "Just restless to get to Weymouth."

"I see. You must be quite eager to unload the truth on me and then be done with this assignment."

He sat up. "No, Lucy. You make it sound as though I consider you a chore. You are not that at all and telling you the truth will bring me no relief whatsoever. Nor will it end my assignment. If anything, we are likely to remain together for weeks. Perhaps months."

"I'm sorry."

He met her gaze. "I haven't minded a moment of the time

spent with you. My worry is for your safety and preventing these killers from getting their hands on you. Be assured, I will fight to protect you to my dying breath."

Gad, he'd said that with too much feeling.

But it was true.

He was not going to deny she mattered to him. The only question was how much?

However, she was also his assignment, and this was his role as an agent of the Crown, to risk life and limb in order to keep England and the monarchy safe, even if the attack was not directly aimed at them. Until they understood what was going on, the attempts to murder Wooton and Lucy had to be treated as a threat at the highest levels.

Lucy cast him an impudent smile. "You are far more useful to me alive. Try not to get yourself killed."

He managed a laugh. "I will keep that in mind next time someone points his pistol or tosses fire at us. Put away your book now, Lucy. I would like to be off before the other guests begin to stir come morning."

"All right." She set the tome back in his travel pouch and then doused the lamp by which she had been reading. "It really is a very interesting book, Donal. You ought to read it."

"I know all there is to know about love. I do not need a book to tell me how to please a woman."

She sighed. "It isn't about the act of coupling. It is about making a happy life with the right person to love. It is all about knowing who is right for you and who may appear to be right but is not."

He was not going to get mixed up in that conversation.

He was already struggling with his growing feelings for her.

"Have you ever been in love?" she asked him, the question escaping in the intimate darkness and striking him with a jolt. This is not what he wanted to think about as he fell asleep. He wanted to give her a quick denial but could not seem to form the words or make them pass through his lips.

"Be quiet, Lucy. Turn off that clever brain of yours and get some rest."

He felt her disappointment as though it were a palpable weight upon the air. "All right. But I have never been in love, in case you were curious to know."

"I wasn't."

"I see. Good night."

He heard her ragged breaths.

Blessed saints.

He shut his eyes as though the gesture could make her quiet hurt disappear and not be his problem. She wasn't crying. She was just…he did not know exactly what she was doing other than fighting off a lifetime of hurt. And he had just piled onto it. How could he be so callous to this girl with a heart full of love that no one other than Eliza had ever reciprocated? Eliza, who was not her sister.

And he had just kicked her in the teeth when she tried to open her heart to him.

He could not give in, or he'd end up in bed with her, holding her in his arms and whispering who knows what admissions as he kissed her and explored her body.

The sky was overcast when Donal awoke in turmoil the next morning just before sunrise. Lucy was still asleep. He took pains not to disturb her while he readied himself for the day's ride ahead. However, she must have heard him or sensed him moving about.

She sat up sleepily, her eyes still shut and her mouth in a kissable pout. The sleeve of her shift had slipped off her shoulder to expose the soft warmth of her body. She had taken the pins out of her hair and not bothered to braid it before falling asleep. The lush mane tumbled around her shoulders.

His gaze dipped to her bosom as she emitted a heavy sigh.

The swell of one breast was visible now that the sleeve had slipped down.

She sighed again, and he held his breath, for that gown was

precariously held up at the moment and…no, he could not allow his loins to perform a happy dance. Not now. Not with Lucy.

He cleared his throat. "I wasn't going to disturb you just yet. But since you appear to be awake, how about readying yourself? If we get an early start, we'll reach Weymouth before nightfall."

Her eyes were still closed as she nodded.

"Lucy?"

"Give me a moment. I'm awake, just not all of me yet."

He stifled a smile as he settled on the bed beside her, an utterly bad idea, but his brain did not seem to be functioning with its usual clarity at the moment. "I'm sorry if I was curt with you last night. I did not mean to be so abrupt." He ran his thumb softly over her cheek. "I don't do well when speaking of love, as you may have figured out by now."

She smiled back at him and casually raised the sleeve back over her shoulder. "It was my fault. My question was inappropriate."

"No, Lucy. Once we are in Weymouth, we'll have time to speak of many things." He should not have sat so close to her on the bed. But now that he had, he could not seem to pull away. He could not seem to get enough of her.

Bollocks.

She was doing nothing, and all he could think of was nudging that sleeve back off her shoulder and lowering it further because…why was he suddenly fascinated with her breasts? The swell of them peeking out from the scooped neck of her shift had his body in aching torment.

They were lush and round, perfect for the cup of his hands.

She heaved again lightly, accentuating her cleavage whenever she took a breath, which left him—ironically—breathless.

Gad, was he getting too old for this agent of the Crown work?

His wits were obviously turning dim.

He could not seem to stop stealing glances at her bosom. Perhaps it was that necklace and the way it disappeared into the magnificent valley between her soft mounds that kept pulling his gaze there.

"Donal, are you all right? You seem to be in pain."

He rose and turned away to peer out the window. "No. Just restless. I'll head downstairs while you ready yourself. I'll be back in ten minutes to help you lace the gown. Latch the door behind me."

He could not tear out of there fast enough.

It was too early for a stiff drink, nor could he be so reckless as to guard her while drunk. He ordered a mug of coffee in the hope the brew was strong enough to jolt him out of these unwanted lustful feelings he was having about Lucy.

She was an unassuming bluestocking.

Why did he suddenly feel the urge to ravish her?

It must have been that ill-considered kiss, a necessary ploy to save their lives. That smuggling innkeeper had been thrown off the scent.

Job done.

Kiss served its purpose.

Now all he had to do was forget how splendid her lips had felt against his.

He lingered over his mug of coffee until he'd managed to calm himself down sufficiently. Lucy needed to trust him, and that trust would be shattered if he made an arse of himself over her. Perhaps this was the problem, sharing a chamber with Lucy. It created an intimacy between them that he'd never felt with any assignment before.

But he dared not be apart from her. Separate chambers were not a viable option while those assailants were so close on their heels.

Keeping sight of her was crucial for her safety. Speaking of which, he knew he had better return to her now.

He shook his head to clear the cobwebs in them as he walked out of the inn's still empty common room to return upstairs.

Lucy was ready and waiting for him when he strode in.

She cast him a fragile smile. "I just need to be properly tied up."

"Yes, I'll tie you up…lace you…that is…" His mind immediately filled with thoughts of her that he should not be having.

Base. Crude.

Go-straight-to-hell sinful.

He blinked to regain control of himself.

Silently cursed his inability to expunge them.

Blinked again because Lucy in a state of undress and awaiting his pleasure was now etched in his dissolute mind.

He quickly turned her away, tightened her lacings as though they were burning and his hands were on fire, and then crossed the room to gather their meager belongings. "Are you hungry?"

She nodded.

"The common room was empty a few minutes ago. Most of the guests are not yet up and about. It ought to be safe enough. Let's grab a quick bite while the ostler readies our horses."

Within the half hour, they rode from the inn, now on the final leg of their journey. Donal dared not relax his guard until they were settled in his grandfather's house in Weymouth.

Only then would he tell Lucy about her true identity.

How could she not be devastated by the revelation?

He would have to watch her closely afterward to make certain she did not run off. But once she managed to calm down and accept the truth of her parentage, what were they to do next? Just sit and wait for news the assassins had been captured?

What if those villains remained at large for months?

Worse, what if they figured out where he was hiding Lucy?

Bollocks.

He was never going to let anyone harm her.

If these men were trained professionals, they would know how to wage an assault. They would take him down first and then go after Lucy.

He ran a hand through his hair in consternation.

Please let them be rabble off the London docks, for if they operated like a skilled army regiment, he'd be dead within seconds and unable to protect her.

"Donal, you are frowning again."

"No, just thinking."

She shook her head as they rode along the little-traveled roadway. The sea breeze was cool off the water and dampened the early morning air. "No, Donal. It is more than that. You are worried. I am learning to read your expressions, the little of them you choose to show. Please tell me. Am I not better off knowing what dangers are about to befall us?"

He nodded. "I'm not trying to hide anything from you, Lucy. Just stay close and do not question my orders when I issue them. The slightest hesitation may have disastrous results. Think of this as a war. Them against us. It is a matter of kill or be killed."

"I understand."

"But not everyone has it in them to kill."

"Oh, I see your concern now. You think I do not have it in me to harm another soul."

He regarded her doubtfully. "Are you suggesting that you do?"

"I think I do. I could if they meant to harm you." She shook her head. "However, you are right to be skeptical. I have never hurt anyone before. I don't even know how to use a pistol. Will you teach me?"

"Maybe."

His response obviously surprised her. "Why won't you teach me?"

"I did not say I wouldn't. Only that I might not. Giving you a weapon is only helpful if you intend to use it."

"Oh, I see."

"Do you? Lucy, can you coldly point your pistol at a man's chest and fire it?"

CHAPTER EIGHT

L UCY WAS TIRED and her back, sore, from all their days of hard riding. They were now the only riders on this perilous stretch of road, which was little more than a narrow cliff path. Donal had mentioned it was a back way to his grandfather's home.

She understood, for one had to be a mountain goat to risk using it otherwise.

"It won't be long now," he assured, sensing her fatigue.

But as twilight fell and she caught a view of the brightly colored sky above the windswept wave crests and blue waters swirling perilously below, she took in a breath. There was something quite magnificent about the sun's fading brilliance. The pink and lavender sky reflected on the water, which now resembled a bed of glistening diamonds. The distant rooftops in the town of Weymouth shone with golden splendor. "Donal, it is so beautiful here."

"I always thought so," he murmured as they paused a moment upon the heights. "Wait 'til you see the house. I know you'll like it, as well."

"I'm sure I will. But you are frowning again. Are you worried it has fallen into disrepair? I'm sure it will be fine. The staff wouldn't stay on if they feared the roof would fall atop their heads."

He slowed his pace, no doubt to make certain she would not

have difficulty keeping up with him. "Look, Lucy. There's the place. Do you see it?"

"Yes." It had just come into view, a charming manor built of warm, red stone the same color as the cliffs they had just ridden past. Ivy ran up the facade, and smoke filtered out from one of the chimneys to indicate the place was occupied.

It appeared well kept, but who could tell for certain in the twilight? Everything looked beautiful amid these half shadows of approaching night. She paused a moment to marvel at the colors cast upon the manor's facade and the golden gleam off its roof.

"It is stunning, isn't it?" Donal brought their horses to a halt beside a grove of trees. "Wait here, Lucy. Hold Fancy's reins for me. I'm going to scout the area first. I'm sure there's no danger, but one can never be too careful."

He helped her dismount, gave her hand a little squeeze for reassurance, and then crept off toward the house, disappearing from view in less than the blink of an eye.

Honestly, the man moved like a shadow.

She did not like to be left on her own, but mostly she worried for his safety. However, she knew what he would say if she expressed her concern. *I am a professional, Lucy. I am trained for this assignment.*

The horses restlessly pawed the ground, but she held firmly to their reins and gave each a stroke on the nose to keep them quiet. "He'll be back soon, Rose Petal," she murmured, soothing herself more than her gentle mare.

By the time Donal returned, the colors of the sky had turned a fiery red to signal night was about to fall. "All clear, Lucy."

"You were gone a very long time."

"Sorry if I worried you. It really wasn't that long, but I will admit I took a second turn around the manor house just to be certain I had overlooked nothing." He helped her back onto Rose Petal and then mounted Fancy with such ease, one would think he had been born in the saddle. "Cook's putting supper on for us. Are you hungry?"

She nodded. "Very. You spoke to the cook?"

"Yes. Once I was certain it was safe." He cast her an affectionate grin. "You look tired."

She nodded again. "I am, just a little."

"You've been wonderful. I want you to know how much I appreciate all you've endured. You've been an angel despite how harrowing it has been for you. Not once have you complained."

His comments surprised her. "Why should I complain when you are trying to save my life?"

He shook his head and chuckled lightly. "You have no idea how difficult some people can be. Or how stupid and vapid. We'll have plenty of time to spend at leisure now that we're here. I'll tell you stories that will curl your toes."

She cast him an appreciative smile. "I look forward to it. You've led such an interesting life. I've done nothing of note until you came along and took me from the Duke of Edgeware's party. But this is a little too much excitement for my liking."

"For mine, too, believe me. This is one of the most difficult assignments I've ever had."

"Truly? You've handled everything so adeptly. Nothing seems to rattle you."

"Do you not think that flaming torch tossed in the carriage upset me?"

"I'm sure it did. But you kept your wits and reacted quickly. You've shown concern. Caution. Sometimes irritation. But never fear."

It was obvious the Duke of Wooton counted upon him for these very reasons. Who else could be trusted with the most delicate and often dangerous tasks? "You were also quite splendid while protecting my sister and the Earl of Monkton from his dastardly brother."

He shrugged. "My brothers did most of the work in capturing him."

It was true the fiend was caught before he could pose a serious threat to her or her sister, but this did not detract from the fact Donal had been there, ready to protect them with his life if the need arose.

She had been in utter terror of Monkton's brother killing them all. Donal had kept them calm as he went about his business with icy confidence and assurance.

Nothing scared this man.

They rode directly to the stable which was situated behind the house and downwind of it.

"Horace," Donal said to an older, barrel-chested man with thinning gray hair, who hurried to assist him while they dismounted, "this is Miss Lessing, the young woman I was telling you about."

He nodded. "A pleasure to have ye with us, Miss Lessing. Horace Gentry at yer service. We'll keep ye safe. Never ye fret."

She smiled at Horace. "I appreciate that very much, Mr. Gentry."

"Aw, ye needn't be so formal. I'm just Horace, although on occasion when in town, I do like to tell everyone I'm Gentry. Get it? It is a play on gentry, as in the finer folk, and m'name, Gentry."

Lucy cast him a sincere smile. "I do, and it is quite clever of you. As for finer folk, if you ask my opinion, what you are doing for me is quite heroic. There is no one finer than you and your family in my eyes."

The man blushed. "Ye rest assured, no one's going to harm ye while I'm around."

Donal cleared his throat to remind them not to dawdle.

Even though the place appeared fairly isolated, Lucy understood the need to get into the house before they were seen.

"Horace's wife is our cook and also serves in the role of housekeeper," he said while leading her out of the stable. "I'll introduce you to her next."

"She's an excellent cook, and ye'll want for nothing." Horace patted his rotund belly to emphasize his point.

"Do you go into town for your supplies, or are they delivered here?" Donal asked as they headed toward the kitchen entrance of the imposing manor.

"Wednesday is our delivery day. I'll have my boy take yer horses into the woods that morning and hide them there until the carts have all come and gone. Just make certain to keep away from the windows so ye're not seen, and ye should be all right. No one else comes here. If ye need anything on the other days, one of us can go into town for it."

Donal nodded his approval.

A portly woman with a flushed face and dark hair sprinkled gray was tossing logs onto an already roaring fire in the massive hearth as they entered the kitchen. Her hair was drawn back, a few wisps escaping as she toiled in the heat.

Donal introduced her as Horace's wife.

"A pleasure to meet you, Mrs. Gentry," Lucy said, casting the woman a winning smile. "I am so grateful to you and your husband for harboring me under this roof."

"Please, call me Blanche, or else my husband will never stop with his silly pun about us being gentry and all. I'm sure he's told ye already."

Lucy giggled. "He has."

Blanche rolled her eyes as she hoisted a pot of stew over the blazing fire with surprisingly little effort. "Ye just ring for me if ye need anything, Miss Lessing. Petrina is my daughter and helps out here as a maid. I've sent her upstairs to prepare yer quarters. Have ye met our son yet? His name is also Horace, but we call him Ox. Ye'll understand why when ye see him."

"Thank you, Mrs. Gentry. I mean…Blanche. Since I expect we shall be in close quarters for a while, please call me Lucy. Um…" She turned to Donal to make certain it was all right, for she did not wish to countermand any rules he had set out for the staff. But he merely nodded in approval, so she smiled and continued. "I was never one for formality either. And as you say, we will all be here for a time."

The woman wiped her beefy hands on her apron and cast her a beaming smile. "Master Donal said ye were a sweet thing.

Clever and pretty, too. That's what he said. I can see why."

Lucy turned to Donal in surprise.

He tossed her an appealingly wicked smile and shrugged. "The place has a nice library, Lucy. I'll show it to you after we've settled in."

She tossed him a glowing smile in return. "Be still my heart. I am in love." Then she realized what she had just said, and her stomach curled with embarrassment. "I mean…not that you are my…I love books. I am in love with books."

He ran his knuckle lightly across her cheek in a caressing motion. "I know. It is part of your charm."

Her cheeks turned hot.

She was going to prattle like a squawking goose if she opened her mouth again, so she said nothing and crossed to a quiet corner of the kitchen. Donal was no longer paying attention to her anyway. He'd turned away to dampen a clean cloth at the water pump and now returned to her side while Blanche lumbered out of the kitchen and into the larder to fetch more vegetables. "Tip your head up, Lucy."

She did, looking up into his steel-gray eyes.

He had a wicked glint in them as he tucked a hand under her chin and began to wipe the dust of their day's ride off her face. He paid particularly close attention to her lips, leaning in close as he ran the cloth gently over them.

Was he going to kiss her?

He certainly made it seem as though he was contemplating it.

"Donal," she said quietly, "my mouth is clean now. I think you have removed every last speck of dust from my lips."

"Have I?" He had a naughty expression as he now pressed the cloth to her neck and lightly ran it along her nape. All the while, he kept his face close to hers, his lips a mere hair's breadth from hers.

She felt his warm exhale of air against her mouth.

"Tilt your face up a bit more, Lucy," he said in a husky murmur as he slid the cloth slowly down her throat. Heavens, he was not stopping there but heading lower when Blanche walked back in, and he casually drew his hand away before he was caught doing something naughty.

His back was turned to Blanche so the woman could not see that he was grinning wickedly and concentrating his gaze on the swell of her breasts. No, he couldn't…

Did he just gaze into her cleavage?

Good grief!

He did it again.

Was it possible he was responding to her in a typically low-brain way? Truly? *The Book of Love* seemed to think this low brain was common to all males. But Donal? In a lustful frenzy over her? Or was he merely having a little amusement at her expense? Releasing some of his pent-up tension? They had been on the run for days. Even though he had not shown it, the strain of protecting her must have been quite wearying.

"Give me that cloth, you fiend." She cast him a chiding glance which might have been more effective had a smile not escaped her lips. "I'll take over from here."

He raised it out of her reach. "No."

"No?" He was utterly shameless. "Are you always this irritating? You are having far too much fun at my expense."

"No, Lucy. I am in agony if you must know," he said softly against her ear.

Her eyes rounded in surprise.

Was he really?

How could she possibly be as exciting to his senses as he was to hers? She was a bookish wallflower, and he thought her gowns were ugly. But there was something unmistakably hungry in his expression. "I can tell you why you feel the way you do if you are interested. It is all explained in *The Book of Love*."

"Not that blasted book." He grunted and turned away to pump more water onto the cloth. "Maybe later. Maybe never."

"Fine, remain ignorant." But it did thrill her to see him exhibit these low-brain behaviors over her. She had not expected it, and her body would not stop tingling.

He took her hands in his to wipe off the dust and sweat from her fingers. She had been holding the reins for hours, and they were dirty and beginning to form blisters on the delicate skin.

His hands were rough from years of riding and other labors.

She liked the rugged way they felt against the softness of her palms.

"Now, who is staring?" he teased.

"I was studying your hands. You were looking at…there is a difference in the direction of our gazes."

"Yes, I suppose there was." He tweaked her nose. "Are you hungry?"

She nodded.

"Me, too. How long until the stew is ready, Blanche?" he called over his shoulder. As he spoke, he ran the damp cloth over his face, neck, and hands before casually tossing it into the sink.

"I'll ladle it out now. Why don't ye escort the lovely lass into the dining room and—"

"No, we'll eat in here." He turned to Lucy as though he believed she might need an explanation.

She understood his concern. "I have no problem with it. The staff should not be using the dining table, so anyone looking at the house would be suspicious if they saw light emanating from any of the more formal rooms. Are there drapes in the library we can draw to hide the light?"

He laughed heartily. "Yes, Lucy. You shall have unimpeded access to my grandfather's books. It is merely a matter of securing those drapes and the window shutters, so no light escapes out."

She settled across from him at the kitchen table and cast him a purposefully sweet smile. "Thank you, Donal."

He shook his head and laughed.

Donal knew he was no coxcomb, but he also knew women considered him handsome.

LUCY WAS EBULLIENT because he was going to show her a few library books.

This charmed him more than any attempts at seduction. He was no green youth and had romped with beautiful, sophisticated women who knew how to pleasure a man.

But he did not think anything could please him more than seeing the look of happiness on Lucy's face just now.

Bollocks.

It was safest if she kept that look for her books and not him.

He was already in hot, roiling turmoil over her, wanting to hold her in his arms. Lord help him, wanting desperately to bed her.

But one did not take a girl like Lucy outside of marriage. He could never walk away from her if he ever did. She wasn't like the others.

She was Lucy.

His Lucy.

He wouldn't hurt her for the world.

"Donal," she said as he stared into his stew, "what's wrong? Have we overlooked something important?"

"No, I was merely planning ahead."

She nodded. "I'll leave you to it. I didn't mean to interrupt."

"You're not. It's all right. I am being rude."

"Not at all. You are very good at what you do, and I have no wish to interfere."

He shook out of his musings. "No, Lucy. You are never a bother. I enjoy your company. I also trust your opinions and never mind speaking to you about our next steps. In truth, I owe you an explanation for why you were dragged into this intrigue. You and I both know it is overdue. Have you finished your supper?"

She set down her fork and nodded.

"We'll talk in your bedchamber. I'm going to spend the night in there with you. On the floor, of course. I'll set up a pallet by the hearth."

Blanche, who had clearly overheard him, cast him a scathing look.

He did not owe his staff explanations but hastened to do so because of Lucy's reputation. "I am a professional. Miss Lessing is my assignment. I need to be sure we were not followed. These men who are after her are not doing this for their amusement. They are hired killers. I've kept her safe this far, and I mean to do whatever is necessary to make certain she remains that way. I am not letting her out of my sight, especially on this first night here."

In truth, he meant to sleep in her chamber every night.

It was no business of Blanche's.

Nor would he tell Lucy his intentions yet. She would not like the idea, and he had no wish to argue with her about it. They had too much else to discuss to be distracted by this bit of nonsense.

And it was nonsense.

Yes, he ached to have her.

But he ached more to keep her alive.

He wasn't going to touch her.

He wasn't going to climb into her bed, no matter how much the idea tempted him.

He was going to protect her, and that was all.

"Come on, Lucy. Let's get you settled, and we'll talk." He glanced at her and the sad state of her gown. It wasn't even hers but borrowed from Lorcan's London apartment. "Blanche, did my grandfather keep any of my grandmother's clothes?"

"Yes," she said, immediately understanding the reason for the question. "But they'll all need altering. Yer grandmother was a big woman. I'll sort through her gowns after I clear away the supper plates."

He nodded. "Pull out several that can be easily adjusted for Miss Lessing. We'll deal with them tomorrow morning. Would your daughter mind—"

"I can sew," Lucy said. "I'll need help with the fittings, but that's all. I can do the rest myself." She regarded Donal with a wry arch of her eyebrow. "This is what genteel women are trained to do. Other than hiding amid my books, this is how I spent my days at home."

"It is a practical talent." He returned her wry look with one of his own. "I can sew, too. I'll show you tomorrow."

She laughed. "Seriously?"

He nodded. "I am a man of many gifts."

"It is a good thing you are as handsome as you are," she muttered, "or everyone would hate you. Is there anything you cannot do? Perfection can be quite irritating, you know."

He placed her hand in the crook of his arm and led her upstairs. "You think I am handsome?"

"Oh, stop. You know you are. Shall I imitate your arrogant stride? That 'Here I am, ladies. Worship me' strut you have perfected."

"Gad, say no more. You are making me out to be a monumental arse."

"No, you aren't at all. I couldn't resist teasing you just the littlest bit. How did you learn to sew?"

"My mother again. As her illness began to ravage her body, it affected her eyesight, as well. My brothers and I did our best to stop home more often to help out. It was not nearly as much as we would have liked. Whenever I was there, I would assist her with the household duties that were traditionally hers. Mending clothes, darning socks. She would also knit woolens for us."

"She sounds like a lovely woman."

"She was, but she could be stubborn. Often. To the very end, she would not give up her chores, and none of us had the heart to stop her. We would just roll up our shirt sleeves and help out."

"She was very fortunate to have you to help her. But Donal, I shall punch you hard if you tell me you can also knit."

He laughed. "Then I won't tell you."

She groaned. "You are a wonderful man, you know. Your

mother must have loved you very much."

He opened the door to her chamber and drew her inside quickly because tears were starting to form in her eyes. "Lucy, what have I said to upset you?"

"Nothing, I promise." She emitted a ragged breath. "You obviously grew up in a household filled with love. I noticed it when I was in Taunton helping Eliza as she was about to deliver the Earl of Monkton's heir. You were there to protect us from his crazed brother. But once that threat resolved, I got to see you with your own brothers, Shayne and Lorcan. There is so much love among the three of you. You would die for each other."

He cast her an affectionate look. "We would risk our lives to save each other, but the point of any rescue is to save the person while also keeping yourself alive."

"Yes, of course. My point is, what you did for your ailing mother…it is wonderful beyond words."

"It is no less than she would have done for us. In truth, she did so much for us as we were growing up. Three boys. We were too much to handle most of the time. But she never lost her temper. We were always shown love even when we deserved to be taken to the woodshed to have our backsides tanned raw. She did not even send us upstairs without supper, which to a growing boy is the worst sort of punishment. We ate like beasts. Blanche was always chasing us out of her kitchen whenever we visited our grandfather in our younger days. We would casually saunter in to steal food. She would come after us with her wooden spoon. She was never fast enough to catch us."

Lucy laughed. "I wish I had grown up in a family like yours. My parents are completely the opposite. I wish…I…" She shook her head and sighed. "Truly, I do not think they ever liked me. Not a moment in all the years of my life."

"Then they are fools," he muttered, knowing this was the right moment to tell her the truth about her parentage. He crossed to the drapes to make certain they were securely drawn, then strode to the bureau and lit the lone candle that sat atop it.

This small flame was hardly enough to illuminate the room, but it shed enough light to allow Lucy to see where she was walking.

He led her to the bed and had her sit on it, then drew up the one chair in the room and placed it beside her. She gripped the edge of the soft mattress and stared at him with sorrowful eyes as he sat and stared back at her. "I never understood why they felt nothing for me. I've been thinking about it for the past few days now, Donal. All this talk of home life and the love you shared with your parents has gotten me thinking. Mine were never warm to me. Is their behavior toward me somehow connected to us being on the run now?"

CHAPTER NINE

DONAL WAS NOT surprised Lucy's nimble brain had been working through the possible reasons for her involvement in this intrigue. He'd worried the truth would come as a shock to her, but she had obviously been spending her nights sorting through all the reasons why these villains were after her.

At first, she was convinced the assailants had made a mistake.

Donal had assured her they hadn't.

This must have confused her all the more.

"Please, just tell me the truth."

He sighed. "Yes, Lucy. One could say they are connected."

Being Lucy, she had explored the reasons and would have considered all logical possibilities.

"How are they connected? Must I keep guessing, or will you tell me?"

He expected his next words would be more of a confirmation of her suspicions than come as a complete surprise to her. Perhaps this would help soften the blow.

Still, he knew it would be bitter news to take.

She was seated at the edge of the mattress, her hands gripping the sheets so tightly her knuckles were turning white.

He took her hands in his, swallowing them up in his warmth because hers were cold and lightly trembling. "I don't have all the answers yet, Lucy. But this is what I do know...and from what you've told me, it is something you must have felt all of your life.

You are not the daughter of the Lessings."

Her face drained of color, and she reeled slightly. "They always made feel an outcast. I should have realized the reason long ago."

"How could you possibly know? I'm sorry they made you feel this way. I'm so sorry they never showed you the love you deserve. You are wonderful in every way."

She gave a bitter laugh as her eyes began to fill with tears.

"Wonderful?" She was obviously struggling not to cry. "The Lessings certainly did not think so. But why should they? I wasn't their daughter, as you've just confirmed. I was never more than a stranger to them. Were they being paid to keep me? They must have been. I think I would have been tossed onto the streets the moment the funds stopped coming in. Or they might have kept me on as their drudge and allowed me to sleep with the scullery maids."

He tried not to show his anger at the behavior of her so-called parents. His quiet fury would not make her feel any better, nor was it professional behavior on his part.

But he was mad as hell. "Your sister would never have allowed them to turn you into their servant. She loves you."

Lucy gave a sniffling snort at his words. "I know Eliza loves me. We will still maintain a close friendship once she finds out we were never truly sisters. You do not have to coddle me, Donal."

"It is not coddling. You truly are—"

"Wonderful in every way?" She laughed softly. "I am quite certain I'm not that. The best to be said about me is that I am as unobtrusive as a mouse and manage to keep out of everyone's way."

Anger shot through him once again.

It was not aimed at her, of course. "I mean it, Lucy. You are a diamond."

She laughed again. "Diamonds are made from lumps of coal. Did you know this? I think that is a more accurate description of what I am. Coal. A thing that is plain but useful. It provides warmth. It is far more efficient than wood. The Romans used our Yorkshire coal to keep their soldiers warm when they invaded us eight hundred years ago. Those Roman legions were masters at efficiency."

This is why he found himself drawn to the girl.

She was a font of knowledge, some of it useful and some of it not. She was also achingly vulnerable. Every time she spoke, she sparked his protective instincts. All he wanted to do was wrap her in his arms and hold her forever. "Lucy, you are not a lump of coal. You are a treasure. I am not saying this because I think you want to hear it. You know I am not soft and tender."

"Yes, you are. What you did for your ailing mother was the kindest thing imaginable."

He shook his head to dismiss her comment. "She was my mother. That is different. You've seen me kill. You've seen me protect you. You know I would not hesitate to slit a man's throat if he tried to harm you. What is soft about that?"

She simply stared at him with her big, trusting eyes.

He gave her hands a light squeeze. "You will only get the truth from me, no matter how brutal it might be. If I compliment you, it is because I mean it."

Lord, her eyes were like starlight.

He cleared his throat. "The Duke of Wooton hasn't told me everything. In truth, all he told me is that you are…his…"

"His daughter? It is the only thing that makes any sense, the only reason anyone would chase me, and why he put his best man to protect me."

Donal nodded.

"It all seems so farfetched. Parents who never cared about me. Wooton suddenly assigning you to hide me. I assume then, I am his illegitimate daughter?"

"That part I do not know. Since I've never heard of him having a wife, it is possible you may be that. Honestly, I cannot give you an answer to this question. Knowing Wooton, however, I would not rule out a secret marriage on his part."

"Then I could be legitimate?" She began to nibble her full and luscious lower lip. "Or whoever is after me is worried that I am. Why else would I matter to anyone? But even if I am his daughter born in respectable wedlock, I am still just a female. I cannot inherit his dukedom."

"Likely, it is his wealth they are worried about, not the entailed properties. Perhaps he made arrangements to leave all of his unentailed assets to you, and his relations got wind of it. Nor do I know anything about your mother's side. Who is to say they are not the ones after you because of what you could inherit from her?"

She eyed him in confusion. "What could I possibly inherit? She must have died when I was a baby—likely giving birth to me. Why come after me twenty years later? Why not simply kill me at birth? It would have been easy to accomplish back then."

"They may not have known about your existence until now. And what makes you think your mother is dead?"

She gasped. "Are you suggesting she is not? That she abandoned me...that she and Wooton just gave me over to strangers...and..."

Seeing her about to fall apart, he lifted her off the bed and drew her onto his lap. "They would never have let you go unless they were desperate to keep you safe."

"How can you know for certain? Is it not more logical they were not married, and neither of them wanted me?"

"No, it is not logical. Of course they wanted you. Wooton sent money to the Lessings all these years."

"To ease his conscience?"

Donal laughed at the notion. "The man does not have a conscience. He is doggedly loyal to the Crown and will do anything to protect the royal family. I suppose he would do anything to protect you, too. Especially now that you've been discovered. The point is, he is cold, hard, and ruthless. I cannot imagine him being a father and dandling a baby girl on his knee. But that does not mean he won't protect you with all his being."

She wrapped her arms around his neck and buried her head against his shoulder. "Donal, how can Wooton possibly be my father? I am a cringing, fearful nobody. I don't know how to use even the simplest weapon. I have no skills at defense. I am nothing like him. What if I am someone else's by-blow? Someone very powerful. What if he lied to you about our connection?"

"The resemblance between you and Wooton is unmistakable. Also, I saw the worry in his eyes when he assigned me to guard you. It was the look of a father concerned for his child. You are his daughter, and he will be ruthless in protecting you. I won't pretend to agree with what he did in turning you over to the Lessings. He must have had good reason. Obviously, he knew it was imperative to hide you since someone is now trying to kill you."

He could feel the silent tears pouring out of her. That she was in his arms and holding onto him with all her might meant she trusted him.

This girl who had been lied to all of her life trusted him.

This meant more to him than all the treasures of the world.

But in the next moment, she tried to squirm out of his arms. "What you must think of me," she said raggedly. "I—"

"I've told you. You are wonderful in every way."

"Oh, for certain." She rolled her eyes. "My parents sold me off. The strangers who took me in did it only for the money. They never showed me an ounce of love. Perhaps if Wooton had been more generous, they might have been more pleasant toward me."

"He did pay them handsomely."

"And they still disliked me? No, that is too harsh. They would have had to feel something for me to dislike me. They felt nothing. I could have dropped dead in front of them, and they would have merely summoned a footman to dispose of my body before it left a stain on the rug." She buried her face against him again and burst into tears.

He did not know what to say to soothe her. There were no

words to ease her anguish.

So he simply held her while she cried herself out.

They remained this way, he was holding onto her as though she was his treasure, for at least a half-hour. Perhaps it was a full hour. It did not matter. He was ready to hold her through the night if it came to that. All he cared about was Lucy and keeping her safe from harm.

When she had no more tears left in her to shed, she lifted her head and looked up at him. "I've soaked your shirt."

He ran his thumb gently across her cheek. "It'll dry."

"I'm sorry I turned into a watering pot. I know you were trying to talk to me about these assailants. I...you see...it's all been building up inside me for years. The never knowing. Always feeling unloved. Always trying my best to make them love me. Never understanding why they did not."

"I know, Lucy. And you owe me no apology. We're in this together from here on out. I won't be leaving your side until the danger has passed."

She wiped the tears from her cheeks by running her sleeve over them. "How will we know it is over? Did Wooton tell you anything about those villains?"

He could see she was trying to regain her composure. "No, he only confided you were his daughter, and I needed to get you out of London as fast as possible. He won't communicate with me again until he has destroyed the villains."

"How will he send word to you if he doesn't know where we are?"

"Coded messages in the London Times. We won't be getting any for a while yet."

"What makes you so certain?"

"A bombing incident earlier in the day. Then someone got close enough to shoot him. Fortunately, they could not get off a clean shot. However, he was wounded. Do you know how hard it is to get past the Home Office guards and into his office? Then our carriage was attacked, those assailants seeming to be in wait for us. He has to know there is someone working against him on the inside."

"Does this mean we are left on our own to figure this out?"

"Yes, pretty much. However, I'm not sure we can do anything other than hide while he goes after these villains. We have nothing to go on, not a single clue."

"Wooton...do you mind if I call him that? I cannot think of him as my father. He must have told you something more, revealed who he thinks is behind these attempts?"

"He wouldn't tell me. As I said, he is determined to destroy these assailants himself."

"Stupidly prideful of him. They will kill him if he tries to confront them on his own."

"He'll be careful. He purposely refused to tell me more because he did not want me trying to work that part out. He needs me fixed on the task of protecting you."

"Would I not be better protected if we knew who was after me?"

"I tried to convince him of it, but he would not budge from his stubborn position. Yes, Lucy, I agree with you. But Wooton does not. So, where does this leave us? I wouldn't even know where to start. I don't know anything about his past or that of your mother's. He's traveled the world and could have met her anywhere. She might not be English."

"That narrows it down quite a bit," she said, casting him a sardonic grin. "Now, we only have to consider every other country in existence."

He sighed. "In truth, we don't have to consider anything. We just have to stay in hiding and hope Wooton rounds up the villains before we die of old age."

"I think I may have a clue," she said, her hand digging into the space between her breasts to lift out her necklace.

His eyes widened, and his heartbeat quickened because...just because his brain seemed unable to think of anything but her breasts at this moment. Yes, they were beautifully shaped. But did he have so little control over his body that his eyes had to pop wide at the merest provocation?

This was not professional behavior at all.

"You think this necklace is a clue, Lucy?"

"I do." She held up the charm that dangled off the gold chain. He had noticed the chain and its unusual charm earlier, his body turning hot because of the way it plunged into her divine cleavage.

Was it his fault she was luscious?

He leaned closer to inspect the charm, one obviously of finest quality gold and precious stones. "It is an odd shape. Looks like a lion rampant, its claws outstretched to grasp a crescent moon."

"Does your grandfather have any books on heraldry in his library?"

"I'm sure he does. But I do not think this is an English crest, certainly none I've ever seen." Her eyes were still infused with pain, but there was also a gleam in them at the thought of solving a puzzle. "Bollocks, Lucy. You and I are going to remain here until the danger has passed."

"But what if we could help? How can we sit here twiddling our thumbs and staring at each other when we could be doing something useful?"

"Useful? That is exactly what Wooton does not want us to do. He needs to know you are out of harm's way. Those men are savages who may do worse than merely kill you. And what of that woman, Andrea? She did not blink an eye when shooting Mel. I want your promise not to run off no matter what we find out."

"Donal!"

"I mean it, Lucy. I'll burn down the damn library if you plan to take this further."

She scowled at him. "How could you do such a cruel thing?"

He moved her back onto the bed because she was squirming on his lap and giving him fits. He could not touch her without fire shooting through him. "I thought I made myself clear. I will do anything to protect you."

"Even prevent me from learning the truth? Are we not safer if we know who is coming after me?" She tried to stare him down but quickly saw that it was useless. "Very well. You have my promise. I will not run off without you."

"Not good enough. Promise me you will not run off…period."

She was scowling at him again. "That is a foolish promise to make. What if they find us, and I have to run for my life? I never wish to lie to you, so do not make me give oaths I have no intention of keeping."

He drew her back onto his lap for no reason other than he simply wanted to hold her.

She put her arms around his neck and gave him a heartfelt hug. "Help me solve this puzzle, Donal. I need to know who I am and why I was abandoned. We'll plan our next steps once we've discovered what everyone has hidden from me all these years. I won't go anywhere without you. I am not an idiot. I know I need your guidance and protection. But I also cannot just sit here and wait for them to find us."

"Lucy…"

"Please, I feel so empty inside right now. I thought it would be a relief to learn the Lessings were not my parents. I used to dream of this when I was young, and they'd particularly hurt me. Oh, never a physical beating. I was never worth that much bother. They hurt me with their indifference. They doted on Eliza and looked through me as though I was invisible. I would lie in my bed at night and silently cry, look up at the heavens, and wish I did not belong to them. I used to make up stories in my head, make believe my true parents would show up to claim me one day."

She shook her head and emitted an anguished breath. "I made up the most elaborate tales. They were captured by pirates. They were royalty. I imagined a royal procession to the Lessing townhouse and the king's chamberlain kneeling before me, holding a satin pillow with a crown atop it just for me. But no one ever came for me."

He stroked her hair, not knowing what to say to make her feel better.

Obviously, there were no words.

She sniffled. "Hearing the truth now, knowing it is what I had wished for throughout the years, I ought to be rejoicing. But I am not. It doesn't feel good at all."

"I know, sweetheart."

"It makes me desperately sad, Donal. I feel as though I've fallen into a dark hole and cannot find my way out. Two sets of parents, and none of them wanted me."

"We don't know that about Wooton or your mother."

"That's right, we don't. But it doesn't hearten me. It only adds to my misery. I need to find out the truth. What is so awful about that? To know who I am. To know if I was ever loved. Where is the harm in helping me learn about my past?"

"All right, Lucy. I'll help you investigate. But no matter what we learn, you cannot run back to London. They will kill you before you are two minutes back in town."

"I understand. Let's just take it a step at a time, then. We can start in the library and read through whatever records your grandfather kept about the noble families of Europe. Perhaps one of them is attached to the charm."

He ran his fingers lightly through her hair to brush back a few stray curls and then kissed her on the forehead. "Agreed. But you are to do nothing about it once we find the answer. You need to let me protect you."

"I know. I am not trying to be a burden."

"You have never been a burden to me, not even for a moment."

She laughed. "I suppose you say that to all your assignments."

"No. Most of them are pompous oafs, and I spend most of my time on duty wanting to throttle them."

"Ha! How is that any different from what you wish to do to

me?"

"It is very different. I've told you, you are a treasure, not a chore."

Her laughter died as she noted the smolder in his gaze. He watched the movement of her throat as she swallowed. "Um, Donal…"

"Yes, Lucy?"

"If you don't want to throttle me, then what is it you spend most of your time wanting to do to me? That is…because you say I am a treasure. What does that mean exactly?"

He cupped a finger under her chin and lifted her gaze to his. "It means this."

He took possession of her mouth in a crushing kiss.

CHAPTER TEN

S WEET MERCY.

Lucy had no idea what was happening, but she quite liked the sensual feel of Donal's lips on hers and the heat of his hard body as he drew her up against him in an utterly possessive and enveloping embrace. This probably violated every agent of the Crown rule and could not possibly have been a part of his training…or perhaps it had been, and this was his way of binding her to him by means of seduction so that she would not run off.

She wanted to push him away in anger, knowing he could not possibly be admitting his ardent affection for her but was manipulating her with glorious kisses. Instead, she held onto his muscled shoulders and surrendered every bit of herself to the magic of his touch. When would she ever experience such a moment again? "*The Book of Love* said it would be like this."

"Hush, Lucy. Don't analyze it, just feel."

How could she not think about it?

Well, perhaps she ought to have waited until he was through kissing her before she started talking.

But who could blame her?

She was excited.

No one other than Donal had ever kissed her. Who else would? Perhaps others would if she turned out to be an heiress. Not that it mattered. She doubted anyone would ever kiss her as magnificently as he was kissing her at this moment.

Nor did she desire to be kissed by any other man.

He had her senses reeling.

Dear flames of heaven.

Her body was lit up like a torch.

"Lucy, you are still thinking too hard," he said in a husky chuckle against her lips. "Stop chattering while I am trying to kiss you."

"You mean there's more? I can't help it. You kiss beautifully, but I suppose you know this. And it also got me thinking that it seems an awful waste…"

He sighed. "What is an awful waste?"

She eased back the littlest bit to meet his gaze. "Do you ever make lists of things you hope to do before you turn a certain age? Or before you die?"

"No."

She cleared her throat. "No? Oh. Well, the thing is, I do. And I find myself thinking that there is one thing very urgent that I have not done, and I certainly must do before I die because it would be extremely wasteful not to experience this particular thing. But I do not want you to get the wrong impression…because I know you are doing this to keep me biddable and manageable…calling me your treasure. It is nice if I pretend it's real. But I know you kissed me and are saying these nice things to me, so I won't run off. I know I do not suit you."

"What are you trying to say, Lucy?"

"I have something important to request of you, and I do not want you to make too much of it or think it is something more than it really is…or think me common. I hope you won't think that, and I would not ask it of you unless I was under threat of death."

His arms were still wrapped around her body, and he appeared utterly confused by what was happening here. "Go ahead, ask it."

"Well, you see…no one has ever kissed me like this. Or held me like this. Or ever spoken to me as though I mattered. Well,

Eliza has. But I don't mean my sister…which I suppose she is not. Well, not anymore. But we shall still remain the best of friends."

"Lucy, what are you trying to say?"

She swallowed hard. "I don't want you to sleep on a pallet by the hearth. I want you to join me…that is…"

Was her face on fire?

"You want me in your bed?" He looked as though his heart had just stopped. "Lord, this is my fault. I should have realized what my kiss would lead to. But it was you I was kissing and…"

His voice simply trailed off.

Did he think she did not have womanly yearnings? That she was a cold, bookish spinster? First of all, she was too young to be a spinster.

How dare he consider her one!

"What I mean to say," he added, his voice quite gritty. "I understand why you might feel this way. You almost died. Everything you believed was true has turned out to be a lie. You feel lost and adrift, in need of something to pull you back to steady ground. And this is why you want to be kissed in bed."

"I want more than kisses, but I suppose you are just putting it politely. Yes, that is what I would like. But I would never make this request of anyone else. Only you."

"You cannot tell me that, Lucy."

"Should I not be honest with you? Oh, perhaps I was a little too honest. You look as though you want to slit your throat…or mine. I did not realize it was such a repulsive request. You kissed me as though you meant it, and I thought perhaps it would not be a chore for you to take that next step. Never mind. Forget I said anything."

"A chore? Do you know nothing about men? I suppose you don't. The request is not repulsive in the least. Quite the opposite, it is very dangerous."

"Why is it so dangerous?"

"You would not ask me that if you knew anything about men."

"Obviously, I don't. Which is the very reason I am humiliating myself by asking."

"Even after reading that book on love?"

"It is your book, and you really ought to read it. But I suppose I am missing the most important points if I have to beg you to—"

"No. Don't say anything more, Lucy. You are overwrought, and the truth about your parentage has hit you hard. I should not have kissed you."

She shook her head in disagreement. "I am glad you did. Your instincts were right. I needed your kiss. I'm sorry if I mistook it for something more."

"You did not mistake it. I wanted to kiss you."

"You needn't be kind to me and tell me what you think I want to hear. Would you have kissed me if I weren't overset?"

"Yes. Perhaps not at this very moment, but eventually, yes."

"Why? Because I was aching, and you could not bear it?"

"I would have grasped at any excuse to press my lips to yours. There's something very kissable about you, Lucy. But I did not mean it to go this far. Indeed, to take it further would be another mistake. It is dangerous for us to get too entangled."

She nodded, trying to sound unaffected by his refusal, even though the reasons were sound. However, she was mortified by what she had asked him to do. Whatever possessed her to think he might want to bed her?

Worse, how could she want to bed him? Well, she did. But to state it aloud? To proposition him as though she were some desperate virgin looking for a night of frolic?

She was exactly that.

Desperate and unwanted.

Pain tore through her. "The candle is about to burn out. I had better climb into bed. You still need to make a pallet for yourself. Just grab one of the pillows. Oh, but there is only the one blanket."

"I'll be fine. I'll use my jacket if I get cold in the night." He held her back as she tried to wriggle out of his arms.

Which only made her more desperate to get out of them. "I'm sure you could take one from any of the other bedchambers."

"It isn't necessary," he said, still refusing to release her and casting her a tender glance as she pushed against his chest. "Here, turn around. Let me unlace you."

Oh, was this all he had in mind?

"All right."

She removed her gown the moment he loosened it and then fumbled with her corset. Her hands were shaking, but she turned away so he would not notice. Still too mortified to look him in the eye, she scampered under the covers.

She felt his gaze on her and ignored it.

What was he looking at?

She was more or less properly clad since she still wore her shift which would have to serve as a nightgown for one more night.

Her hands were still trembling as she removed the pins from her hair and set them on the small table beside the bed.

She did not know if she could fall asleep, not only because her body ached for Donal's touch but because her mind was racing about more important matters. She could not stop thinking of the Lessings or the Duke of Wooton or her unknown mother. Who was she? Why had the woman never attempted to contact her?

Was she dead?

Or still alive and just uncaring?

And what of Wooton? He was alive and obviously never saw fit to claim her.

She tried to muffle her sob and failed. Now she was about to cry again. Perhaps Donal was right; she was too overset. Why else would she brazenly proposition him?

Only, she had meant it.

She trusted him and liked him.

More than liked him.

His kisses were magnificent and tender.

He would give her an unforgettable night of pleasure. Why should she not experience this splendid union of their bodies before she died?

Who better to induct her into womanhood?

She buried her face in the plump pillow and willed herself to fall asleep.

But it was impossible.

Her heartbreak and the questions swirling in her head had her on the verge of tears again. How would she look to Donal after a night spent sobbing? Come morning, her eyes would be red and her face a splotchy mess. When he looked at her, would he lose respect for her and regard her as a pathetic, love-starved burden?

She was now a watering pot, utterly devastated and unable to control the flow of tears that dampened her pillow.

"Lucy, hush." The mattress dipped as Donal settled beside her, his body solid and warm. He drew her up against him and circled his arms around her. "I'm here. I won't leave you tonight."

It took her a moment to realize he had taken off his shirt. He'd probably been preparing to stretch out on his pallet when her moans and sniffles became too irritating to ignore. So he'd climbed into bed with her to silence her.

She was now lying in his arms.

Her damp cheek rested against the warm bands of muscle on his upper arms.

She dared not turn to face him, dared not put a hand to his broad chest and trail it lightly across the dusting of dark hair or run her fingers down his firmly rippled torso.

Why did he have to be so gorgeous? She inhaled his masculine scent, that of heat and island spices.

She found this scent ridiculously arousing...whatever that meant, because she truly did not know where these feelings of ache and yearning were supposed to lead.

He was a big man.

His arms were the size of tree trunks, and his fists could strike a man with the force of twin boulders.

Yet, he was so gentle when he touched her.

He traced a finger along the curve of her jaw.

"I thought you did not want to share the bed with me," she said in a breathless whisper.

"And you believed me?"

She blinked to clear the teardrops from her lashes. "Yes, was I not supposed to take you at your word?"

"Never believe a man when it comes to such matters."

"Does this mean you have accepted my proposition? Is this what is about to happen? Will we have…a torrid encounter together now? I've never done anything like this before. Will you teach me?"

"Torrid?" His laugh was mingled with a groan.

It was not the response she had hoped for.

"Lucy, I am not going to…we are not going to couple. Put it of your head immediately. I am only going to hold you in my arms. This alone is bad enough. I should be on a pallet by the hearth."

"Then why are you here?"

"Because you are irresistible. Because you are hurt and aching. Because I like having you in my arms. Don't respond to that comment. Just keep your head on my shoulder and close your eyes."

"All right. Have you lost all respect for me?"

He laughed again, a soft, affectionate rumble. "No, Lucy. I have tremendous respect for you. If I didn't, that shift would be off you, and I would be kissing my way down your body."

"That sounds nice."

"Go to sleep."

She wanted to say more but was afraid he would move from her bed to the pallet if she continued to prattle. A thousand questions still whirled in her head. Those would have to keep until tomorrow.

She turned to face him and snuggled against his powerful

frame, rested her hand upon his chest. The reassuring warmth of his body lulled her. She listened quietly to the steady beat of his heart.

Hers was beating wildly.

His was slow and measured.

She did not mean to play with the sprinkle of hair across his chest but had never seen an unclad male body before other than statues in a museum. She ran her fingers in a gently whirling motion. He put his hand over hers. "Stop that."

"I'm sorry. I was just curious."

"I know. But I am not carved of stone, Lucy. Your touch affects me."

She inhaled sharply, surprised by his admission. "I had no idea."

"I thought your book had an entire chapter on the power of touch."

"It is *your* book, and it did. I just…I never thought a man like you would ever be tempted by someone like me. Or is it merely that we are together in a bed, and I am touching you? Is it only your low-brain response that I have stirred?"

He groaned. "What are you talking about?"

"Read the book, Donal. It is truly enlightening."

He surprised her by caressing her cheek. "I think I had better if only to be sure it isn't leading you down the road to ruin."

She laughed softly. "I am hardly at risk for that. Not even you want to touch me in a more intimate way, and I am lying in bed with you. I wouldn't want anyone else touching me anyway. It simply would not feel right. I'm not sure why I feel it so urgently with you."

"I am your anchor at this moment, the thing you need to hold onto while all you thought was real in your life has slipped away. You don't want to let go of me because I am the only person you dare trust."

"I did not realize agents of the Crown were philosophers as well. But you are right about my feelings. Everyone but you has lied to me. My entire life has been false. I even wonder if Eliza knew and never had the heart to tell me. I suppose she felt it did not matter since we do love each other as sisters." She sighed. "I'm sorry. You want me to be quiet and fall asleep."

"For your own good. Your mind is reeling with questions, most of which cannot be answered yet. Rest that active mind of yours tonight. We'll look through my grandfather's library in the morning."

"Will you stay with me even after I fall asleep?" He was right about her needing him to be her anchor. She felt so adrift amid a vast ocean of lies.

Those waves of deception kept crashing over her and threatened to drown her.

"Yes, Lucy. I won't leave you tonight."

"Thank you. I am truly sorry for propositioning you. I won't ever ask it of you again."

She hoped he would say something back, something romantic…admitting he desired her, and it was only his professional duty that prevented him from ravishing her as he desperately wished to do. But he remained silent, no doubt hoping she would finally stop talking and allow him to sleep.

Well, it was kind of him to remain by her side and promise to hold her through the night. And kind of him to softly caress her body in the hope of lulling her to sleep. In truth, she was exhausted both in mind and body.

She ought to have turned once more to face away from him but could not bring herself to move. Instead, she remained half atop him, her body scandalously pressed to his. It could not be comfortable for him. Who wanted to sleep with someone clinging to them like a limpet snail to a rock?

This is how she fell asleep, in the comforting cocoon of his arms.

His naked arms.

She could not overlook that exciting part.

After all, it was all the excitement she was likely to have tonight…or any other night of her life.

This is how she found herself waking the next morning, the delicious heat of him surrounding her as he held her in his protective embrace. She dared not move and disturb his slumber, especially since she was not certain of the time. The drapes were drawn, and there was only the slightest light filtering into the room. For all she knew, it could be the middle of the night.

Or the middle of the day.

But it felt like morning.

Fairly early still because the house was quiet.

She'd had a restful sleep, which surprised her since she'd done nothing but gush tears before finally drifting off.

Donal could not have gotten much rest while she lay beside him. He had to be exhausted. Indeed, he'd gotten almost no sleep the entire time they had been on the run, and then last night having to listen to her as she prattled and questioned the meaning of her existence.

Perhaps if she slipped ever so quietly…and eased ever so gently…

"Lucy, what are you doing?" His voice was a soft growl as he tugged her back to his side.

She emitted a defeated sigh. "I was trying not to wake you. Is it morning yet? I wanted to peek out and see for myself. Don't worry, I would not have drawn the drapes aside. Just nudged a slat. All I wished to do was steal a glimpse."

"All right." He released her and then rolled onto his back, letting out a manly roar as he stretched that exquisite body of his. Truly, such a fine body. Sleek and powerful as a predator. Muscled. Lithe. "Are you going to gape at me all morning?"

She shook out of her trance. "I'm sorry. No…I…it's just that I've never awakened to a man in my bed before, and I…you never put on your shirt…and…" She stifled a groan and scurried to the window, nudging a corner of the drapes aside just the littlest bit. The shutters proved to be more difficult. She could not move one slat without the others opening up at the same time.

"Drat, I can't do it."

He rolled out of bed, tossed on his shirt and boots, checked that his knife was securely tucked within the sheath hidden in his boot, grabbed his pistol, and wordlessly strode to the door.

"Donal, where are you going?"

"Next door first. That was my grandfather's bedchamber. The shutters were not closed there."

"Let me go with you."

"All right, but you cannot simply run in. Stay next to me and follow my every instruction."

She nodded.

"Then you are to come back in here while I take a look around the manor before everyone begins to stir."

She nodded again to mark her consent and was surprised when he took her hand. He must have noticed the expression on her face, for he quickly said, "I don't want you tripping over anything. You're not familiar with the house yet, and your eyesight in the dark is not as good as mine."

"That is true." But the excuse felt made up. There were streaks of early morning light filtering into the hallway as they stepped out of her bedchamber. She expected the sun would break through the gray dawn and shine in soon enough. There was easily enough light to make her way without stumbling.

But he kept hold of her hand.

She supposed he was acting on instinct, that ingrained need to protect her. *The Book of Love* spoke of this protective nature in a man, attributing it to the function of his higher brain.

She wanted to think this is what she was becoming to him, a woman acceptable to his higher brain, the one capable of love. However, she was not so deluded as to believe he was falling in love with her or ever could. He was not singling her out as someone special to him. This strong need to protect was in Donal's blood. This is why he was such an effective agent of the Crown.

He took his assignments seriously.

He was always successful in his task.

Was he as kind and gentle to others under his charge?

He had said he wasn't.

Did she dare believe him?

"Come stand beside me, Lucy." He released her hand only to open his arms to her so that she could nestle against his body.

She hastily complied.

Could he feel the rapid patter of her heart?

His expression revealed nothing as he eased the drapes aside. "I think it is about five o'clock in the morning. The Gentry family will soon start their day."

She glanced up at him, caught up in the beauty of his face and its intense look. "Anything of concern?"

He scanned the woods beyond the manor's garden, his gaze alert.

"What are you looking for, Donal?"

"Anything that seems out of place. A glint of light amid the trees. An unnatural quiet. Birds often chatter at this time of the morning but will suddenly go still if there is an intruder in their midst." He continued to peer out the window as he spoke. "Also, there's dew on the ground at this hour. Footprints will show."

"Do you see any?"

"No. Only the tracks of a foraging deer."

"You see things so clearly," she remarked. "This is another thing your book explained, the importance of really seeing whatever it is you are looking at and understanding it for what it is, not for what you wish it to be. Sometimes people are so desperate to fall in love or be connected to someone in a permanent way, they will convince themselves their partner has no faults. They will purposely ignore any intolerable traits and make every excuse to continue ignoring those failings."

"Go on, Lucy. This sounds interesting."

"It does? Yes, I thought so, too." She cast him a quick smile. "What the book says is that even if two people are pleasing to each other's senses, it may not be enough to forge a happy union.

They have to be compatible in certain important ways, willing to accept each other's flaws. But they must first be honest about what they perceive as flaws and not minimize them."

She glanced at him, surprised he was listening and not merely allowing her to prattle while he studied the grounds for trespassers.

Clearing her throat, she continued. "There are many reasons people lie to themselves about a potential partner. Perhaps they are miserable at home and wish to escape. Perhaps that partner is wealthy or has standing in the community, and this is something they want. A man is able to make his own way, but a woman is looked upon as nothing unless she is married."

Donal frowned. "I don't look upon you as that."

"You are not like other men, surely that is obvious. But most of society ignores the spinster. My point is that people often ignore warning signs of unhappiness because they want a thing so badly. If a woman thinks she will change a man after they marry, this will likely be an unhappy marriage. He may be a heavy drinker, a gambler, a womanizer. But marriage to such a man may also give her the prestige in society she hungers for. She may be quite content to live a separate life from her husband and still reap the rewards of their union."

She sighed and shook her head. "I suppose this is why so many dukes, earls, and others in the nobility accept marriages designed to add to their wealth and power. It is the rare instance when they marry for love. The Duke of Edgeware is such an exception, isn't he? He is obviously deeply in love with his duchess. Dillie was a Farthingale. Your brothers married her cousins, Willow and Cammy. I assume they were love matches as well."

He nodded. "We Braydens marry for love. Come on, Lucy. I'll walk you back to your bedchamber before I scout the rest of the property. I'd like to get it out of the way before others are up and going about their business."

He took her hand, once again surprising her since he seemed

to be doing this on instinct and not for duty or other calculated purpose. She had just lectured him on the importance of truly seeing someone for who they were and hoped she was not deluding herself into thinking he liked her.

In truth, how could she trust anything she saw? Had she not spent her entire life blind to who her parents truly were? Had she not accepted the Lessings's lies and put the blame on herself for their failure to love her?

"Lucy, are you listening to me?"

"Oh, forgive me. My mind wandered." She had been distracted and paying little attention as they returned to her chamber. She glanced at the bed, and her heart sank. The sheet and counterpane were in disarray. Anyone walking in would immediately notice both sides had been slept in.

Was it not bad enough Donal thought her a wanton?

She drew in a breath, trying to remain calm, but her face immediately turned to flames. "I had better make your side of the bed. I mean…because we were both…there."

He cast her an affectionate smile. "You are thinking too hard again, Lucy."

"Please. I've humiliated myself in front of you and would rather not do the same in front of your grandfather's staff."

Sighing, he helped her put order to his side of the bed and then set out a pallet by the hearth to make it appear as though he'd slept on the floor. "There. All done. I'll take you down to the library when I return. Stay here, and do not leave this room or open those drapes for any reason. I'll be back within the hour."

He gave her cheek a light, lingering caress before striding out and leaving her on her own.

She quickly washed and dressed, unable to do up the laces of her gown, but Donal would do them up for her when he returned. Once she had done all she could, she picked up the red leather tome, that precious book about love, and dove into the chapters on connections and expectations.

Donal said his family only married for love.

She believed him because she had seen both of his brothers, Shayne and Lorcan, fall in love with their wives. These were tough men, obviously used to battle and not afraid to face the most hardened of criminals. But their expressions immediately softened when looking upon their wives. One could sense the love flowing between them, feel it as a palpable force.

Shayne and Lorcan were not the only Braydens to make love matches with Farthingale ladies. Four of their Brayden cousins had met and married these Farthingales. She had read the gossip sheets daily and followed their adventures.

In truth, those scandal rags were one of the few things she enjoyed in a day that was otherwise filled with drudgery and boredom. Of course, she did not believe half of what was printed.

What was obvious is that Brayden men married for love, just as Donal had told her. Of course, not all of them had married Farthingale women. Nor had the women from that family married only Brayden men.

But it could not be overlooked that both were big, loving families. They were close-knit and supportive. This was one of the obvious ways the Brayden men and Farthingale women were instantly connected. Each of them understood what it meant to grow up with boisterous and meddlesome relations.

She wanted this so badly.

But she had been raised differently…well, not so much raised as merely tolerated. What did she have to offer Donal? What connected them other than lies about her parentage?

She placed a hand over her heart to stifle her dismay.

It was in her nature to think about problems and try to work them out. She would make her lists and write down every way in which she and Donal were connected. Every hope and dream they might have in common. Every way he pleased her senses and what strengths in her might please him.

He had said she was a treasure and that she was pretty.

He held her hand when it was unnecessary.

Was it significant?

She needed to get down to the library and pull out paper, ink pot, and quill pen.

But she could not go wandering the halls with her gown unlaced, and she had promised to stay in her chamber.

Which left her frustratingly trapped until Donal's return.

Was there any chance Donal might fall in love with her?

CHAPTER ELEVEN

DONAL TOOK A quick look around the manor house and then scouted the grounds as well. All appeared quiet, as it should be. The house was not far from the water, so he took another moment to walk toward the beach. However, he was not going to clamber down to the sand for fear of being seen by a local fisherman or farmer on his way into Weymouth.

The woods provided sufficient cover for him to make his way down the nearby hills to several caves he and his brothers had discovered when visiting here as boys. He, Shayne, and Lorcan used to pretend these were pirate hideouts.

In truth, this is exactly what they were, well-hidden lairs used for smuggling that had fallen into disuse sometime in the prior century. He would bring Lucy here sometime within the next few days because these caves would make a perfect hideout for her if the need ever arose.

"Did you notice anything?" she asked the moment he strode back into her bedchamber.

"No, all is quiet. Here, turn around and let me lace you up. I thought Mrs. Gentry or her daughter might have come up to check on you. I'm glad they didn't. It is better if we go down to them."

"Won't they have to come up sometime?"

"Yes. But the less often they do, the better. After breakfast, we'll grab needles and thread, then go through my grandmother's clothes." He held up a hand when she opened her mouth to protest. "Stop, Lucy. We'll grab a few of her gowns and work in the library so that you may also search through my grandfather's books."

She cast him a delicate smile. "Sounds perfect. I'll read while you sew."

He laughed. "Don't be impatient. We'll have days to work on both together, altering the clothes as well as hunting for a similar design to your necklace."

"I can't help it," she said quietly, her smile slipping a bit. "Not knowing who I am or where I truly come from has left me shaken. I need answers more than I need another gown or two. Let's start on the books first."

He wanted to take her in his arms but resisted the urge. He was far too involved, his heart too much engaged with this girl already. "Gowns and then books, Lucy. Even if we discover the identity of your mother and her family, we will not leave here. You must stay in hiding until Wooton eliminates the threat."

"Or it eliminates him."

"That is his problem, not ours. There will be no next steps. What do you not understand about this? And don't glower at me for trying to keep you alive. These men are not playing a game. There is even a woman assassin on your trail who is as ruthless as any of the others. She will shoot you on sight as she did Mel. Promise me you will not run off no matter what we find out."

She did not appear pleased but nodded. "I already gave you my word of honor, and I shall keep to it. I won't go anywhere without you."

He arched an eyebrow. "Even if I refuse to leave here?"

"It shall be my job to make you see reason."

He groaned inwardly, knowing the ideas were spinning in her head, and he would have his hands full containing her if she wanted to go in search of her mother. He doubted the woman was still alive, but this entire affair was so murky. He could not be sure of anything other than Lucy was innocent and in danger.

"Come on, you must be hungry."

"Famished," she admitted.

He took her hand and kept her close as they made their way down the back stairs to the kitchen. Lucy was now regarding him oddly, and he finally realized why. He'd taken her hand again and not let go of it, even after they'd entered the kitchen.

He released it before Mrs. Gentry turned around from the porridge she was mixing and looked over at them. "Ye're both up bright and early," she said cheerfully.

Donal nodded. "I wanted to look around before settling in for breakfast."

"I wake early when at home," Lucy remarked, noticing where the dishes and silverware were stored and setting two bowls and two spoons out for them. "I enjoy the morning sun, and one gets so much more accomplished when one has an early start to the day. Blanche, where do you keep the table linens?"

"Oh, my dear. Ye just sit down and make yerself comfortable. Would ye like tea? We also have coffee and cocoa. I know Master Donal likes his coffee."

"I would love tea." She scooped up the empty kettle, pumped water into it, and set it on the stove beside the pot of coffee already brewing.

Donal tried to keep his anger hidden. Lucy wasn't one for idling the day away, but it was clear by her ease around the kitchen that the Lessings had used her as an unpaid servant over the years. Not for heavy labor, because Lucy did not have the muscles on her. No, she was soft and heavenly to the touch.

But they'd piled chores on her, nonetheless. Less rigorous ones, but still chores. Perhaps they had grown overly confident the duke would never acknowledge her. They must have been rubbing their greedy hands together, totaling up their savings over the years, and knowing they would have a lifelong income if they kept Lucy as their drudge at home.

If Lucy were ever to marry, it would disrupt their plans.

Bollocks.

He should have proposed to Lucy when they were at the Earl of Monkton's estate in Taunton. He'd liked her at first sight, but his thoughts had been on the earl's crazed brother and how to stop him, so he'd never done anything about his feelings for her.

To his regret, he had never approached Lucy other than to make certain she was not in any danger.

Perhaps he'd sought her out more often than his duties required.

He knew he had.

Even then, there was something so charming and sweet about her, he simply could not look away.

He shook out of the thought.

Wooton would now recognize her as his daughter. With that connection to wealth and power, she could have any man she wanted.

Besides, hadn't he decided she was not his type?

That he could not stop thinking of her and enjoyed being around her, loved holding her. Perhaps he did not know a rat's arse about love and ought to read that book.

"Donal, how do you take your coffee?"

He stared back at Lucy while she looked up at him with her gorgeously innocent eyes. "Just as it is. Nothing added."

She set it down on the table beside his place setting. "I suspected as much. This is you, direct and unadorned."

He stopped her when she started toward the tea kettle to pour the boiling water into her cup. "Let me do it."

She laughed and shook her head. "You needn't."

"I know. Let me spoil you a little. How do you take your tea?"

"With honey, if there is any."

Donal grinned. "My grandfather put honey on practically everything he ate. I'm sure the larder is filled with pots of it." He strode to it and emerged a moment later with a full jar. "He used to keep bees for this purpose. What has happened to them, Blanche?"

"I'm afraid they abandoned the hive and moved on. We didn't know how to tend them once he passed. Indeed, I think the bees sensed he was gone. But they left behind a year's supply of honey in those abandoned honeycombs. Master Donal, you sit down. I'll tend to both of ye. Although I think it is quite charming the way the two of ye like to fuss over each other."

Lucy's cheeks turned scarlet.

He winked at her and sat down beside her. "Have your tea and porridge, and then we'll settle in the library for the day. The sky's overcast and threatening rain, the sort that lasts into the night. All the better if we were somehow followed. I don't want to make it too easy for those villains. I hope they will be drenched to the bone."

Lucy began to nibble her lip. "Is there something you are not telling me? Did you notice them on our trail?"

He covered her hand with his. "No, I would tell you if I thought they were close. I never understood that nonsense about keeping women ignorant of dangers. How can you protect yourself if you do not know what is happening?"

"I heartily agree. This is why I am so eager to find out the truth about my parentage."

"But I still do not want you running off on your own, Lucy."

She glanced at his hand that was still covering hers.

Lord, he had to stop doing that.

However, he awaited her answer and had no intention of moving it away. "Lucy?"

"I've already promised you. Why won't you trust me?"

"Because the news hit you like a towering wave, and you have not yet recovered your bearings. Nor do I expect you will any time soon. But your logical mind needs answers, and your heart does, too. I just don't want you talking yourself into doing something dangerous because your need to know is more compelling than the promises you've made to me."

"The incident on the night of the Duke of Edgware's ball left me in no doubt," she said with a shake of her head. "I am not capable of defeating those men without you by my side. I gave you my promise, and I will keep it, Donal. If ever you find me gone, it is because I have been taken against my will."

He nodded and finally released her hand.

The thought of losing her was not something he wished to consider. He simply had to do all in his power to keep her safe. Later, he would worry about his feelings for her and what he intended to do about those.

After breakfast, they followed Blanche into the attic and searched through the trunks of gowns stored up there. "These will do," he said, pulling out four gowns from a pile they had taken out. One was an emerald green, another a dark blue, and the last two were in shades of brown.

Blanche held up several gowns of lighter colors.

Donal shook his head. "Not those."

"Why not?" Lucy asked.

"Aye, Master Donal. Why deprive the lass? Those you selected are all dark and of plain muslin. Well, that last one's all right. A very pretty tea-gown and the color looks lovely on ye, Miss Lucy. Brings out the rose in yer cheeks and the honey-brown of yer hair."

"We aren't selecting them for style. If Lucy needs to hide, I want colors that blend in with the woods and hold up sturdily while she's in hiding. She'll look as beautiful as an angel no matter what she wears." He winked at Lucy and cast her a rakish smile.

She blushed. "You needn't flatter me."

"It isn't flattery. It's the truth."

Bollocks.

Now both women were smiling at him.

Lucy's smile was so sweet and hopeful, it touched his heart.

"We'll need scissors, pins, needles, and thread next," he said, silently kicking himself for these small compliments that seemed to tumble from his lips without thought. But how could he not? This vulnerable girl had no idea how beautiful she was, and it ate him up inside that no one had ever told her.

Blanche held up an old box with a handle on it. "Here's yer grandmother's sewing basket. Ye'll find all ye need inside there. We left it untouched and brought it up here along with the rest of her possessions. Yer dear grandfather could not bear to have them in the room they'd shared throughout their marriage. It broke his heart to be surrounded by her belongings and know he would never see her again. Nor could he bring himself to give them away. But…"

Donal arched an eyebrow in response to her expression. "What is it? Why are you frowning?"

"The lass…Miss Lucy…will have to be fitted first. She'll have to remove her gown."

"Oh, that. I've already seen her in her undergarments." He put a hand on Lucy's shoulder as she began to squirm. Not only squirm but blush and stammer. "I am a professional. Lucy is my assignment. I am not leaving her side. Obviously, we have been on the run for days. We've shared sleeping quarters."

Lucy groaned.

"We have, Lucy. Blanche knows this. She also knows I remained on a pallet in your bedchamber to guard you last night and will do the same every night for as long as the danger exists. There is no other way to protect you, so let's have no more discussion on the matter. Blanche or her daughter can assist with the fittings if it will make you feel more comfortable. But I would rather they went about their daily chores on the chance someone is watching."

"All right," Lucy said quietly. "Whatever you think best."

"It is for the best. The slightest slip can be fatal."

Blanche returned to her duties while Donal led Lucy to his grandfather's library. It was not a large room by any means, but the polished, cherrywood shelves were crammed with books, and there was an overly large desk of the same wood dominating the center of the room. A round table and chairs were tucked in a corner. A large rug of oriental design covered most of the dark wood floor.

Lucy's eyes lit up as though she had just walked into an enchanted garden.

He smothered a grin and shut the door behind them.

The girl was so predictable, in a very sweet way.

"Where do we start?" she said, more to herself as her gaze swept the bookshelves.

"Gowns first." He set them and the sewing basket down on the table, then crossed to the shuttered windows to make certain they were secure. Fortunately, the day was turning cold and nasty, which worked in their favor. The locals would be too busy protecting themselves against the drenching downpour to notice anything different going on at the manor house.

The cold would allow them to keep the windows and drapes tightly sealed without turning the room into an oven.

He made certain the drapes were secure, then crossed to his grandfather's desk and lit the lamp sitting atop it. His breath caught as he gazed at Lucy in the soft, amber glow. She looked ethereal, like a magical wood sprite gliding from shelf to shelf and lightly touching the books as she now read their spines aloud. "Did your grandfather keep them in any order? By author? Or subject? I hope he shelved them by subject, or it will take hours for us to find the heraldry books we need."

"Gowns first, Lucy."

She sighed. "All right, but let's be quick about it."

"I'll work as fast as I can without sticking you with pins."

"Blanche or her daughter, Petrina, could have done this. I know what you said, but it is pouring rain and not yet Wednesday, so there will be no delivery wagons, and it would not raise alarms if they came in here to help me."

He frowned. "Do you want me to summon them, Lucy?"

She shook her head. "Whatever you think best. I'd rather go by your instincts. Mine are obviously useless."

"They are not useless. You were purposely lied to by everyone around you. How can you trust anyone or anything under those circumstances? In time, you'll gather friends who deserve your confidence."

She snorted. "Time. Yes, that is the crux of it. How much time will I have before those villains catch up to us, do you think?"

"I don't know. But it doesn't matter. I am never going to let anyone hurt you." He came to stand by her side. "Let me unlace your gown, and let's get started. Put on that brown one first."

"There are two. Do you mean the muslin or the tulle?"

"The what?"

She grinned. "The sturdy fabric or the delicate one?"

"Sturdy. You aren't going to be sipping tea with your attackers." His fingers trembled as he helped Lucy out of her garment.

Trying to remain a gentleman was harder than he realized. His body was in torment, and it took all his concentration to keep his mind on his task and not on the fantasy going on in his brain.

That Lucy felt so comfortable around him made matters worse.

She stripped down to her shift, completely trusting his honor.

Well, he was honorable.

He was also on fire.

She paid him no attention as she donned the ridiculously oversized gown, then turned to him with a grimace. "We'll have our work cut out. Your grandmother was much larger than I am. Everything has to be taken in. The sleeves. The waist. Bodice. Hem."

Yes, he'd noticed her bodice and nothing else because he'd been staring. To him, she was just perfect in every proportion. "You are lost amid the billows of material. I'm not sure I am adept enough to fix this."

"What? Am I hearing right?" She emitted a gentle trill of laughter. "Donal Brayden stymied? It is impossible."

He tweaked her nose. "Very well, I confess. I may have been a bit thickheaded when refusing Blanche's help. Shall I call her in? Or do you think you can manage these alterations on your own?

Everything needs to be taken in."

"You needn't call anyone in. I am handy with needle and thread. Just finish pinning this one, and I'll take care of the rest." She raised her arms as he took in what felt like yards of fabric along the sides from her shoulder to her waist. He could not believe he was doing this, and quite ineptly too. Were he guarding anyone else, he would never have put himself in this situation.

But this was Lucy, and he wanted her all to himself.

So, he had to be a know-it-all hero.

Helping his mother darn a sock or do up a hem was a far different thing than reconfiguring a gown into something entirely new.

"Is it too late to change my mind?" Lucy asked with a giggle when he dropped several pins on the rug, spent five minutes picking them out of the weave, then stuck himself twice as he resumed pinning the gown.

"No," he said, joining her in a chuckle. "I have it under control."

She arched a delicate eyebrow and smiled. "Are you certain?"

"Yes. Nobody touches you but me." *Blessed saints.* Why had he said that? Obviously, his brain had turned to pudding.

He was behaving like a possessive ape over her.

"Done," he muttered, setting the last of the pins in place at the hem.

"I'm sure it will be perfect." She slipped the gown off her body, her bosom and slender hips once more clearly outlined beneath her flimsy shift. She donned her old gown, the one taken from his brother's London apartment, and continued to chatter while he stood quietly burning. "I'll finish this altered gown today and use it as a measurement for the others. Good thing your grandfather was a big man. You'll probably fit into his shirts, but his trousers will have to be taken in for you."

He gave a snort of laughter.

"I don't need his trousers. You are not going to touch me."

He would erupt like a burst of lightning if her hands were anywhere near his privates.

"Prickly, aren't you? Lace me up, and let's start looking through the books on heraldry."

Of course, he had no issue with touching her.

She had such a sweet, little body.

He fastened her laces, then drew out the latest *Debrett's Peerage* and several older tomes his grandfather had acquired during his travels through continental Europe. "Let's start with these."

She glanced up at him, her eyes vivid and gleaming.

Lord, she was pretty.

Those incredible eyes of hers were framed by long, dark lashes.

He studied her features.

Everything about her was achingly beautiful, but he could not place her looks to a particular country. She took after her father, the Duke of Wooton, who was decidedly English. How were they ever to figure out her maternal parentage? "Let's see the necklace again. Take it off and place it on the table while we look through these drawings. Here, let me help you."

She put her hand protectively over her chest. "Must I? I would rather leave it on."

"And I would rather you didn't. I will need to look at it closely, and I would prefer not to be sticking my nose between your…well, you know." Not that he minded, but he doubted she would appreciate his nose poking where it ought not to be.

"I see." She blushed, then sighed and arched her neck, angling it so he could unclasp the chain. "It feels odd to have it off me."

"How long have you had it?

"The Lessings gave it to me when I turned sixteen. It was the only gift of quality they ever gave me. I should have known it did not come from them. They were never generous to me before or ever since. Donal, what if it was just a gift from Wooton and has no significance to my mother's family?"

"It is too unusual a design. And Wooton is not the sort ever to do anything without a purpose."

"Then you believe it has to be a clue?" That seemed to please her.

He began to sort through the books while she attended to the sewing. Of course, she constantly stopped to peer over his shoulder and ask questions. "I know most of the English and Scottish crests," he said. "I think we can rule those out. Perhaps it is Welsh. Or Turkish. Or Saracen. Or Moorish. But I'm still going to start with the English ones first."

"Why?"

"Just my investigative method. I don't want to overlook anything. I'll move to the Scottish crests next. I like to work methodically, searching from a central focal point and expanding outward. You were raised in England. Your father is English. And you were attacked in England. As for those assassins, I wish I had gotten a better look at them. They could have been hired from anywhere."

"I was attacked in England because this is where I live. Don't you think they would have struck at me in France if I were living there?"

"I suppose. But this affair feels English to me. There seems to be an army of scoundrels after you and Wooton. All I am suggesting is that if the villain behind these attacks is foreign, I think he would have sent only one or two ruthless assassins to take care of the task. Men who could slip in and out of the country unnoticed. I don't know. My instinct tells me this assault is not a foreign matter."

"Well, we know that horrible woman who shot the ostler was English, born and raised. Her accent gave her away." She pursed her lips and frowned. "She did not strike me as anyone's lackey. Yet, she was obviously sent to find us."

"No, not a lackey at all. She was too finely dressed and carried herself with an air of entitlement one finds mostly among the nobility."

"Then you think she is of the Upper Crust?"

He shrugged. "I cannot rule anything out."

She returned to her sewing while he returned to poring over his grandfather's books.

There was something quite wonderful about having Lucy near him. From time to time, he glanced over at her and was amazed by how deftly her fingers worked on the gown. Her stitches were neat and even, far better than anything he could have done despite boasting of his skill with a needle.

They were nearing the end of their first day in Weymouth and no closer to finding any clues about the necklace. However, Lucy had finished alterations on the first gown and was now using it as a pattern for the others as she pinned those.

He'd left her a couple of times during the day to scout the house and grounds and each time returned to find her nose buried in his grandfather's books. He knew she was jumping out of her skin to find answers. For this reason, he never remarked upon her discarded sewing or her fascination with those books.

Much of the day passed quietly in this way.

They had supper when he returned from his early evening scouting tour. Afterward, they returned to the library to continue their task.

But even he was getting tired as the evening wore on.

His eyes were bleary.

He rose with a soft growl and stretched to relieve the ache in his back from sitting for so long. "Lucy, it must be nearing midnight. Leave the books and sewing as they are, and we'll pick up both in the morning."

"Must we? Can we not read a little while longer?"

"No," he said with a determined shake of his head. "Sometimes when we study at a thing too long, we overlook important clues staring us in the face. Things will fall into place after a night's rest. Trust me, I've been through this before."

She cast him a wry smile. "Do you never get tired of being sensible?"

He laughed and shook his head. "I was an idiot when pinning

your gown. I'm sure half the pins are still on the rug. Come on, let me take you up to bed."

Bollocks.

That had sounded too good.

Not only good but completely natural.

Lucy did not seem to take it as anything more than a suggestion to get some sleep. Had she turned to look up at him in that moment, she would have noticed the smolder in his eyes and the taut coil of his body.

It was a struggle not to take her in his arms and kiss her into sunrise.

But she was gazing with longing at the pile of books.

Chuckling, he took hold of her hand again, muttering some lame excuse about it being too dark for her to make her way through the house without tripping over some item or other of furniture.

"Surely a candle—"

"No light, Lucy. Not even the tiniest flicker of a flame. This house has to appear deserted save for the Gentrys. As for your precious tomes, they'll be here in the morning, exactly as we left them. Let me take you upstairs. I'll unlace you, and then I am going to search the house one last time before retiring."

"All right." She looked up at him as they entered her bedchamber. "I cannot imagine anyone standing out there. It has been raining all day."

"Nor can I, but I don't like to vary from my routine." He noticed she held the necklace in her hand. "Here, let me put it on you before I leave to search the grounds."

"Thank you. It felt odd having it off. I almost feel as though it is a magical talisman designed to keep me safe. But I know that necklace has nothing to do with my protection, just as *The Book of Love* cannot magically make people fall in love. Still, it is nice to believe such things are possible."

"There, done." He kissed her on the neck, a light, quick kiss that should not have happened but did. *Bollocks.* He hadn't even been thinking about it, just acted on instinct because everything felt right with Lucy. "Get into bed and dream your magical dreams."

He silently cursed himself, for his voice sounded raw with need.

The last thing he *needed* was to kiss her again.

But this is what he ached to do.

He strode from the room before his brain turned completely soggy. Cursing silently, he shut the door behind him and took a moment to calm down.

He had to stop behaving like a besotted arse.

As the storm continued to rage, rain pounding the roof and shutters, and wind whistling through the trees, he quietly prowled around the house to make certain all remained secure. He had checked all the doors and windows after the Gentrys returned to their cottage for the night but tested all of them again after doing a final inspection of the barn and stables.

Almost an hour had passed by the time he returned to Lucy.

She was still awake, as he suspected she would be, since her mind had not stopped racing with excitement. Searching through the books on heraldry had given her hope they would find clues to her parentage.

He thought it was unlikely, but miracles did happen on occasion.

In any event, keeping her occupied in the library was better than having her run back to London or off to some foreign location where he might never find her.

"You were gone a long while, Donal. Any problems?"

Other than his usual worries about keeping her safe? "No. How are you feeling tonight? Do you need me…"

"In my bed?" She cast him a wry smile. "I think you had better not. I'll be all right knowing you are in the room with me. But if your pallet is uncomfortable, then—"

"I'll be fine on the pallet," he said in a rush, intent on settling the matter before he ended up atop her and grinding his big, oafish self into her exquisite, little body.

She cast him a grin. "We'll both be safer if you keep your distance, won't we?"

He came to her side and planted a kiss on her forehead. "I would never do anything to hurt you, Lucy. Sweet dreams. I'll see you in the morning." He left her side and took a moment to fashion his pallet by the hearth. "Lucy…"

"Yes?"

He rested on his haunches as he regarded her from across the room. She was comfortably nestled under the covers. "Do not leave this room for any reason without waking me first."

She tipped her head up to peer at him. "Even if I have to…tend to my necessaries? I cannot…while you are here in the room with me."

"I'll give you privacy. The important thing is that I need to know where you are at all times. Wake me. I'll be the one to step out. I don't mind. But I will be angry if you sneak off, no matter how innocent the reason." He felt a bit like an ogre, especially since they were probably safe here. But he had not become the Crown's best agent by taking anything for granted.

"I'll do as you ask, Donal. Good night."

He stretched out beside the hearth and closed his eyes while absorbing the sounds and scents of the room, listening for an unexpected creak upon the stairs or scratch against the window-panes. He eventually drifted off to the rhythmic pounding of the rain.

The steady patter of raindrops ought to have lulled him to sleep, but he remained on edge. Perhaps he was overly worried because of these growing feelings for Lucy. But his instincts were rarely wrong, and he sensed trouble approaching.

How long before their hiding place was discovered?

Could he protect her from these trained assassins?

Who was she to the villain behind it all, and why did he want her dead?

CHAPTER TWELVE

L UCY WAS STILL sleeping, her body curled in a little ball, as Donal looked down on her. She reminded him of a kitten nestled on a bed. He smiled, liking that she seemed more at peace than she had the night before. He expected she was still in torment over the news of her true birthright, for one did not get over such a thing in a day.

However, the distraction of poring over his grandfather's books must have made her feel as though she was accomplishing something, giving her a sense of control over her destiny. That control was illusory, but he was not about to tell her that.

Did anyone have the power to change their fate?

Well, it was no time to get philosophical about it.

If her studies calmed her, he was not going to do anything to dampen her hopes. "Lucy," he said in a whisper, "I hope your dreams come true."

He stared at her a moment longer, but there was not much he could make out in the dim light. He had kept the drapes and shutters tightly sealed and dared not open them even at this early hour.

Nothing was safe, not while the unknown brute had his agents scouring the countryside for Lucy.

Someone could be watching even now.

He grabbed his knife and made his way next door to his grandfather's bedchamber. Those shutter slats were loose and could be moved imperceptibly to allow him to peer out.

He saw that the ground was still covered in a hazy mist. However, the sky was clearing, and the sun would burn through the layers of gray now covering the damp grass as the morning wore on.

He also expected Blanche to lumber into the kitchen at any moment to begin her daily chores. She had a key to unfasten the latch, so he did not need to worry about having locked her out. He watched from his grandfather's window as she left the caretaker's cottage, where she and her family resided, and walked to the manor house.

Her husband was beside her and gave her a kiss as they parted ways, she for the house and he for the stable.

Donal shook his head and sighed.

Would he ever have this with Lucy? "Bah, don't be a dolt."

He returned to Lucy's bedchamber, quietly washed and shaved, then slipped on a fresh shirt he had borrowed from his grandfather's wardrobe. It was a simple work shirt and a little snug around his chest, but it would have to do for now.

Lucy began to stir as he was about to put on his boots. "Good morning," he said softly, loving the sultry look of her as she awoke.

She cast him a sleepy smile. "What time is it? Did I oversleep?"

"Not at all. It's not even six o'clock. No need to get up."

"But you are already washed and dressed." She sat up, her eyes half-closed and her hair an attractively rumpled mess. "Will you give me a few minutes to take care of myself?"

"Of course."

"Then I'd like to return to the library to finish going over the books." She touched a hand to her heart, or rather to her necklace that rested over her heart. He noticed her relief to find it still securely around her neck.

"Take as long as you need, Lucy. I know you're eager to resume where we left off last night. Books, then breakfast, then

I'd like to show you some hidden caves on the property, now that the rain has stopped. I want to leave some supplies in one of them on the chance we need to make a fast escape."

She nibbled her lip. "Do you think it will become necessary?"

"I hope not. I just like to be prepared. I'd also like you to keep sewing those spare gowns. I want to store one in the cave when you've finished altering it. One less thing to worry about if we happen to get soaked or muddied while on the run. Hard to keep alert if you're suffering from a lung infection because you had no dry clothes available."

He left her to ready herself for the day while he went down to the kitchen to greet Blanche. He would return in a few minutes to lace her up, but there was no urgency to anything they did today.

"Good morning, Master Donal," Blanche crooned, smiling up at him. "How is the sweet lass?"

"Awake and eager to get back to the library." He assisted her in lighting a fire in the massive hearth and, at her request, carried several pots over to it while she poured out the oats for their morning porridge.

"Can't blame the poor dove, wanting to know where she belongs and who she belongs to. Everyone seems to have abandoned her. I hope you won't."

He arched an eyebrow. "She isn't abandoned. The Duke of Wooton will acknowledge her as his own as soon as the assassins are apprehended. She'll enter society as the daughter of a duke and won't need me to—ow!" Blanche smacked him hard on the shoulder with a wooden spoon. "What did you do that for?"

"She won't need you? Is that what ye think? And what of you? Don't ye dare pretend ye have no feelings for her."

"Did you ever stop to think she might not want me?"

She smacked him again. "Stop that ridiculous talk at once. Ye're not blind. Surely ye see the way she looks at ye. I'll not have ye abandoning her as everyone else has done in her life."

He rubbed his shoulder and scowled at her.

The old woman packed a wallop.

"Who appointed you her protector?" he grumbled. "She won you over remarkably fast."

"I am always on yer side, Master Donal. But it is not right of ye to hurt her. One has only to look at the girl to see she has laid her vulnerable heart out before ye. Do ye understand how difficult it must be for her to trust ye with it? How crushing it will be if ye reject her? I will beat ye senseless if ye do."

"You don't even know her. Why am I made out to be the rogue?"

She rolled her eyes. "Typical man. Ye think marriage will be the death of ye and find every stupid reason to avoid it. But did ye ever think of how happy ye might be if ye accepted the lass into yer heart? It will not make ye a weaker man for it. But if ye cannot see that, ye will miss out on a lifetime of joy."

"Why does every woman think a man cannot be happy as a bachelor?"

"Rot and nonsense. Is that what ye want to be? A tired old man living alone in a musty house, no wife or children to bring fulfillment to yer life? And what about her happiness? I know ye like her. But are ye going to treat her like rubbish just as everyone else has done? Shame on ye, Master Donal."

He groaned. "Leave it alone for now, Blanche. My first priority is keeping her alive. I'll give consideration to what you have said once she is out of danger. I'm not going to let anyone hurt her, not even me. Especially not me. I'm not a complete oaf. May I trouble you for a cup of coffee? Or are you going to hit me again and tell me to get it myself?"

"I'll do it for ye, ye wicked man." She lumbered to the stove and set a pot of coffee to brew and then put water in the kettle to heat for Lucy.

"I had better go see how she's doing," he muttered, about to rise when Lucy walked into the kitchen.

Donal shot to his feet in alarm. "Who helped you lace your gown?"

He knew she could not have done it on her own.

"Petrina did. She came up to tidy the room and—"

"How did she get upstairs? I didn't pass her on the back steps."

Lucy's eyes widened in the face of his mounting anger. "She didn't mean any harm. What has she done wrong? Obviously, she must have come up the main staircase."

"No, she would have had to come into the house through the kitchen first and…" Donal raked a hand through his hair. "Blessed saints! Blanche, is there another way into this house?"

The woman hemmed and hawed and then glanced down at her toes. Anything to avoid meeting his gaze. After a moment, she sighed and nodded. "A secret passage. But I don't use it. The steps are too steep and narrow for me."

"Damn it. Why wasn't I told about this third entrance? Where is it?"

"Please, Master Donal. I cannot manage those stairs. Petrina will show ye."

"Bloody right she will," he muttered and left to go in search of the girl.

Petrina looked up as he entered the bedchamber he and Lucy shared. Lord, that sounded awful. He wasn't sharing it so much as…*bollocks*. What did it matter? "Put aside whatever it is you are doing and show me how you got up here."

The girl had just made Lucy's bed and was grasping the chamber pot in her now trembling hands. "Why, it was just through the old servants' passageway," she said, her eyes as wide as those of a frightened doe. "Should I not have used it?"

He rubbed the nape of his neck in consternation. "Show it to me."

How did he not know of its existence? He and his brothers had run amok on their visits here as children and yet never discovered this third staircase…a hidden passage, the sort often found in medieval castles. But this house was not more than a hundred years old. He needed to know where the access points were and if any of the passages led out of the house.

Lucy had scampered after him, no doubt concerned he might shout at Petrina or do worse. No, she could not think he would ever strike a woman.

Petrina led them into his grandfather's room, then pushed a spot on the wall that silently slid open.

Dank air filled his nostrils.

Lucy inhaled lightly. "Oh, my."

"I didn't see no harm in using it, Master Donal," the girl said, her voice shaking. "I didn't mean to do wrong."

The girl appeared ready to burst into tears, and he quickly sought to calm her. "Petrina, don't fret. I am angry with myself, not you. I had no idea this secret door existed. But now, thanks to you, I do. You've done us a great favor. Set your chores aside for the moment and show us through the passageway."

"As ye wish." She led them along a narrow walkway and down a set of steps that circled back to the kitchen. However, before they reached the kitchen access, there was another narrow passage that led to a tunnel running beneath the house and grounds.

"Where does this end, Petrina?"

"In the woods."

"Of course." He shook his head and laughed. "How stupid of me."

Lucy tipped her head in obvious confusion. "What am I missing?"

"What is the one profession no one talks about but everyone does?"

Lucy eyed him, still confused.

"Smuggling, of course. The former owner must have been up to his eyeballs in the trade to have built this elaborate tunnel. He would have used it to avoid encountering the king's men. While they watched the house, he carried illicit goods in and out through here under their very noses. Do you know if my grandfather carried on the tradition?"

Petrina hesitated. "Um, yer grandfather may have used it a time or two."

Donal arched an eyebrow. "May have used it? I knew there was mischief in the old goat. He must have been thrilled when he found this tunnel and did not waste a moment developing a robust business bringing in French goods during the war years. Lord, how could I have been so stupid? He always said he'd built his wealth on the import and export trade. Some of it was honestly made, which must have served as a convenient cover. He made his real money on the contraband trade."

"I hope ye don't think less of him, Master Donal. He was a good and decent man, never did anything really bad. He was generous to the townspeople and paid off the local king's men, so their pockets were quite full. No one ever came to harm. He brought in the loveliest French lace, perfumes, and wines."

"I suppose your father and brother still dabble in this from time to time?" No wonder they hadn't disclosed the existence of this tunnel earlier. Perhaps they assumed he knew of it. No matter, he knew of it now.

She nodded. "It is harmless, really. Ox and m'father rarely bother with it now that the war is over. Ye won't turn them in, will ye?"

"Of course not." But he would give them a private talking to since he was an agent of the Crown and could not have smuggling going on in the home he and his brothers now owned. He expected they would vigorously shake their heads and assure him their activities would stop.

But he knew they would not.

The moment he and Lucy were out of here, the illicit trade would resume.

In truth, he did not care. The taxes imposed on foreign goods were ridiculously steep, and who was harmed? Even the royal family routinely enjoyed these forbidden goods.

More important, this hidden passage was the perfect escape route if he and Lucy needed to go on the run again. Not only did it let out in the woods, but the woods backed onto the stable. They would be able to get to their horses and ride off.

Even if they could not grab the horses at that moment, they could make it to the safety of the caves and wait for a better moment to escape out of Weymouth.

He thanked Petrina for the tour, then led Lucy back to the kitchen, where they had their breakfast. Blanche eyed him cautiously. "I am not angry," he said, "but you should have told me. Lucy's life is in danger, and I need every weapon at my disposal to keep her safe."

She cast a sheepish glance at Lucy. "I'm sorry, truly. We would have said something if those men found ye here."

Donal frowned. "It would have been too late by then. These are ruthless assassins. I cannot stress enough how dangerous they are. There happens to be a woman among them, too. So, you are to trust no one."

Frustrated, he escorted Lucy to the library and sank into the chair beside hers. "I thought I knew every nook and cranny of this house."

She placed a hand on his arm. "It upsets you not to be in control of a situation."

He started to shake his head in denial, but she was right. "I am not a tyrant; however, this was an important miss on my part. The Gentrys should have told me about it when they knew I was prowling around the house checking all the access points."

"Don't blame them. They were afraid you would turn them in for smuggling. After all, you are an agent of the Crown. How were they to know you'd keep quiet about it?"

"I suppose, but I cannot let it go. Your life is at stake, Lucy."

"And they have put their lives at risk by sheltering me." She was still holding onto his arm and now spoke softly to him. "They must understand the danger, and yet they have not complained or urged us to leave. Do you not think it is very brave of them? So, do not be too cross with them. It isn't their fault. They are not trained as you are. Besides, no one cares about me as you do."

This only made him feel worse.

"Donal, it turned out well. Now you know how to get me out of here unnoticed."

"Assuming the opening to the tunnel is well hidden in the woods. We'll walk by it today, as soon as the mist lifts."

"You're going to take me with you?"

"Yes, I want you to know every rock and twig on this property, all the escape routes. All the hiding spots. There is a good possibility you'll need to flee on your own."

"No! Not without you." She stared at him, obviously horrified by the notion.

"Yes, without me. Keeping you alive is all that matters. But as long as there is breath in me, know that I will find you."

She emitted a pained groan. "Where should I run? We ought to agree on a location now. Do you have a place in mind for a rendezvous point?"

"I do. You know my brother, Shayne."

"Of course. He is the magistrate in Taunton. You want me to run to him?"

He nodded. "Taunton isn't too far from here, and you are familiar enough with the area not to get lost."

"What of the Earl of Monkton? Eliza is married to him, and I know she would hide me. His estate is in the next town over. Why shouldn't I go to them instead?"

"That is the worst place to hide and likely the first place anyone hunting you will look. Don't involve them. In fact, don't even think of contacting them. They aren't trained for this sort of danger and will make mistakes. Besides, they now have a child to worry about. I can tell you for certain, if it is a choice of protecting his wife and child or keeping you hidden, the earl will give you over to them without hesitation."

She stared down at her hands, no doubt hurt by the reminder she was not a part of that family.

"Lucy," he said gently, "I know the earl is not an ogre, but he loves Eliza and will do anything to keep her safe. Go to my brother. He will know what to do until I reach you. If you have any difficulty along the way, my cousin Rafe Quinton is the magistrate in Exeter. Try to get there if you cannot make it all the way to Taunton. He will deliver you safely to Shayne. All right?"

She nodded. "All right."

Having settled that business, they resumed studying his grandfather's books. Lucy also took up her sewing, although he could see that their conversation had left her troubled. There was no help for it. She had to be ready to escape without him if necessary.

With nimble fingers, she managed to keep her attention on fashioning a perfect seam, all the while also studying the emblems and family crests found in the pile of books. Perhaps burying herself in both tasks kept her from thinking of being on the run without him.

They worked in silence for almost two hours until Donal rose to take a sheaf of paper, quill pen, and inkpot from his grandfather's desk. "I want to expand our search."

She set aside her needle and thread. "What do you mean?"

"We've only been looking at family crests, but I think we should also be looking at important homes. Those places with the words 'crescent' or 'moon' in their names or built into the design of the house. We'll start with those in England."

She stared at him. "You really think we'll find the answer here? Why not in Italy or Constantinople or Russia?"

"I'm not ruling them out. However, this is how I like to work my investigations, as I mentioned yesterday. I prefer to start inward and work my way out. Also, while the design of your necklace appears to be foreign, the manufacture of it strikes me as English. Not that I am an expert, for I am not by any means."

"There are no markings on it, so we can never know for certain. Goldsmiths and silversmiths often place their signature marks on anything they design, but I've looked for one on this necklace and haven't found anything."

"I couldn't find any either," he remarked.

"And yet, you still think it came from here?"

He raked a hand through his hair in frustration. "I don't know. I also want to read up on whatever we can find about the Duke of Wooton. I know nothing of his early years or his ancestors. Maybe it was one of them who started a feud that is flaring up again. We cannot ignore looking at this mystery by delving into the past of the one party whose identity we do know."

"I wish we had gossip rags from back then. Those would provide a more accurate account, I'm sure. Lurid details. I am twenty years old, so if we could get our hands on newspapers from about twenty-one or twenty-two years ago and work forward…can you think of anywhere nearby where we might get our hands on those archives?"

"Probably any town hall or library of note. Many towns in the area would have them, even the Weymouth magistrate might keep copies of the more important London newspapers. But I am not taking you into town."

"Well, certainly not in broad daylight. But what if we went there at night?"

He arched an eyebrow. "As in breaking in?"

"We wouldn't be stealing anything, just reading," she said in utmost earnest. "We ought to pull out the issues starting about nine months before my birth since this is when any scandal would likely have occurred. But we should also look for reports of any international incidents around that time. Who knows? The Duke of Wooton's name might be mentioned in those." She shook her head. "I cannot think of him as my father. But neither can I think of Mr. Lessing as my father now that I know he is not."

Donal put his hand over hers. "We'll sort it out when the time comes."

She slipped it out of his grip. "Let's go through the tunnel and make certain it is well hidden. I don't think I can sit here any longer."

"Nor can I. The books will be here after we check out the

woods and caves."

"I hope the walk will help clear our heads. I like your idea of digging into Wooton's past, starting with what we know and working outward. I'm sorry we wasted our time hunting for a crest resembling my necklace."

"It wasn't wasted. We've ruled out a lot of families." He grabbed a lamp and matches, then returned to her side. "Stay close to me, Lucy."

She tucked her arm in his. "I will cling to you like a limpet snail to a rock."

Yes, don't ever let go.

What was it about Lucy that spoke to his heart?

❦

CHAPTER THIRTEEN

WERE IT NOT for the fact that people were trying to kill her, Lucy would have been in raptures over the time spent with Donal. She had never been one to fawn and giggle over the handsome men present at the few balls or assemblies she had attended. Most were too elegant for her tastes, too much caught up in the fashionable style of their clothing or the sound of their own voice as they spouted erudite opinions.

Donal was cut from a different cloth.

Handsome as sin, of course. But he was not out to impress anyone.

He did not care how elegantly his cravat was knotted.

He wasn't even wearing a cravat.

He simply was the man he wanted to be. Honest. Protective. Compassionate. It was this quiet compassion she liked best about him. He did not care what others thought of him, yet he was quite valiant in the care he held for others. If someone was in trouble, he would be the first to rush to their aid.

"We're almost to the end," he said, regaining her attention. "Good thing, too. The air is so stale, I can hardly catch my breath."

They had made their way slowly through the smuggler's tunnel, which was surprisingly large and sturdily built. There were no fragile beams to hold up loose soil since there simply was no loose soil. The entire length of it had been carved out of stone.

"It must have taken years to chisel through all this rock," Lucy remarked.

Donal held up the lantern and nodded. "For certain. The original owner must have felt it was worth the effort. This had to have taken a decade to accomplish. But once done, he made a fortune in smuggling his wares. Judging by the size of this tunnel, he was smuggling in shiploads of merchandise. I'm a big man and can stand to my full height along its entire course."

Lucy watched him as he studied the impressive structure.

The lantern light illuminated his features as he held it up. She noted the manly line of his jaw, the elegant slope of his nose, the fine angles of his cheekbones…the wry curve of his lips as he smiled at her.

He was half cast in light and half in shadow.

He looked powerful…ethereal…like a dark angel.

She put a hand to her stomach to still her butterflies as they began to flutter inside.

When he glanced at her and smiled again, heat coursed through her body.

Goodness, he made her insides melt.

"The tunnel is surprisingly dry," she commented, trying not to look like an addlepated fool as she gazed at this splendid man. "Not a single puddle or muddy patch. One would think the dankness would carry throughout the tunnel after all the rain we just had."

"With this access point so securely sealed, I expect very little air or moisture seeps in. Let's see where it lets out. Stay close to me, Lucy."

She laughed. "I have not let go of you the entire time. Am I not like an unpleasant mist breathing on your neck?"

"Nothing at all unpleasant about you," he murmured, now shoving lightly against what looked like a door. "Hold the lantern while I try to get this open. Step back. I don't want you hurt if anything falls on me as I push it wide."

He put his shoulder to it, his honed muscles straining as he shoved at it with all his might.

"Ye won't get it open that way," a deep voice said from behind her.

Lucy gasped and almost dropped the lantern as she turned to face a young man the size of an ox. She emitted a nervous trill of laughter. "You must be…Ox. Mrs. Gentry's son."

He nodded and cast her a surprisingly gentle smile. "M'mum sent me after ye to give ye this key. We keep the door locked when…well, it's locked, and ye'll never get it open without this. Ye'd better hold onto this key for now. I hope ye'll never have the need to use it."

"Thank you," Lucy said with genuine gratitude. "Is this the only one?"

"No, there's another. But this spare is important on the chance we lose the one my da is holding."

"Or if it is confiscated by the authorities." Donal came forward to take it from Ox's outstretched hand. "Don't worry. I am not about to report this to anyone."

Lucy nodded earnestly. "We'll take the secret to our graves…that is, not that we plan to die anytime soon." She blushed as she turned to Donal. "I wish for a long and healthy life for both of us."

He grinned. "So do I."

The key turned easily in the lock with a soft click. "Good. You keep it well greased."

"Yes, we try. Most nights, the owls hunting or the sound of waves crashing against the rocks drown out these little noises, but one can never be too careful. Well, I'll leave ye to it unless ye need me to serve as yer guide."

Lucy nodded. "Yes, I think that is an excellent idea."

"No," Donal said at the same time. "I don't want you straying from your daily routine. I remember this place from my childhood. I may even show you a cave or two later that you have not discovered."

Ox shook his head. "Doubtful, but I'm sure m'da will be

eager to talk to ye about it. Have ye seen the old maps?"

Lucy's eyes rounded in excitement. "What maps?"

The young man groaned. "My parents didn't tell ye? Now my da's going to tan my hide but good. Yer grandfather has maps of this property. Every structure, cave, and tunnel. They're kept hidden under the floorboards in the room Miss Lucy's sleeping in."

"Where exactly?" Lucy's heart was pounding so hard, one would think she had just unearthed a pirate's treasure.

"Under yer bed. Ye'd have to lift the bed aside to get at them."

Donal was frowning. "I'll help you move that massive thing once we return to the house. Lucy, we'll study those plots and charts before supper. It is helpful to know what else is hidden here, but I don't want us distracted from our more important search for clues. Finding the identity of the man trying to harm you must come first."

"Certainly, but is it not also wise to know this place and all its hiding spots? Is it not the very reason I am here with you now? We'll have plenty of time for both over the coming days."

He made no further comment before turning to Ox. "Just go back about your duties as though we are not here."

Lucy waited for him to trot off to the house before she turned to Donal. "He could have been helpful. You haven't explored here for years. Why didn't you want him to come with us?"

"An abundance of caution on my part, perhaps." He led her out of the tunnel, locked the door behind them, and tucked the key securely in the lip of his boot, where he also kept a sharply honed knife. He kept a loaded pistol in his other boot. Who knew what other weapons he had hidden on his person?

She stood aside as he removed all trace of their footprints and other traces of the tunnel's entrance. Once done, he took the lantern from her hand, doused it since they were now in broad daylight, and then led her through the woods to the hidden caves he'd told her about earlier.

The ground was still muddy from yesterday's hard rain, requiring them to step around the dampest areas and hop over some lingering puddles. She kept her gown drawn up to her knees, trying to protect the fabric. But she still managed to get splotches of mud on it. "Drat."

"Mrs. Gentry or Petrina will attend to any stains. Don't worry about it now."

Lucy gave a little bob of her head to acknowledge his comment as they continued traipsing through the underbrush.

The sun was out in full strength now, the sky unusually clear and blue. A warm breeze blew gently through her hair and carried the salty tang of the sea. In the distance, she heard the crash of waves against the rocks. They walked in silence until they reached the edge of the woods where it met the cliff face. From there, it was a steep drop to the small strip of sandy beach that lay nestled between two massive outcroppings of stone.

"Perhaps I am being too cautious," Donal repeated as they stood together, looking out across the swirling blue waters. "But it still troubles me that those villains seemed to know our every move. They were lurking in wait for us everywhere we went."

She nodded. "You've told me you believe there is someone working on the inside, someone close to Wooton who is betraying him."

"It also means this someone knows more about me than I like. This informer will be angry when he learns you and I were never on our way to Dover."

"But it is quite a stretch to know we did not leave England and be able to track us here."

"I know. Still, I cannot take anything for granted. Should your assailants pass by here, I want them to move on and rule out my grandfather's place as our hiding spot. The only way to do that is to keep the Gentrys to their usual routine unwaveringly. It is for their own protection as much as ours." He rubbed the nape of his neck and sighed.

She looked up at him with worry. "What is agitating you

now?"

"This blasted prickle at my neck. I can't shake it. I *feel* their foulness in the area."

Lucy inched closer to him. "Do you think they will see us if we climb down to the caves?"

"No. We are only visible from the sea, and there's no one out on the water. Even if someone was out there, they'd need to be looking through a spy glass to see us." He put his arm around her waist. "This is just me being on edge. Have you made note of our path? Do you think you could find your way here in the dark?"

"I think so. However, there isn't much space between the end of the woods and the cliff's edge. That is my greatest fear. If I had to run away in the dark, I might just leap straight off and fall upon the rocks below because I could not see where the tree line stops."

"You won't make that mistake if you use all your senses."

"What do you mean?"

"Close your eyes, Lucy," he said softly against her ear. Once she did, he continued in that same soft, husky rumble. "*The Book of Love* spoke about these senses. You told me so the other night. Did you take any of it in? Or were you just spouting what you'd learned but not really understanding what it meant?"

"I find that highly insulting," she shot back teasingly, her eyes still closed. He did have a point, she reluctantly admitted to herself. If she ever found herself running in the dark, she had to use more than just her eyes to "see" what was before her. "What else should I be doing to stop myself from tumbling off this cliff?"

"Use the sense of sound. What do you hear?"

Beyond the pounding of her heart because he stood so close and smelled so insanely good? "Um, I hear the rustle of the wind through the trees."

"What else?"

"The waves crashing against the rocks. Oh, and some of those waves are also gently *whooshing* against the sand."

"That's right. You'll know you are close to the edge when

you can also hear that soft whoosh. That is the sound to listen for. It will alert you to the cliff drop." He turned her to face him, her eyes now open as she waited for his next instruction.

He told her to close them again. "The scent of the air will also give you clues. Take a deep breath, Lucy."

She laughed. "I am breathing you in."

"I'll step away," he responded with a chuckle. "Don't move. Just give it a minute, and then take another breath. Tell me what scents you notice."

She had been irritated with his disinterest in *The Book of Love*, but it was obvious he had already mastered the five senses. Not only mastered them but used them every moment of every day for his survival.

This revelation was humbling.

She had thought herself superior in knowledge and was ready to chide him for ignoring the book. But she was the one who needed chiding. Having read it, she still hadn't understood its teachings as well as he had done without reading a single word. Despite her bluestocking ways, her love of learning and eagerness to absorb everything she could, it turned out she was wholly lacking in the matter of the senses.

"Breathe in," he said, standing downwind of her so she would not inhale his glorious scent. "Keep your eyes closed. What strikes your nostrils?"

"The scent of the sea. A little salty. A hint of fish…rotting?"

"You are probably noticing the stench of dried kelp on the sand." He put an arm around her and led her back into the woods. "What scents do you notice now?"

She was surprised by the difference the short distance made. "Damp leaves. Pine. Also, a little of the sea."

She opened her eyes and smiled at him. "How did I do?"

He grinned. "Top marks, Lucy. Do you think you can keep all of it in your head and notice these subtle changes? It takes training to be able to stay aware of everything around you and immediately pick up on the slightest variations."

"I'll try my best."

"You're doing beautifully." He took her hand and kept hold of it as they made their way along a hardly noticeable trail that led between rocks. "Here it is."

"Here is what? I only see more rocks."

"Look closely," he prompted.

"And some scrawny bushes. Obviously windswept."

"What else?"

"I give up. Oh, I see a few nests, too. What sort of birds does one find here?"

"The usual. Swallows, kestrels. Warblers. But none of them build nests like these. They are fake. Lift up the biggest one."

She attended to the task carefully. "There are more rocks beneath it."

"We'll move a few of them out of the way." He helped her draw the larger ones aside until they'd cleared what appeared to be a small hole.

"Is that the entry to the cave?"

"One of the caves. Be careful. The steps are slippery. Wait until I light the lantern again. I'll go first and help you down this time. If ever you should have to hide in here, you cannot panic. Make certain you slide a few stones over the opening after you are inside, or if you cannot, then do your best to pull the nest over it. Stick one of the smaller rocks in the nest to keep it from blowing away. Then carefully make your way toward the entrance. If they should find this one and follow you down that little hole, then run out the front and hide in one of the other caves. I'm going to show you the rest of them next."

"You make it sound so simple."

He gave her cheek a light caress. "I know it isn't. But awareness of the hiding spots on this property gives you the advantage should they find us. I would train you in firing a weapon, but the noise would draw too much attention."

She shook her head. "I don't think I would be very good at it anyway. Fading into the shadows is what I do best. I'll use my wallflower ways to my advantage."

"You are a beautiful, glowing light." He made a grumbling sound of displeasure. "Not in the least a fading shadow. Only a fool would ever overlook you. Do not bother to deny it. I'll hear not a word of protest from your lips. Come on. Let's explore the caves."

They spent the next several hours climbing over rocks and down openings that seemed no larger than rabbit holes. Lucy was tired by the time they made their way through the last of the caves and walked back to the tunnel entrance leading to the manor house.

Donal had put her in charge of guiding them through the woods to be certain she knew her way. "I have a good sense of direction," she assured him.

"You did that flawlessly, Lucy," he said with a broad smile to mark his satisfaction. "But be aware it is easy to get turned around in the darkness."

"I've made note of markers and where each is in relation to the others. I'll know at once if I'm headed the wrong way."

"Well done, you clever thing." He smiled again and traced a finger along the line of her jaw. "Your cheeks are pink, and so is your nose."

"It is all the adventurous climbing. I've never done this before, but I enjoyed it immensely. I also like that it gives me power. For the first time in my life, I feel as though I have some control over my fate. Not that I intend to leap down from the trees and punch my assailants. I know I am no physical match for them and all I must do is hide. But it enables me to do something useful to save my own life."

He unlocked the hidden entry to the tunnel, then cleared all trace of their footsteps and put the shrubs back in place before shutting the door and locking it again. Lucy had been holding the lantern while he tended to the task, and he now took it out of her hands. "I hope Blanche prepared a hearty meal for us. I'm starved."

She laughed. "So am I. The bracing sea air definitely helps one work up an appetite."

"We'll return to the books right after we eat, unless you're tired and—"

"I do not need an afternoon nap to restore my delicate bones. I may not look like much, but I am hardy."

He took her by the elbow and turned her to face him. "Stop saying that, will you? I've told you, you are beautiful. Don't let anyone ever convince you otherwise."

"But this is precisely what I have been told all of my life," she said with a dismissive shake of her head. "I am no one special. I am plain. Merely to be tolerated. Mostly ignored. You are the only one who has ever made me feel worthwhile. You called me...beautiful." She had never been in love and wasn't certain what it ought to feel like, but she imagined it would be very much like how she felt about Donal right now.

Being with him, never mind that she was only an assignment, felt exquisitely good.

"Lucy," he said in an aching whisper.

She cut him off before he said anything more. Oh, she knew he liked her to some extent. He certainly liked her enough to kiss her and not mind having to hold her hand. But he would leave her once this assignment was over, and her heart was already breaking over the thought of never seeing him again...or worse, seeing him with another woman on his arm. "Let's eat and then return to the library."

Needing something to hold onto, she took the lantern back out of his hands and quickly led the way to the kitchen. But she paused as they were about to open the secret doorway and enter it. "Once this is over, assuming we survive...I promise you I will not be Lucy the dull dish rag again." She cast him a wry smile. "I will still be a bluestocking and run to the library when at a party, but it will be because I like to do this, not because I am hiding or ashamed."

He wanted to say something to her, had reached out for her,

but she quickly opened the secret door.

Blanche was working alone in the kitchen.

Lucy hurried in and set the lantern on one of the side tables. "Smells delicious," she remarked, trying to ignore the fact that Donal had not taken his eyes off her, and his gaze was boring into her back. Of course, he wasn't angry with her but irritated that she did not consider herself a fascinating woman.

What a jest!

Even he had called her gowns ugly and thought of her as a bespectacled, boring bluestocking. Well, his regard for her may have softened, but he was hardly enraptured by her siren ways. First of all, sirens did not wear spectacles. He'd worried about her loss of them on the night they were attacked. She ought to have confessed they were fake, just another prop to hide behind.

She had hinted at it.

He probably realized it anyway because nothing ever got past him.

Still feeling the heat of his attention on her, she busied herself helping Blanche set the table.

The others joined them in the repast of a hearty stew, and then Ox and Donal slipped upstairs to retrieve his grandfather's old maps. Lucy scurried after them and watched in amazement as these two brawny men lifted the bed that must have taken twenty men to carry up here. Ox then removed the floorboards and withdrew a dozen yellowed papers. "This is everything," he said, looking up at Donal.

Lucy took the papers while the men secured the floorboards and put the bed back in position. Ox then headed off to resume his daily routine while she and Donal went back to work in the library.

The sweat of his labors lingered on his body, but it was a hot, manly scent that shot a pang of awareness through her. She wanted so badly to touch him, to put her lips to his skin and taste his warmth.

He would think her mad.

She turned her attention to the papers instead and heard his soft chuckle as she stared at them. "Your eyes are glowing as bright as full moons."

"These maps are amazing." Afraid to look at him for fear of melting into a puddle, she took in the architectural plans, the tunnel drawings, and the various cave sketches. "Are you aware of all these caves, Donal?"

He nodded. "I didn't take you to all of them because there wasn't time today. We'll go out again tomorrow if the weather holds. I even know of a few more that are not shown on this map."

"Where?"

He pointed out two more not far from the first cave they'd explored today. They pored over the house plans and made note of which rooms had access to the secret passages. After a while, Donal began to fold them back up. "Lucy, I think we should consider who wants you and Wooten dead. These maps might prove to be a distraction we don't need."

"All right. We'll put them aside in a moment, but what is that last map?"

He shrugged. "I'm not sure why it is in here. It seems to be a general sketch of the southwest coast of England. Probably shows the best inlets between Portsmouth and Plymouth for smuggling goods and where the king's regiments are situated."

She pursed her lips. "No, look. It shows more than that."

He peered more closely at the markings. "You're right. This is not about the regimental posts. Each mark represents…a family. This map is a detail of the consortium of noble families in the area involved in this specific smuggling enterprise. They joined forces for this purpose. No wonder this tunnel is so big. The former owner was supplying the entire southeast of England. Supplying them and probably taking a cut of anything that came in or out."

Lucy suddenly gripped his arm. "Donal, am I seeing right? What is this?"

❦

CHAPTER FOURTEEN

Donal stared at the spot where Lucy was pointing. Emblems had been drawn on this map of southeast England stretching from Portsmouth to Plymouth. He had no doubt each emblem designated a particular noble family.

These were not the actual family crests but served a similar purpose to identify the participants in the smuggling operation.

"Here. Look here," Lucy said breathlessly.

To the north of Plymouth and a little to the east was the important market town of Exeter. He knew the town well because his cousin, Rafe Quinton, was magistrate there. Between Plymouth and Exeter was the area of Dartmoor, and drawn immediately over the word "Dartmoor," was the emblem depicted on Lucy's necklace.

The crescent moon.

The lion rampant.

Rings of gold circles around both.

"Blessed saints," he muttered, although he silently swore much saltier oaths to himself which were not proper for Lucy's ears. Indeed, an entire string of oaths ran through his head because he knew what was about to happen next, and he meant to cut off all discussion. "Lucy, we are not going to Dartmoor."

"But why not? If we leave early enough and the weather holds up, I'm sure we can reach Exeter in a day. The town is large enough for us to risk spending the night at one of the lesser coaching inns. You've mentioned your cousin is magistrate there, but we should not stay with him. He has a small boy, does he not? I would never put a child at risk. Perhaps we are better off stopping just outside Exeter. From there, it is a short ride to Dartmoor. We—"

"Do you seriously expect me to take you into the jaws of this beast who is trying to kill you?" He stared at her incredulously. "Do not toss me that soft smile and say you trust me to keep you safe."

"Why not? You are wonderful, and I do trust you."

He groaned, loving the starlight in her eyes and knowing she did think the world of him. But he was not invincible. He could not protect her if they were outnumbered. "I am going to tie you up…bind you hand and foot to your bed if you dare suggest this again."

She gasped. "You wouldn't."

"Try me." He tried to look fierce, as though he would reign fire, and she had better not cross him. But Lucy had a way of looking at him that softened his heart, so he doubted that stern glare was effective at all.

Now she was staring back at him, her eyes so wide he could see into her vulnerable soul. "With or without my clothes?"

His heart hitched. "What?"

"Will you bind me with my clothes on or without them?"

Was she serious?

"Do you know what I think?" she said in a sultry purr that now had his heart completely stopping. "It would be ever so much fun if you bound me with them and then slowly peeled—"

"Damn it, Lucy." He blinked and shook his head. "I am not your biddable servant. Do not use seductive tricks on me out of that love book. They will not work."

Which was an outright lie.

One sexy purr out of her, and he was on fire, every pulse on his body throbbing. He was a professional. She was his assignment. How many times had he repeated those warnings to keep himself from stripping the gown off her delectable body and kissing his way down the entire length of her?

The urge to plant himself inside her sweet, soft warmth was growing unbearable. But her body was not enough; he wanted to plant himself inside her heart.

He blinked again.

He wanted to marry her.

"Donal, do you have something in your eye? I know you well enough to realize what those blinks mean. I affected you. Was it—"

"Do not say another word." He placed his hands on the table, palms flat, and leaned forward so that his face, which once again held his sternest expression, was inches from hers. "You are not going to seduce me into taking you to Dartmoor."

She stared back at him with those ensorcelling eyes, demolishing all his defenses. "Do you not see? They won't be expecting us. They'll be searching everywhere but under their very noses. It is so simple, it's perfect."

"That thinking is going to get you killed. Wooton knows who is behind these attacks. He'll be on his way to Dartmoor as soon as he recovers from his injury. Perhaps he is there now. Leave him to it. He isn't known as the Duke of Ice for his kind and generous nature. He will go to Dartmoor to destroy his enemy."

"On his own? No one to assist him? All the more reason for us to help."

"Having you underfoot is the one thing he does not want. Indeed, it is the worst thing imaginable. You cannot shoot a pistol. You know nothing of weapons or tricks of defense. You are completely untrained. What if this villain captured you? People like these…cold, ruthless…there are worse things that could happen to you than shooting you dead. This villain might keep you alive and…" He emitted an agonized groan. "I dare not even think what he might do to you."

"Donal!"

"Why are you shocked, Miss Bind-Me-With-Or-Without-My-

Clothes? This villain is filled with hate. Do you think he will pleasantly invite you to tea? All you would do by going to Dartmoor is make it easy for him to do whatever he wishes to you and then kill you? He won't even have to leave his castle. His lackeys will drop you at his feet. Don't you get it? Dartmoor is his stronghold."

"So, we are to hide here and simply wait for that monster's men to find us?"

"Yes." He was still scowling at her, but he was aching on the inside. "I am not going to lose you, Lucy."

"You will never lose me," she said in a choked whisper. "You have my heart forever. Can you not see this?"

Now the blasted girl had turned his own heart upside down.

He came around to her side of the table and drew her into his arms. "I couldn't bear it if you were hurt. I couldn't. I am not speaking as a professional now." He brushed a stray wisp of hair off her brow. "I never kiss my assignments."

"But you've kissed me."

Of course she would point it out as though he could ever forget the taste of her, the silken touch of her skin, or the beauty of her smile.

"And I am about to do it again." He drew her up against him and brought his mouth down on hers.

Huge mistake.

He was in love with Lucy.

Yet, he could not be in love with her and properly protect her. His heart was too engaged with this lovely girl. How could he remain cool, detached? He would turn into a savage beast if anyone ever laid a hand on her.

His lips pressed against those luscious, heart-shaped lips of hers. Sweet. Soft. Plump lips. He loved the way she surrendered to him.

Then she began to talk against his mouth because this was Lucy, always ready with questions and eager to tell him what she was feeling as each sensation washed over her. "Donal, I want you to know…"

He kissed her again more urgently.

"Oh, my…that is very nice."

"Hush, Lucy."

"But I want you to—"

He was not going to allow it. They were going to end up in bed if she said what he thought she was about to say. He did not want her to tell him that she loved him. He was not going to say it back to her.

It did not matter that he loved her. Loved her beyond anything he'd ever known in his life. Feelings had to be set aside, no matter how much this flood of desire overwhelmed him.

He deepened the kiss, pressed his mouth against her pliable lips, and wrapped her in the gentle strength of his embrace. His hands roamed along her body, running up and down her every exquisite curves.

After a moment, he brought up one hand to cup her face. He felt tears on her cheek. "Lucy, sweetheart."

Gad, he was breaking every rule.

"I cannot help it. You overwhelm me. In a lovely way. I never want to be out of your arms. But I know I cannot stay in them forever. Our time together will come to an end soon. Perhaps as early as tomorrow. This is so hard for me, Donal. I'm sorry if this is proving an embarrassment to you."

He wanted to kiss her again.

An embarrassment?

How did she not see he was the one making a fool of himself over her?

She eased out of his arms and brushed aside her tears with a light dab of her sleeve. "Let's keep to the subject at hand. Shall we find out more about whose emblem is a match to my necklace? Do you think it is my mother's family?"

His heart was still in rampant turmoil, but it was best they forget about their feelings for now. "I don't know. But we now have a solid lead. Let's see what else we can find in this pile of books."

She was still sniffling as they returned to their seats at the table. He picked up the *Debrett's Peerage* again and quickly found the name of that noble family in Dartmoor...de Poitiers. There was a current Baroness de Poitiers, who held the title in abeyance. Upon her death, a distant cousin, a young man of fourteen years of age, would claim the de Poitiers barony. At that tender age, he was still too young to formally take on the duties of the title and likely too young to plot Lucy's death.

He raked a hand through his hair. "Blessed saints. It's starting to make sense now."

She shifted her chair closer to his. "What have you found?"

He quickly showed her the pages in the book of peerage. "Does the name de Poitiers signify anything to you?" he asked once she had finished reading.

"Should it? Other than historically, I mean. Poitiers, is this not the region in France where the dukes of Aquitaine had their stronghold? Queen Eleanor, who married the English King Henry II, was Duchess of Aquitaine. She and Henry married in Poitiers, and afterward, they returned to England where she gave him children, two of whom became kings in their own right. Richard, who was beloved, which always surprised me considering he spent almost no time in England. But I suppose he was quite valiant on Crusade. His younger brother, John, assumed the throne upon his death. But he was disliked by his barons, who coerced him into signing the Magna Carta."

She took a breath and continued. "Eleanor was one of our most powerful English queens, although obviously, she was not English. Indeed, she held vast areas of France in her own right as duchess. I suppose this is why England later sought to claim half of France. Um...should I go on?"

Donal grinned. "No, Lucy. Sorry I let you prattle, but I truly like your cleverness. I knew you would be familiar with that name. Now take it the next step. How do you think Eleanor is connected to you?"

Her eyes widened in surprise. "To me?"

She shook her head and laughed, believing he was in jest. But he wasn't. Having digested the description of the de Poitiers line of succession, it all made perfect sense to him now.

She stared at him in disbelief. "How is it…wait…are you suggesting this title, having descended from Eleanor of Aquitaine, can pass directly to a female? And…oh, no. You are mad to believe I could…you cannot believe it. No, it is impossible. I cannot have a superior claim to the title than that boy."

"Not only to that boy but to the baroness who currently holds the title in abeyance." He tucked a finger under her chin and gave her a light kiss on the nose.

"Are you suggesting my mother was related to the baroness?"

"Not just related but was first in line to succeed the old Baron de Poitiers upon his death."

"So that upon my mother's death, I became first in line? Ahead of the current baroness? Ahead of the boy?"

"Top marks for you."

She frowned at him. "That is absurd. This necklace is no proof at all. It could have been lost. Pawned. Sold at auction. It is no more than a coincidence I ended up with it. Anyway, women do not inherit titles in England."

"Now you are purposely being dense. Is there not a current Baroness de Poitiers? Forget about that boy for the moment. It is the baroness who interests me most." He pointed to the pages in the peerage book.

She shook her head. "There must be some mistake."

"Is what you just read completely meaningless? Eleanor of Aquitaine was no mere woman. She was more powerful than most kings throughout history. She was a queen of England and, before that, a queen of France. How many women in history can claim that? I knew there was something special about you the moment I set eyes on you."

"Don't be ridiculous. Even if I were somehow connected, the only way I would have a claim to the estate and title is if the Duke of Wooton had actually married my mother. This also assumes my mother was connected to the de Poitiers family, *and* the original grant permitted women to assume the title."

"Look, there's more here about the family history. Two female cousins who were the right age to have been love interests for Wooton. Blessed saints! Look at the names. Andrea and Olivia."

Lucy stared at him.

"Andrea," he repeated. "This had to be the woman who shot Mel back at the old bridge in Tunbridge Wells. So, we know she is alive, but look at the date of death for Olivia. Five days after your birth."

"Stop, Donal. I cannot take it all in." She buried her face in her hands.

His heart sank as he realized he'd piled all this on her too fast.

These revelations had to be tearing her to pieces.

His growing affection for her was not helping.

He had put her heart in turmoil with those kisses that never should have happened—the result being she considered him yet another person who would walk away from her once the danger had passed.

Pile that atop finding out her family connections and, in the same breath, discovering this woman who could have been her mother was dead and her next closest relative, this Andrea person, was desperate to kill her.

He had been so caught up in unraveling the puzzle, he'd given no thought to Lucy's feelings. This news had to be so difficult for her. A mother she had never known and now would never know.

"Lucy, I'm sorry." This was no mere puzzle for her but a hunt for the missing pieces of her heart. A search for her own identity.

Her head was still buried in her hands, and her shoulders were shaking.

"Olivia must have been as beautiful as you," he said with aching tenderness. "Not only in her physical beauty but in her soul as well. Wooton never stopped loving her. He may be the Duke of Ice to others, but he must have melted the moment he set eyes on his Olivia."

"How can you say that? He abandoned us."

"He must have had his reasons."

"What possible explanation for leaving this woman he supposedly loved and the child she carried to the mercy of wolves?"

"Whatever forced them apart had to have been something over which they had no control. His military duties, perhaps. Family disagreements."

He sighed when she did not respond.

Rather than look up, she kept her face hidden in her hands and was silently crying. Those silent tears just crushed him. "Lucy, I think Wooton chose me to protect you because he recognized how I felt about you."

"That's a lark. I am a bluestocking and a watering pot."

"You are an angel. Wooton knew I would take any measures to protect you."

Her face was still covered, and she would not budge to look up at him. "Because you are a professional, and I am your assignment."

"You must know you are more to me than this."

"You are mistaken. You only believe I am important to you because someone is trying to kill me, and your protective instincts cannot allow it to happen. Things will change once the danger has passed."

"Which brings me back to the reason we are not to go anywhere near Dartmoor. I will get a message to Wooton and Edgeware reporting what we've discovered about this Andrea and warning them of that high-level spy within our London office. Then you and I are going to do nothing but wait until one of them sends their coded message in the papers advising the danger has passed."

"Will you not tell them where we are?"

"Absolutely not. This still remains our secret. Once things

settle down, I will take you wherever you wish to go."

"Assuming Wooton allows it. You are more precious to him than I will ever be. He'll send you off on your next assignment, and you will soon forget me. The only question in my mind is, how soon before he also forgets me?"

"Never, and that applies to both of us. He will acknowledge you as his daughter and provide you with all the benefits of his rank and wealth, as well as ensure you, not Andrea, are properly recognized as baroness in your own right."

Moments went by, and Lucy still would not look at him.

Perhaps it was for the best.

She had gone from being Miss Luciana Lessing, daughter of no one of consequence and therefore considered unremarkable by those in the *ton*, to Lady Luciana, daughter of the Duke of Wooton and perhaps a baroness in her own right.

What could he, a mere agent of the Crown, possibly offer her...other than his love?

CHAPTER FIFTEEN

ALMOST THREE WEEKS had passed since the night Donal fled London with Lucy. He was finding it more difficult by the day to remain in close quarters with her and do nothing about it.

H loved everything about her, from her wry wit and cleverness to the honey scent of her skin.

She set off a yearning deep within his soul.

But an entirely new world was about to open up to her, one of rank and privilege. Would she want him then? Perhaps both of them were making too much of these feelings for each other because they had been thrown together under dire circumstances.

Would he still feel this aching need to protect her once the danger had passed?

He wanted to be done with this assignment and see what would happen next between them.

In any event, he did not like being forced to remain in hiding and unaware of what was going on at the London office. Was Wooton dead? Alive? Had he gone after the de Poitiers villain…or villains since it was possible more than one member of that family had been plotting his and Lucy's demise?

Certainly, the baroness, Andrea, was involved and had likely set the plan in motion. But how could he be certain of anything while he had no idea what was going on outside of this cocoon where he and Lucy were hiding?

A coded message should have been posted in the London

Times by now, but he had found nothing, and this was beginning to worry him.

Of course, these London papers took days to reach Weymouth and then more days before Horace or Ox could go into town on their usual errands and quietly pick up whatever recent issues they found.

He expected some lag in time between an event occurring and the news reaching him. However, this was more of a stretch than he had counted upon.

"Lucy, watch out for that wave," he called to her while standing at the base of the cliff where the rocks met the sand beach. August had rolled by, and they were early into the month of September now. The days were still warm, but the nights were growing cooler.

Twilight came earlier now and would soon be upon them if the arc of the sun was any indication.

"Take off your boots and walk with me." Lucy was standing barefoot at the water's edge, her toes dug into the wet sand, and her gown hiked up to expose her shapely legs. She looked like a water sprite with her hair long and loose, the gentle wind tousling her curls in a swirl about her hips. "The water's lovely. Don't you want to cool yourself down before we return to the house for supper?"

"I am enjoying watching you." He was growing used to this hot and bothered state in which he found himself every time he was near her.

Of course, he was near her all the time.

She smiled and shook her head. "Fine, be stubborn."

He was about to toss back a retort when he heard a gunshot in the distance.

Lucy gasped and immediately ran to his side. "Do you think Ox and Horace are out hunting?"

"At this hour? Doubtful."

A second shot rang out as she hastily gathered her stockings and shoes.

"Those came from the manor house." He hoisted her over his shoulder and began to run to the closest cave.

She pounded lightly on his back. "What are you doing?"

"Stay here, Lucy." He deposited her at the cave's entrance. "Get your shoes on, and don't you dare follow me. I'll come back for you once it is safe. Hide. Do not poke your head out for any reason."

Another shot sounded.

He left her and tore up the cliff path through the woods. He was not a religious man, but right now, he was praying harder than he ever had in his life that the Gentrys were unharmed.

His next prayer was for Lucy's safety when he saw two men on horseback, their backs to him as they studied the house.

Were they alone? Or had they brought others who were now tramping the grounds? Or asking questions in town? Searching the caves? No, only he and Lucy had been anywhere near those caves this afternoon. He would never have left her hiding there otherwise.

Nor had there been any boats sailing into their cove throughout the day.

He moved as silently as a ghost under cover of the trees and circled around to the rear of the manor to scout out who else might be lurking.

But he saw no one other than those two men who were now dismounting by the stable.

"Donal!" a familiar voice called out toward the general direction of the woods. "Can you hear me? Wooton sent me to find you and Miss Lessing. We're to bring you to Exeter. Don't bother hiding. I know you are here."

Lorcan.

"Blessed saints, Lor," he grumbled, stepping out into the clearing with his weapon lowered. He and his brother exchanged hearty claps on the back. He then did the same with the second man who was Shayne, their eldest brother and executor of their grandfather's estate. "I suppose you let Lor drag you along to make sure I did not destroy the house," he said in jest, never happier to see them. "Why did you fire those shots? I thought you might be that bastard Fielding."

Lorcan shook his head in obvious confusion. "Fielding? No, he's dead. Died inside the carriage with an unidentified man, I presume was your assailant. Unfortunately, both bodies were scorched beyond recognition. If not for that ring he always wore, we would never have been able to identify him. What happened? Did he hold the man off while you escaped with Lucy?"

"The bastard did nothing of the sort. Fielding is the traitor and is likely still alive—I've thought on this—know it as fact. He was never inside the carriage. I killed those two assailants when they tried to grab Lucy."

Lorcan frowned. "No...damn it...then what was he doing? Are you sure he cannot be one of those bodies?"

"Certain of it. The flames engulfed the seats and entire interior mere seconds after we escaped. When Lucy and I jumped out, I noticed he wasn't in the driver's seat either. He had been driving the carriage."

Lorcan's expression turned fierce. "Go on, tell me more. Obviously, we got it all wrong at the London office."

Donal quickly went through every detail of what happened. "I wrote to Wooton and Edgeware about this."

"Wooton must have sent me off to find you before he or Edgeware received your report. No matter, they'll have it by now. But that's a serious accusation. Are you sure about Fielding?"

"If he had been killed, you would have found his body on the ground outside the carriage. *Outside.* He must have planted his ring on that second assailant sometime during the chaotic inferno and then fled."

Lorcan gave him another brotherly clap on the shoulder. "Thank goodness it wasn't you and Lucy we found in that burned-out carriage. Cammy and I had just gotten to Wooton when news of what happened reached us. We were told the bodies of two men were found. Still, we were mad with worry. It wasn't until Cammy and I stopped at my old apartment that I saw her gown was missing and Lucy's hanging in its place. I knew then you'd made it out of London unharmed. There would have been blood or some other hint of a wound if you'd been hurt."

Donal grunted. "That gown is an ugly thing, isn't it?"

Lorcan shook his head and emitted a groaning laugh. "Do not ever let her hear you say that. I haven't been married long, but even I know that statement will get you kicked out of bed for a month."

Shayne cleared his throat. "Speaking of which… Donal, she's Wooton's daughter. You haven't *done* anything, have you?"

He frowned at his brother. "You mean taken liberties? Not that it is anyone's business, but no. She's a lady. And I am not referring to her courtesy title as a duke's daughter. Has Wooton openly acknowledged her?"

"Not yet," Lorcan said. "Only a select few were told. But I expect the news will be all over the gossip rags soon. Not even he will be able to keep it quiet once the whispers start."

"But he'll make the formal announcement once Lucy is safe and they've had the chance to reunite," Shayne said.

"Reunite? That would suggest he had a presence in her life." Donal tamped down his mounting anger. Wooton, as much as he admired the man professionally, had not been a father to Lucy. "He…bah! Let me fetch her before this goes any further. She'll be relieved to know you are our trespassers. As for riding to Exeter, she's been aching to go there. I'll tell you why later. We can compare notes over supper."

He led them through the woods and down the cliff path to the sea caves. "Lor, how did you know to find me here? I never mentioned our location in my reports to Wooton or Edgeware, which apparently did not arrive until after Wooton sent you off after us anyway. Not that I wanted to hide Lucy from him or Edgeware, but I was afraid these communications might fall into the wrong hands."

"How could you think I would not find you? I'm the Crown's best tracker, am I not? It was easy once I knew you were last seen in Tunbridge Wells and had fooled everyone into thinking you were headed to Dover. Weymouth and grandfather's estate was the first place that came to mind. We're brothers. I know how you think. Besides, I'm smarter than you."

Donal laughed. "That is hogswallop, and you know it."

"I found you, didn't I?"

"Took you long enough." He laughed again and playfully punched his brother's shoulder in response to Lor's smug grin. "And you got lucky, that is all."

They reached the beach as the tide was coming in. Donal made haste toward the cave since it was beginning to flood. The entrance was high enough that the water would only seep in about a foot at most, but Lucy was going to get her gown and slippers wet if he did not help her out at once. Well, he could carry her out in his arms if he had to.

"Lucy," he called as they entered. "Lucy, it's me."

His brothers exchanged glances when he received no response. "Do you think she's hurt?" Shayne asked.

"No, she's familiar with these caves." But they conducted a quick search to make certain she had not slipped and fallen.

"She must have run to one of the other caves. I've been teaching her about the best hiding spots on the property."

He searched two more of the hollowed-out caverns and came up empty. "Damn it, now I'm truly worried. She would not have run off. Are you sure you weren't followed?"

"No one followed us," Lorcan insisted. "I would have known."

"Do you think Fielding got here ahead of us and has been watching you all this time?" Shayne asked as they expanded their search to the woods. "Would he know about grandfather's place? Maybe overheard a conversation between you and Lor months earlier and put it all together?"

"I don't know. Possible. The bastard has been a step ahead of all of us the entire time." He stopped and put his hands to his mouth to make his bird call.

Nothing.

Lucy, where are you?

He repeated the bird call.

He finally heard the honk of a goose from behind him. "Blessed saints, that's her." He started running in the direction of the sound, his brothers close on his heels. A moment later, he saw Lucy making her way toward him.

But as the sun's rays filtered through the trees, he noticed a metallic glint amid a nearby hedgerow.

"Lucy, no!" he shouted at the same time two shots rang out, his aimed at the shrubbery where he'd seen the glint and the other from that hidden assailant's pistol.

He watched in horror as Lucy grabbed her chest and fell back.

His world spun out of control in that moment.

He raced to her while his brothers took care of the brute who had shot her. He would kill the man later, rip him apart with his own bare hands if he still lived.

Tears clouded his vision as he knelt beside her and tore at her clothes to get to the wound. She had clutched her heart upon the impact. How could she possibly have survived it? But he would not give up, he'd keep pressure on her chest until the flow of spurting blood stopped. As many times as she died, he would revive her. "Lucy, don't leave me. Sweetheart, stay with me."

But as he tore through the last layer of clothing, his mind began to whirl in confusion. Her shift was that last layer and ought to have been soaked with a crimson stain by now.

But there was nothing.

Not a drop.

"What the...?" He blinked away the tears clogging his eyes and put his hand over her heart.

She opened her eyes and moaned. "Donal, what happened?"

His hand still covered her heart.

Her rapidly beating...strong...

He slowly drew it away to reveal her creamy skin and a gorgeous breast with a dusky rose tip. He quickly tucked the torn fabric over her bosom for modesty's sake, his mind still reeling in confusion. "There's not a mark on you. How is it possible? I saw that shot strike you in the chest. You fell back."

She winced. "And I think I bumped my head as I hit the ground. Just against the soft earth, though. It knocked the wind out of me, but I'll be all right in a moment."

Then he saw her necklace, the lion now mangled, and the crescent moon gemstone chipped. Incredibly, lodged within the golden circles fashioned around the moon and lion rampant was a little metal ball. It fell out when he touched it, so he scooped it off the ground and put it into his pocket.

He drew Lucy into his arms and hugged her fiercely. "I thought I'd lost you."

He had never believed in miracles before, but how could one overlook this? Lucy's life had been saved by this symbol of her family…the very people who were trying to kill her. Ironic. Miraculous. "The angels were watching over you, my love."

He kissed her on the forehead, kissed her closed eyes, her cheeks. Her lips. She smiled against the light pressure of his mouth on hers. He then placed his lips to her heart, still unable to believe this was not a mad dream.

Her heart pounded a steady beat.

She would be all right once the shock of this attack wore off.

But would he?

He eased aside the torn fabric, needing another look at the skin around her heart to be certain nothing more serious was developing.

There was hardly a scratch, barely the trace of a welt on her.

He bent his head and kissed her again at the spot where the ball should have entered her body and killed her. "Lucy, sweet heaven…I still can't believe it."

She rested her hand against his cheek. "Your lips feel much nicer than that pistol shot. I heard the sound of it, then felt a light punch as it hit my chest. It made me fall backward, more out of surprise than any pain."

He kissed the palm of her hand. "You had me so worried."

"I hope you're not angry I left the cave. I heard someone by the entrance and got scared. I thought maybe it was just birds. I didn't know for certain, so I climbed out through the cliff opening and hid in one of the other caves you had shown me. But I heard those footsteps again, so I ran into the woods. I wasn't trying to hide from you."

"I know, love."

"I knew you would have called out to me if it had been you there. Please don't be angry, Donal. It wasn't as easy to hide in the woods, and I got scared. I heard your voice, and all I could think to do was run to you. I didn't even consider the danger. How stupid of me. How utterly and completely stupid of me. Everything you'd taught me flew out of my head when I saw you searching for me. I wanted so desperately to be in your arms."

She began to sob. "You are my safe harbor. I had to reach you. That's all I could think about, and it nearly got us both killed."

"No, love. It's all right. You did exactly what you were supposed to do in the caves. Let's get you back to the house, and we'll sort it all out." He secured the clothes at her bosom as best he could.

Lord, he'd been so frantic.

There hadn't been time to do anything but rip them aside.

"Who shot me?" she asked as he rose with her in his arms.

He turned to glance at his brothers, who had managed to subdue and disarm the assailant while he had been tending to Lucy. Although Donal could not get a good look at him yet, it was no stretch to guess his identity.

Fielding.

This was confirmed a moment later when his brothers carted his bleeding body out from behind the shrubs. Donal saw a massive crimson stain at the front of his shirt and realized he must have shot him in the gut.

"Bastard!" Fielding spat at him.

It was an impotent outburst from a man who would spend the rest of his life in a squalid prison or simply be hanged, assuming he survived his injury. A gut shot. It wasn't likely he would last out the day.

But dying was too good for that traitor.

It would allow him to escape hanging.

It would allow him to escape the wrath of a vengeful father.

Fielding had just tried to kill the Duke of Ice's daughter. Never mind that the duke never once attempted to establish a relation with Lucy. That fact was irrelevant. She was his blood kin, and his punishment would be swift and terrible.

Lucy circled her arms tightly around his neck as Fielding tossed more epithets at him.

"It's all right, love. He can't hurt you."

"I wasn't afraid for myself," she said in a shaky voice, still much affected by what had transpired. "He cursed you and looked at you with such venomous hatred."

"Others have done worse." He kissed the top of her head. "As long as you never look at me that way."

She laughed. "I never would."

He kissed her again and waited for his brothers to get well ahead of him before he carried her into the house. He'd taken a moment to assure his worried brothers Lucy was fine. Lucy did the same, and her laughter went a long way toward easing their minds.

Fielding had been stunned into momentary silence when he'd heard her speak. "I shot you through the heart. You should be dead."

Lucy had said nothing.

Instead, she'd buried her head against Donal's shoulder and would not lift it until his brothers had hauled their prisoner away. "Sweet mercy, he's right. How am I still alive?"

He couldn't speak for the lump in his throat, so he just

hugged her to him.

However, she recovered her composure once the fiend was out of sight. In truth, she looked angry more than frightened, much of that anger trained on herself.

"Lucy, if Fielding is here, others could be as well. My brothers and I will have to go out again to scout the area more thoroughly. We spotted no one else while we were looking for you, but it does not mean he came to Weymouth alone."

She nodded reluctantly. "I understand."

"Shayne will remain behind to guard you. I want him to question Fielding. He has a more engaging manner and stands the best chance of coaxing him into giving up information. Lor and I will conduct our search after nightfall. We operate better under cover of darkness."

She nibbled her lip. "Won't the delay give his accomplices time to escape?"

"Doubtful. They are on a mission. If Fielding does not return, they'll just modify their plans and proceed without him. We'll be prepared for them. But I am not leaving you now. You are my priority."

She rested her head against his shoulder a moment longer, then looked up and tugged on his ear to regain his attention when they arrived at the kitchen door. "You can put me down now."

"Not a chance. I'm never letting go of you."

His brothers were just finishing up with Fielding as he strode in. Lorcan assured him they had the traitorous agent securely bound and gagged. "He'll likely be dead within a matter of hours."

Donal glanced over at the man. "I want him guarded until he draws his last breath, Lor."

Fielding was the lowest form of life, lower than a scorpion.

And just as dangerous even when injured.

Shayne looked over at him. "Take a moment to tend Lucy, then come back in here."

Donal gave a curt nod.

He and his brothers had worked together for years, and a mere exchange of glances was sufficient to know they were all of the same mind concerning their next steps. He did not need to relay orders. All of them were trained agents, Shayne only recently having retired from service to the Crown.

Lucy tugged on Donal's ear again as everyone was now watching them. "Aren't you going to put me down?"

"No. I told you. Not a chance. I am never letting go of you."

She blushed.

His brothers grinned.

"I knew it," Lorcan muttered.

"Possessive arse," Shayne added. "She can walk, you know. Thank goodness for that. You scared the life out of us, Lucy."

"I'm sorry."

Shayne shook his head. "Not your fault at all. Glad you're not hurt. Willow will claim it was the magic of *The Book of Love* that saved you when I tell her about this."

"It wasn't the damn book," Donal grumbled. "It was…forget it. I don't know what it was." He tried to ignore all of them as he made his way into the hall. But the Gentrys were also in the kitchen and now rushed to him.

"Is the lamb hurt?" Blanche asked, curious as to why she was still in his arms.

Donal frowned as his brothers snickered. "No, she's fine. We'll need rooms made up for Shayne and Lorcan. They're only staying the night."

"That's all?" Lucy glanced in surprise at the three of them.

Shayne nodded. "We leave for Exeter tomorrow. All of us. That includes you."

She gasped. "We are? Finally! I've been longing to go ever since we discovered that—"

Donal gave her a little squeeze. "Save the discussion for after supper. Horace, have you noticed anyone else on the property recently? Any footprints that did not belong? Traces of a camp in the woods? I'm concerned our prisoner came with more men."

"No," he replied with a solemn shake of his head. "Nothing to report, Master Donal."

"Ox, how about you? Or notice any strangers in town?"

"No, I would have said something if I had."

Lorcan stared at him with a furrowed brow. "We can do some more looking around once you settle Lucy in her quarters."

"I don't need settling. Or more coddling. But I am in need of a change of clothes. Petrina, will you help me?"

"I'll do it," Donal insisted, his scowl giving Petrina pause. "I'll do it," he said more gently, afraid Lucy would vanish into air if he ever let her go.

Lucy sighed and made no further protest. "Mr. Fielding looks badly hurt."

Donal followed the direction of her gaze. "He got what he deserved."

But he motioned to Ox. "I think you had better fetch a doctor. My brothers will do their best to keep him alive in the meanwhile. However, a gut shot..." He turned to Fielding. "Time to redeem your soul. You had better start talking while you can."

He left his brothers to deal with this agent turned traitor while he carried Lucy upstairs to the bedchamber they shared.

He set her down at her insistence but kept his arm wrapped around her.

Lucy eyed him curiously, no doubt wondering why he felt this need to touch her. The pull between maintaining a professional distance and also being in love with her had wreaked havoc on him these past few weeks.

He'd tried his best to keep a distance between them because he was certain it was the right thing to do. His duties as an agent of the Crown and the cold calculation necessary to properly perform them should always win out over matters of the heart.

He had been convinced of it.

But no longer.

Lucy could have died today.

The thought that she might have left this earth believing he did not love her, thinking she was a mere assignment to him...that devastated him.

Blanche lumbered upstairs after them. "Forgive me, Master Donal, but ye both looked as if ye could do with some assistance."

Lucy smiled at her and nodded. "Very much so. My undergarments are in desperate need of repair. They'll have to be cleaned, and then I'll mend them."

"Lamb, did that fiend...were ye...?" Her usually ruddy face turned ashen as her mind obviously leapt to the wrong conclusion.

Lucy quickly sought to reassure her. "Nothing like that, truly. That odious Fielding did not set a hand on me. It was Mr. Brayden's doing. He thought I'd been shot through the heart and was merely trying to stanch the wound. Fortunately, there was no wound, which he realized as he gaped at my—"

"Lucy!" Donal raked a hand through his hair. "Blessed saints. I thought you were dying."

She put a hand on his arm. "I know. I can see you are still in turmoil over it."

He groaned and turned to face Blanche. "Lucy and I will have a quick supper in the dining room as soon as you can have it ready. My brothers, too."

He turned to Lucy. "I was going to refuse the order to take you to Exeter. But after this latest attempt on your life, I think it may be the safer place for you. Not that anywhere is safe yet. But if Fielding is here, then his cohorts cannot be too far behind."

"Oh, ye poor lamb." Blanche was wringing her hands.

"Assuming it is safe, I expect we'll leave at first light tomorrow," Donal said, turning to the worried woman. "But I want you to know how much I appreciate all you've done for me and Miss Lessing."

Lucy, with her typical warmth, gave her a hug. "You and your family have been wonderful to us, and we shall never forget your kindness."

Donal could not help but look upon her with pride. Lucy was sweet and wonderful. She deserved none of the treatment she had been given in life.

But everything would soon change for her.

She would be acknowledged as a duke's daughter and gain entry into the highest circles once the gossip rags broke the news. Would it turn her into someone unrecognizable? He could not imagine her ever tossing a superior glance or ignoring a kind gesture.

But wealth and title did change people.

Not you, Lucy.

Don't let them spoil you.

He stared at her once Blanche left, and they were now alone.

She blushed and glanced down at her torn gown.

Wordlessly, he drew her back into his arms to help her out of it. The corset and chemise as well since he'd ripped them, too. "I'll close my eyes," he said, not wanting to embarrass her as he stripped the last of the garments off her.

"Don't," she said, emitting a ragged breath. "I want you to see me."

"Lucy…I didn't mean to…earlier. I was mad with fear. I thought he'd killed you." He ran a hand roughly through his hair again. "I failed you."

"You? *Failed me?*" She shook her head and laughed, but the sound was curt and held little mirth. "Quite the opposite. I was the one who did not follow the rules you'd taught me. You've never failed me. You saved me from an empty existence. You are the only one who has ever cared about me. Worried about me. Understood my heart. Donal, you see into my soul."

She returned his tumultuous gaze with a loving one of her own. "And now you will know all of me."

She stepped out of his arms, so he could feast his eyes on her.

His heart swelled at the trust she placed in him.

"I never believed I could feel about anyone the way I do

about you," he said, his voice ragged and hoarse. "I am never leaving you, Lucy. Never. I want you to know this. I am so sorry I did not tell you earlier."

He kissed her cheek.

He kissed her on the shoulder.

His heart pounded through his ears.

Every pulse and pore in his body thrummed. His blood turned hot and thick as molten lava. He wanted to toss her on the bed and spill himself inside of her.

He wanted to devour her sweet, little body.

Tonight.

Later.

But there was still so much to do.

"You are the most beautiful girl I've ever...it's as though you were made just for me. I mean it, Lucy. I cannot get enough of you." After a moment, he strode to the wardrobe to fetch one of the gowns she had altered when they'd first arrived. She had taken in some of his grandmother's shifts as well, so he grabbed one of those, too.

"Are you cold, sweetheart?"

She shook her head. "I'm fine. Do you mean it, Donal? Because I don't want you to tell me what you think I want to hear. If you don't care for me, then don't pretend you do. Lies will shatter me. I can bear almost anything. I've lived all my life ignored and unloved. But I don't think I will survive having my hopes raised by you only to see them dashed. If you say all those sweet things you think I want to hear and then walk away after this assignment is over, I will never recover from that hurtful blow. Never."

He wiped a stray tear off her cheek. "I mean it, Lucy. Every word. There is no one else for me. Only you."

Her body was perfection.

He had never seen her completely naked before this.

She was even more beautiful than he'd realized.

Her breasts were ample enough to fill the cup of his hands,

and their tips were the loveliest pink.

Pale.

Soft.

Dusky.

He felt like an utter oaf.

She had almost died today, and he could not stop looking at her breasts. Or thinking about them.

He groaned as he helped her don the shift and gown. The gown was a lovely shade of brown, tinged in rose that highlighted the soft rose of her cheekbones. The material was soft and quite elegant, not one of those drab affairs she usually wore.

But he loved her no matter what she wore.

He laced the ties of the gown. "You have my heart, Lucy. I mean every word. No lie."

She stayed silent.

"Sweetheart…" He cupped her face gently between his hands. "I give you my oath. I am yours forever."

"Even if my father…the Duke of Wooton…even if he forbids it?"

CHAPTER SIXTEEN

DONAL'S BROTHERS TOOK a moment to wash up in their chambers, but soon they all met in the dining room for a hearty venison stew and private conversation. Lucy insisted on joining them, and Donal voiced no protest.

He had no desire to be apart from her even for a few minutes, although he intended to scout with his brothers once darkness fell. Lucy would not like it, but there was no other way to protect her.

He would not leave her for long.

The house itself was secure, and she knew of its hidden passages.

"Fielding has been tended by the local doctor," Lor said casually as they ate. "Nothing could be done to save his sorry soul. He is expected to pass sometime in the night. Shayne and I watched while the doctor treated his wounds, hoping to hear a confession."

"Fielding gave up nothing," Shayne added with a grunt. "Ox is guarding him now. He'll summon us if Fielding has a change of heart. Donal, are you all right?"

He frowned at his brother. "Me? Lucy's the one who was shot...should have been..." He set his fork down with a clatter.

Almost losing her in the woods today still haunted him.

Lucy was seated beside him at the table and now put a hand over his to give it a light squeeze. "I think we ought to let your brothers know what we've learned so far," she said in an obvious attempt to calm him.

"Fine." Donal recounted everything he and Lucy had learned in the weeks they'd spent poring over his grandfather's books.

Shayne stared at him when he finished the retelling. "So, you think Lucy is the rightful baroness? And what of the present baroness? Or should I refer to her as the usurper? She is obviously the one behind these attempts to kill Wooton and Lucy. Now it is all starting to make sense. I wondered why we were told to find you and bring you to Exeter instead of London. It is the closest town to Dartmoor."

"What do you think the baroness promised Mr. Fielding to turn him into a traitor?" Lucy asked, barely nibbling her stew. Most of it remained on her plate, and she did little more than move the pieces of venison around from one side to the other with her fork.

Donal watched her, realizing she was no calmer than he was, but she had spent years learning to keep the hurt to herself.

No matter how badly she ached, she wasn't going to reveal it to him or his brothers.

"You'd be surprised how cheaply some people can be bought," Lorcan said in response to her question. He took a sip of his wine and then set the glass down. "It could have been a pittance."

Lucy shook her head. "You said he was arrogant. Would he not demand a higher price for his services? After all, his task was to kill Wooton and me. Not that anyone would have noticed my demise or particularly cared. But Wooton was never going to be an easy target. And now, all of you may be in danger because you know I am his secret daughter, and the baroness cannot let you spread that information."

"No, Lucy." Donal entwined his fingers in hers since they were still holding hands. "It is over. She cannot prevent the news from getting out. Edgeware knows and has taken others into his confidence by now. This is no longer about the baroness holding onto her title. That scandal will explode soon. All that is left to do is find her."

"Do you think she is here?"

Donal shook his head. "Yes, if Fielding sent word to her. Or she may be back in Dartmoor now, frustrated and anxiously awaiting Fielding's return."

She pursed her lips. "Then why must we go to Exeter?"

"Wooton may believe it is safer there than here. Or perhaps he wants you with him to draw the baroness out of her lair."

Her big eyes took all of him in. "I'm not quite sure I understand."

"I think he may be planning to use you as bait," Donal said. "It is a stupid plan, and I won't ever let it happen."

He'd told her that he was hers forever. Tonight, he would actually say the words she needed to hear. *I love you.* This is how he felt about her, and not even Wooton was going to stop him from marrying her.

Only Lucy held that power.

If she did not want him, then one word from her would silence him.

She cast him a wide-eyed stare. "You would defy him, Donal?"

He nodded. "For you? Yes."

"This is turning into a mess." She glanced at his brothers. "Is there no way to reach Fielding's conscience? Convince him to tell us where she is and what she plans. You mentioned he had been a trusted agent for many years. What makes a man like that suddenly accept to be bribed? Turn to betrayal and murder?"

Donal swallowed a bite of his stew. "As you just said, Fielding always considered himself a superior agent. Perhaps we should have seen this coming after Wooton passed him over for two important assignments. Then Lor and I helped Shayne take down the Earl of Monkton's crazed brother and his nasty crowd. Followed by Lor and Wooton saving Cammy from that killer plaguing London. The Brayden brothers were receiving all the accolades, and he was suddenly shoved aside, no longer the Crown's best."

Lorcan frowned. "Cammy is my wife. I was never going to allow anyone else to protect her."

"Fielding did not see it that way. He was already quietly seething and took it as Wooton favoring the Braydens again, handing us the plum assignments he deserved."

Shayne set down his fork and folded his hands under his chin in thought. "After your report, Wooton has to know Fielding's body was not one of those found in the carriage. Even before-hand, he must have suspected. *Do not presume a man is dead unless you can clearly identify his body.* Isn't this what he taught us? He certainly pounded that into my head when I was an agent."

Donal nodded. "It was the same for me. Well, he'll be glad to know that Fielding is no longer a concern. But he asked you to bring us to Exeter while still suspecting Fielding was out there and a threat. Why bring us out of hiding? Why deliver Lucy to Exeter? We keep touching upon it, but…"

"What is it, Donal? Why are you frowning?" Lucy asked.

"I want to trust his motives, but I cannot. No matter how I look at it, the only reason for us to meet him in Exeter is that he intends to spring a trap for the baroness."

"With me as bait, as you suggested?"

"Yes, Lucy. That he can even consider such a thing…using his own daughter. The Duke of Ice can burn in hell before I'll ever allow it."

Lucy tried to remain stoic, but Donal could see her lips trem-bling. "I'm not going to let anyone hurt you. Wooton can find some other lure to draw the baroness out. Or use himself to do it. They're all thirsting for his blood anyway."

"But I'm already a target, am I not? And I would still be a target if the baroness managed to kill him, would I not?"

Donal saw Lucy struggle with her feelings, much as she had done throughout supper. It had to be so hard for her to listen to him and his brothers discuss her situation with a cold, professional dispassion.

Yet, she did not flinch or falter.

She had a beautiful spirit, a quiet strength that held her together when most others would have come apart.

Of course, this only made him love her more.

The urge to protect her was so strong in him, it was almost unbearable. "Yes, you would be. Which is precisely the reason I hesitate to take you to Exeter. He's your damn father. What sort of man uses his daughter as a lure?"

"You've just given the answer," she replied, her voice tight and her eyes filled with pain. "He is the Duke of Ice, a man whose heart is cold as ice. Why else would he wait all these years to claim me as his child? In truth, why even bother with me now? Unless he has been in a cat and mouse game with the baroness all these years. Do you think it is possible? That he harbored a hatred for her, blamed her for the death of my mother? She may have been completely innocent. Women die in childbirth, and it is sadly the way of things."

"No, Lucy. That woman we encountered was a murderess. You saw her act in cold blood. She will not meekly give up her title. Nor is it farfetched to believe that if she hired Fielding and those vicious assassins to kill you and the duke now, she may have killed your mother back then."

Shayne still had his hands clasped as he leaned his elbows on the table and studied Lucy with obvious concern. "I'm inclined to agree with Donal. We ought to find out more about what happened between the baroness, your mother, and Wooton before we cart you off to Exeter."

Donal nodded. "Thank you, Shayne. This assignment reeks. So, we are agreed? Change in plans? I am not taking Lucy anywhere until I trust Wooton's motives."

"Who can ever know what goes on in that man's mind?" Lorcan remarked.

"Why don't we review what we do know about him?" Shayne suggested. "Let's fix the timeline of his life and see if…if he is lying about Lucy even being his child. That ought to be our first step. Sorry, Lucy. I don't mean to pile on the hurt."

"I understand." She cast Shayne a fragile smile and nodded. "We need to do this. I have to know what happened, no matter how brutal the revelations may be."

She was right, but it still made Donal's soul ache.

"All right." With much reluctance, he pursued the discussion of Lucy's parentage. He and Lucy had already considered the possibility that Wooton had lied about her being his daughter. "We know Wooton was in the army back then, of course rising in prominence because he has always been a brilliant tactician. Every agent knows of his military accomplishments. His father was alive in the year before Lucy's birth. Wooton, at the time, was the second son and not expected to inherit the title. But his brother died of a lung infection, and his father died shortly afterward. Wooton was discharged from his military duties and sent home to assume the title. Lucy and I calculated as best we could. He was in England nine months prior to her birth. Then shipped off on a military mission to the American colonies immediately afterward."

"And returned home shortly after I was born," Lucy added. "That was the period of upheaval in his life, father and brother dying. More to the point, he was not in England in the weeks immediately surrounding my birth."

Lorcan arched an eyebrow. "Are you making excuses for him?"

"No, there is no excuse for abandoning me for all these years afterward."

"We haven't figured out how or when Wooton learned of Lucy's existence," Donal said. "However, we do know he *could* be her father. There is an obvious family resemblance. What we also don't know is why Lucy survived if the present baroness had indeed killed her mother. Why spare the child?"

"The only plausible explanation we came up with is that she did not know I had survived," Lucy said, her voice still tight.

"Nor do we know what happened recently to make the baroness aware of Lucy," Donal said. "Well, that's as far as we've gotten on that investigative trail. What do you think, Lor? Shayne?"

Lorcan rocked back in his chair. "It is like trying to make your way safely out of a maze of poisonous snakes. But I'm still for taking Lucy to Exeter. Wooton is the only one who knows the entire story. You'll never have your answers if you don't take her there."

Donal frowned. "It is out of the question."

"Why? Keeping her here changes nothing. We've taken down Fielding, and that is an important catch, but what's to stop anyone else involved in the baroness's schemes to come after her? Believe me, I went through similar anguish with Cammy. I know exactly what you are thinking and the guilt you are feeling. But you cannot protect Lucy every hour of the day. Wooton was brilliant in taking down Milkwood, and Cammy is now safe because of it. Will you have Lucy spend the rest of her life in hiding? And what if the baroness manages to get another man close to Wooton to take him down? The longer this goes on, the more likely it is that Lucy and Wooton will get hurt. I may find his using Lucy as bait utterly reprehensible, but this could be the only way to draw the baroness out."

"No, Lor. Lucy's situation is different from Cammy's." He glanced at Lucy and saw she was taking Lorcan's words too much to heart. "Wooton is capable of killing in cold blood. There is nothing to stop him from taking this evil woman down now on his own. Our reports and these attempts on his and Lucy's life cannot possibly leave him in doubt of her guilt. Let him catch her without needing to bring Lucy in."

"It is exactly the same as Cammy's situation," Lorcan insisted. "If Lucy is with him, then the baroness will aim all her resources there. But if Lucy remains here, then we are left to wonder where she'll strike first. Not to mention, our resources would also be spread thin."

"Who else besides Wooton would be in Exeter to protect me?" Lucy asked quietly.

"The three of us would," Shayne said. "This is our brothers pact. We stand with each other. You know how it was in Taunton with the Earl of Monkton's brother and his vicious crowd."

She nodded. "I do."

Donal groaned when she turned to him and cast him a determined look. "Donal, please. Let's go to Exeter. I need to learn the truth. You've grown up in a wonderful family. I...I've spent my life always feeling the outcast. I have to find out why he abandoned me all these years ago. I cannot go on like this."

"Lucy..." He spoke her name with aching torment because that was what he was feeling. "How can I toss you to the wolves?"

"To save me. This is why you must do it. This feud, or whatever exists between Wooton and the baroness, has to end. Fielding may no longer be a threat, but what is to stop another assailant from finding me and hunting me through the caves? Is it not likely he brought others along? They might have intended to meet him at some tavern in a town not far from here. What if they decide to come looking for him now?"

Donal gritted his teeth. "You know I plan to search the property after nightfall, and Weymouth, too."

"I'll be going with him," Lor said with a determined look; he was the Crown's best tracker and had no intention of being left out on this hunt.

Donal was immensely proud of his little brother. "Wouldn't think of going without you, Lor. What do you think will turn up once we start kicking over the rocks?"

CHAPTER SEVENTEEN

Lucy could not shake off her worry as Donal prepared to search the woods and nearby town. "Do you not think it is more likely those men will flee once they realize Fielding has been captured?" she asked as the four of them left the dining room.

Donal planted a casual kiss on her forehead. "I won't be gone long. Let me walk you up to your bedchamber and—"

"You are mad to think I will sleep a wink while you and Lorcan are out there. I'm staying down here until you return."

"Fine." He escorted her to the library. "Keep Shayne company. Go over everything we've learned again. The two of you might come up with something you and I overlooked."

"Now you are merely trying to placate me."

He cast her an irritatingly appealing grin. "Is it working?"

"No."

But he was immovable as a mountain.

She supposed his brothers were equally as stubborn, for they were all cut from the same cloth. Clever. Fearless. Determined. If Shayne was irritated to be relegated to the role of nanny while Donal and Lorcan went out into the night, he did not show it.

Instead, Shayne tried to distract her by asking questions about the property and its secret passageways. Of course, it worked. He absorbed everything she told him, and she rather liked being treated as an equal instead of a piece of furniture to be ignored in a corner. "The maps have all been returned to the box kept hidden under the floorboards beneath my bed."

"Then I'll inspect them on my next trip here," he said with a nod. "You have told me most of what's important. Stop pacing, Lucy."

"How can you be so calm?"

"My brothers are trained for this. I swear they have the eyes of night predators, and they'll move through the woods like phantoms. Unseen. Unheard."

Several shots rang out.

Lucy put a hand to her throat and gasped.

Shayne leaped up from his chair, his face pale. But he quickly recovered. "They've got Fielding's cohorts."

"Or those villains got them."

"No, Lucy. They are excellent at what they do."

But she could see he was worried, for he now had his pistol in hand.

He cast her a wry smile. "Perhaps I am fretting a little. They may be England's best, but they are still my younger brothers. A part of me will always worry for their safety. But I know how efficiently they work as a team. They'll be back soon."

"Shouldn't we go out there to make certain? I know the secret passages and can lead you in the dark. Donal taught me. Please."

"Out of the question."

"What if they are lying out there wounded? They may be the best at what they do, but wasn't Fielding as well? By all accounts, I should be dead."

More shots rang out.

"Mother in heaven, we have to go out there, Shayne. Hand me a rifle. It sounds as though they are taking on an entire army."

Shayne grabbed her around the waist when she tried to run past him. "Lucy, stop. Do you not think I am feeling the same worry? But to take you out there? Or leave you unguarded while I run off to find them? It is the worst thing I can do right now."

"Then give me a weapon, and I will guard myself. Or we can fetch Ox and Horace to watch over me while you—"

"Stop. Hush!" Still retaining a grip on her, he crossed the room to open the window just a crack and cautiously peer out of it.

"What are you doing?" she asked in a whisper, sensing he was listening for something in particular. Of course, the bird calls. This is how agents communicated. These brothers probably had their own secret language.

As the shooting stopped, she heard the trill of a particular bird and recognized it as Donal's call.

Shayne eased noticeably and responded with a call of his own.

Lucy closed her eyes and released the breath she had been holding. "Thank goodness."

"Indeed," Shayne muttered, his expression one of obvious relief.

"Do you think it is safe to go to them, Shayne?" Her words came out breathlessly for the wild thumping in her heart. She was still apprehensive, for who could know yet whether the danger had passed?

"No, we'd better wait for them to return. Be patient, let him do whatever is needed to make certain all is clear."

"Then you think there may be more assailants lurking in the woods?"

"Possibly." Shayne drew the drapes back into place but kept the window open a crack to listen for more bird calls.

It felt like an eternity before Lucy heard noises, and then someone called out in the hallway.

Donal.

She flung open the library door and ran into his arms. "We heard the shots. Are you hurt?"

He drew her back inside the library, giving Shayne a quick nod of acknowledgment before he began to tell them what had happened. "I'm fine. Lorcan is, too. But you were right to be concerned about Fielding's accomplices. We...got them...all."

The way he said it, she realized he meant they had been per-manently stopped. A shiver ran through her. "They are dead?"

Donal had been nothing but gentle and protective of her, but he was still one of the Crown's top agents, which meant he was a ruthless predator when he needed to be. She would not be alive now if not for him.

"Blessed saints, Lucy. I'm sorry. I wasn't thinking." He held her so delicately in the circle of his arms. How could he be exquisitely soft with her and at the same time uncompromisingly effective against these villains?

"I'm glad you're all right, little brother." Shayne handed him a glass of the brandy he'd just poured from his grandfather's stock. "What happened?"

Donal accepted the drink with a nod of gratitude and took several quick gulps before setting it aside. "We identified ourselves as agents of the Crown and asked them to surrender their weapons. They refused and tried to shoot us. We shot back. All five of them are dead, including that man we saw with the baroness by the old bridge that day."

Lucy gasped. "Who is he? And what of the baroness?"

"She's still at large. Who knows if she's even here? I cannot imagine her hiding in the woods with those men. Likely, she's sitting in comfort in some Weymouth inn awaiting a report. We won't stop searching for her, but we have to deal with these men now. Stay in the library, Lucy. There's still too much going on for you to be wandering about the house. Lor's telling Fielding about his friends now, hoping the news will get him talking before he takes his last breath."

Shayne poured a quick brandy for himself, drank it down, and slammed the glass on the table. "Lord, I'm getting too old for this. Let me go help Lor and the Gentrys."

On his way out, Shayne cast her a wry smile. "Death is never taken lightly, but sometimes it cannot be avoided. It takes a particular sort of ruthlessness to kill a stranger merely for coin, especially an innocent young woman. These men did not think twice about coming after you, Lucy. When facing vermin like these, compassion serves no purpose. The moment you lower your guard, they will find a way to kill you."

She gave a reluctant nod.

"I suppose we had better advise the Weymouth magistrate about this mess," Shayne muttered. "I'll talk to him. The news is better taken if given by a fellow magistrate."

"Send Ox off to fetch him. Good thing he's built like an ox. We've had him riding back and forth to town all day. But I want to speak to the magistrate once you are done. I'd like him to do a little investigating for us, approach the local tavern owners and see what they know about these dead men and the baroness. I'd go myself, but I hesitate to leave Lucy again, especially with that viper still at large. I'd also like to know if there are more assassins out there."

"More?" Lucy asked. "It seems to me if the baroness and that companion of hers were here, then it must mean they had no reserves left. Do you not think the assault you fended off tonight was meant to be a last, desperate attempt on their part?"

"I do. My gut tells me we've got them all, but we still need to be certain."

Shayne nodded. "I'll ask the Weymouth magistrate to send a couple of his men out tonight for this purpose. I had better go with them. In the meantime, I'll search the bodies and saddle pouches to see what else might turn up."

"Their horses will need to be rounded up and put in the stable. That's a low priority. Questioning Fielding and finding the baroness comes first."

Shayne put his hand on the door. "I'll see if Lorcan's had any success getting Fielding to talk. The man hates you and Lor. Maybe he'll open up to me this time. The minutes are ticking away to save his soul."

As the door closed behind Shayne, Lucy cast pleading eyes at Donal. "We need to find this evil woman who destroyed my family."

"We?" He shook his head. "My brothers and I will do all we can. That woman certainly is a bringer of nightmares. If we do find her, you are to keep as far away from her as possible."

"Why? Do you not think seeing me might rile her into confessing? Might she not then tell us what she did to my mother?"

"There is no remorse in her, sweetheart. All your presence would do is give her another opportunity to verbally stab you through the heart. Why are we arguing the matter? We do not have her in custody yet."

"You're right." Her insides were already roiling so badly, she felt ill. But a part of her also needed to show this fiend that all her plotting had failed. Olivia, the mother she had never known, lived on in her heart.

Wicked Andrea could never destroy this.

She turned away and sank into one of the overstuffed chairs beside the hearth, wishing she had the training to find her and bring her to justice on her own. But she would never be so foolish as to go out on her own.

Being shot in the heart by Fielding had taught her that lesson.

Donal knelt beside her. "It's been a rough day. Let me take you upstairs."

She shook her head. "No, just leave me here. I won't interfere with whatever it is you need to do, but I cannot wait in my chamber. I cannot, Donal."

He raked a hand through his hair, obviously not pleased. "All right."

"Donal, what about Wooton? Should someone not send word to him?"

"I was thinking it may be best for all of us to ride to Exeter tomorrow. But we'll see. No firm plans yet. There's quite a mess to sort through with the Weymouth magistrate first. I also want to hear what Shayne and his men report once they've questioned the local innkeepers."

"Let me know if there is anything I can do to help." Donal and his brothers were the trained agents, and she was not going to jeopardize their safety by getting underfoot.

"I will, love."

She had brought *The Book of Love* down to the library earlier and now crossed to the desk to retrieve it.

Donal noticed the unmistakable faded red binding and cast her a wry smile. "That book is not magic, Lucy. No matter what anyone thinks, it will not save you. Nor will wishing over it somehow change the wicked baroness. The rot is too deeply rooted in her heart."

"I know. I only meant to stow it back in our travel pouch, so I do not accidentally forget it here. But Donal…"

"Yes, sweetheart?"

Despite her turmoil, she could not contain her smile. "I have been your *love* and your *sweetheart* ever since Fielding tried to shoot me."

He leaned forward and gave her a light kiss on the lips. "You were my love and my sweetheart long before that. I was too much of a fool to let you know it."

"No, you were a professional, and I was your—"

"Oh, blessed saints!" He emitted a groaning chuckle. "You are going to plague me with my stupid remark into our dotage, aren't you? Surely, you know. You have never been a mere assignment for me."

His words warmed her heart, but she was afraid to have this conversation with him yet. She understood the sort of man he was. The greater the danger, the more his protective instincts were aroused.

How would he feel once the danger had passed? Would she bore him to tears with her bookish ways once they settled into a quieter life?

Had he not considered her a boring bluestocking when they'd first met?

Donal was staring at her intently.

Was he worrying about the same thing?

"Lucy…"

"Yes?" She gripped the edges of her book, waiting for him to take back the words of love he'd spoken when he thought she had been shot and was going to die.

Well, she had been shot.

But not injured.

He released an anguished breath. "As dangerous as it has been here today, it could be worse in Exeter. Not physical danger, because this is the end of the baroness. We'll catch her soon. She is likely on her own without resources left. But you will be meeting Wooton…your father. That's a deep and longstanding hurt, and I have no idea what he will reveal to you."

She nodded. "This is why I held you back a moment. I wanted to ask you about him."

"I am probably as close to him as anyone in the Home Office is, and I would hardly consider him a friend. He allows no one close. Even knowing the danger to you, he saw fit to tell me almost nothing. I only know that you are his daughter, and I was ordered to keep you safe."

"Are you afraid he will play games with my heart?"

He brushed a stray curl off her brow. "He may try. But I think you will melt his solid wall of ice. You've certainly gotten to me. You have strength, Lucy. I was so proud of the way you managed to elude Fielding in the caves. He may have been corrupted, but he is still one of the best agents ever to work for the Crown, and you bested him."

"Until the encounter in the woods."

"You would have succeeded in hiding from him if my bird call had not drawn you out."

"We can argue this back and forth for hours and never agree. You trained me to answer your bird call and then remain in place until you reached me. Instead, I ran to you. I ran when I should have remained where I was and let you come to me."

"Lucy, it's all right. Do not blame yourself for—"

"We both know this is what I should have done. This is how you taught me to respond. Instead, I blindly ran to you. I promise

I will be more careful. I know I still have a lot to learn. And I will take everything you've taught me to heart. I'll hide when I have to, listen for subtle changes to the air, not lose my wits. I will truly make you proud of me."

"Sweetheart, you are brilliant, and I have always been proud of you. That is entirely my point." He eased back, releasing her to set her book aside and then cup her face in his hands. "I am going to kiss you now."

She smiled up at him. "Do you need to announce it?"

"I don't suppose I do. Perhaps you are rubbing off on me with your need to explain everything you are thinking or feeling." He laughed and then brought his mouth down on hers with magnificent intensity.

Warmth flooded through her.

She loved this man so deeply.

Did she dare tell him?

In this, she was still a coward. Having never known love, she simply did not have it in her to be the first to admit how she felt about him.

He'd called her his love. His sweetheart. But had not simply said *I love you*. That ruse at the smuggler's inn purposely meant for the maid Maisi to overhear did not count. Their kiss and all the dialogue that followed were mere pretend.

But here and now…if he could not bring himself to speak those simple words, her soul would be crushed.

Crushed and never repaired.

As for her, she was ready to surrender every last drop of herself to this man who overwhelmed her with his strength, courage, and decency.

His mouth moved over hers with possessive ardor, slanting across her lips to claim them and conquer her, although he had to know she had long ago surrendered her heart and was already his.

Oh, his kiss felt so sweet.

He ran his tongue lightly across the seam of her lips. She opened to him, allowing him to plunge and probe, to plunder all she was and all she possessed.

He filled her heart with such deeply intense longing.

Dear heaven.

He had a way of holding her, touching her that engulfed her soul. Flames shot through her, carried on her thick, hot blood. She dared to respond similarly, touching her tongue to his and gave a little *eep* when he sucked on hers and began to swirl his in what felt like a naughty dance.

Naughty and wonderful.

Trying to talk was impossible while her mouth was thus occupied.

Perhaps words weren't necessary, but this kiss felt different from the others that had come before it, more…erotic seemed to be the best way to describe it.

She felt his grin against her lips because he knew what she was thinking. She wanted to tell him anyway. Which she started to do the moment his lips eased off hers. "Oh, Donal. That was—"

He kissed her again in that hot, raw way and did not let up for the longest while. "Splendid," she said the moment he eased his mouth off hers. "I've never—"

He laughed and kissed her again, this time even more boldly. His hands roamed up and down her body in a light, tracing motion that left her aching for more…aching for him.

She told him so.

"Bollocks, don't tell me that." He cupped her breast and softly kneaded it, swirled his thumb across the hardening bud of it.

She gasped.

He was breathing hard and staring at her with the smoldering look of a famished beast who wanted to devour her. Was he that aroused by her?

The notion set off more fires inside her.

Is this what passion felt like, a stream of molten lava?

An unstoppable torrent of scorching heat?

She was now up against the bookshelves, somehow wedged there by his magnificently big body as he continued to kiss her senseless.

Would it not be perfect for their union to occur right here in the library between the two things she loved most…him and books?

He must have read her thoughts, for he began to laugh again. "Sweet mercy! Lucy, you are a treasure. *My* treasure. I love you."

He kissed her fiercely, held her against those precious bookshelves that were rocking perilously as their bodies ground against each other.

He loved her!

She wanted to say it back to him, but his mouth was pressed too tightly to hers, and she was mindless anyway.

Who would not be while caught against this big wall of muscle?

She ran her hands along his body, felt the heat of his skin through his shirt.

Even his scent was hot…hot spice and maleness.

She tried to speak, but these fiery sensations overwhelmed her, ravaged her senses. She could not fashion the simplest words.

"I will love you always. Forever, Lucy." His voice was deep and husky, and he punctuated his words with kisses along her arched neck and down her throat. "But I don't want you to say it back to me."

"Oh, blessed heaven. Why not?" This is what she had been waiting for, aching for from the moment her eyes met his all those months ago in Taunton.

"I'll lose all control and take you here and now if you say it back to me. I'll take you against your beloved bookshelves. Yes, I know this is what you want. Your eyes hide nothing."

She stared up at him. "I would never hide anything from you."

"I know, love. This is one of the things I treasure most about you. Tell me to stop. We need to talk about Exeter. I need to get back to the kitchen and our prisoner."

"Your brothers and the Gentrys are handling matters."

"I shouldn't be kissing you…breathing you in…running my hands along your breathtaking body. Things are going to move very fast there."

"Where? On my body?"

"No, Exeter."

"Oh." She immediately sensed the change in him and tried to squelch her disappointment when he eased away. He shook his head and took several ragged breaths.

She sighed.

He gave her cheek a light caress. "I shouldn't have done that to you…or to myself. But I was so wound up, afraid someone would get to you next time because I wasn't there to protect you. It devastated me. But I meant what I said. I love you."

"And I lo–"

He kissed her again. "Don't say it."

She frowned, not understanding why he persisted in denying her this pleasure when her feelings had to be obvious, and she simply had to tell him.

He drew back, no longer deliciously squashing her against the shelves. "We have to talk about what happens after things resolve in Exeter. Everything will be different for you."

"How? You said you loved me. Are you now going to leave me?"

"No, it is the other way around. You will be brought into the world of elevated society. However, one thing will remain constant…my love. You have all of my heart, and I will never stop loving you."

"And I—"

He put his fingers to her lips. "Don't, Lucy."

"Why can I not say it back to you?"

She was surprised by the flicker of anguish in his eyes. "You may not want me after Wooton acknowledges you as his daughter and sees you made Baroness de Poitiers. I was enough for Luciana Lessing…"

She gasped and threw her arms around him. "There is no one

else for me. It does not matter if I were made Queen of England tomorrow. My heart would never change."

He leaned his forehead against hers. "It will, Lucy. Perhaps I should not have revealed my feelings."

"Then why did you?"

"Not to stake my claim on you, but to give you confidence in yourself. No one has ever given you this. I want you to know that you are a gem. A treasure. A diamond. The man who claims your heart will be the luckiest man alive. Believe it, Lucy. Don't ever let anyone tell you otherwise."

This man was going to make her cry.

"You will soon have a line of suitors out your door. Wooton may push you toward one or another of them. Stand your ground. Take your time. Come to me for help if you ever need it. I am yours. My heart will never belong to anyone else."

"As mine—"

"No, do not commit to me until you've seen enough of *ton* society to be sure."

She wanted to hit him over the head at this moment, she surely did. Had he not just marked her as a beast marks his territory? His divine scent was on her. In truth, all over her. He'd claimed her with his touch and tasted her on his tongue.

How could he do this and then give her up?

A knock at the door brought an end to their conversation.

Donal crossed the room and opened it.

Blanche poked her head in. "That Fielding knave is talking to Master Shayne. Your brothers wanted me to let you know."

"Thank you. I'll be right there." He turned to Lucy, his gaze exquisitely tender. "Stay here, Lucy. I'll be back as soon as I can. Blanche will stay with you. Is that all right?" he asked the older woman. "Fielding is talking, and I need to concentrate on this right now."

"Yes, Master Donal."

Lucy struggled to hold down her frustration. She wanted to listen in on that deathbed confession, but there was no way possible other than joining him in the kitchen, and that would immediately distract Fielding.

She was the reminder he'd failed in his mission.

If he was ready to give up information, there was no way she would interfere with that.

She nodded to acknowledge she would remain behind. "Don't forget me."

He laughed and shook his head. "Not a chance of that, Lucy."

Once he'd left them, Lucy walked to the desk to retrieve her book. "Blanche, do make yourself comfortable. You've been on your feet all day. Please, do not stand on formality with me."

She nudged the woman into one of the cozy, overstuffed chairs beside the hearth.

"Oh, bless ye, lass. I will admit to being exhausted. All this excitement is too much for me."

"Then rest, Blanche. We're stuck here for now anyway. I have a book to read. You needn't entertain me." She sat in the companion chair by the hearth and had only been reading for a few minutes before she felt a light breeze.

Shayne had left the window open a crack, but as she was about to rise to close it, she caught the scent of perfume in the air. It wasn't Blanche's for certain, for her scent was of the kitchen and whatever meal she happened to be cooking.

Her heart shot into her throat.

She'd felt the breeze because someone had opened the window wide and drawn the drapes aside while climbing in.

The baroness!

She had to be in here with them, but where was she standing?

Blanche's eyes were closed, and she was unaware.

Lucy wanted to keep her that way. Screaming would bring disaster down upon them, for the baroness was likely armed and would start shooting the moment she realized she had been spotted.

She strained to hear the slightest movement, afraid to so much as turn her head for fear of alerting the baroness.

She heard a creak by the door and then its soft click as the woman shut it…and another click as she locked it.

With pounding heart, Lucy reached over and silently lifted one of the fire-irons from its holder. She wasn't certain what good it would do unless the baroness came close enough for her to hit this fire shovel over her head.

She had no better plan at the moment.

Then Blanche snorfled.

At the same moment, Donal pounded on the door. "Lucy, why did you…hell!" He began to ram his shoulder against the thick wood to batter it down.

The distraction was all the time she needed to lunge out of her chair and wallop the baroness over the head with the iron hearth shovel. Then she brought it down on the woman's hand, eliciting a cry from her as the pistol slipped out of her grasp and fell to the floor with a thud.

Lucy kicked the weapon under the sofa and hit the baroness again so that she fell to her knees with a moan. "Don't get up, or I'll split your head wide open."

Donal smashed the door to pieces and tore into the room with his pistol drawn. "Lucy! Love, are you hurt?"

"I'm fine. Your presence is most timely and welcome." She stepped away from the baroness, afraid the woman might have a knife or other trick to harm her. "I did everything you taught me," she said proudly, hoping he could hear her over the baroness's shrill shrieks.

Her heart was still racing as she watched him bind their captive's hands.

"Where's Blanche?" he asked, his gaze remaining on the baroness who was fighting him for all she was worth.

"I'll kill you! I'll kill you!"

Donal remained calm as he searched her for hidden weapons.

Lucy turned to their dear housekeeper, who was hiding behind the chair. "She's right here. Are you all right, Blanche?"

"Yes, Miss Lucy." Her eyes were wide, and her mouth gaped

open, but she managed a nod. "I am, dear lass. Thanks to yer quick thinking. Oh, ye should have seen her, Master Donal. Miss Lucy was magnificent."

Lucy tried to appear nonchalant about her accomplishment but couldn't. She cast Blanche a beaming smile. "It was my training."

Donal laughed softly. "Top marks for you, Lucy."

Ox and Horace ran in to see what was happening.

"We heard a crash," Horace said, then his gaze fell on the baroness who looked like a coiled snake about to strike. "Well, doesn't that beat all. Ye got her, Master Donal."

"Lucy did. I merely arrived in time to tie her up." He glanced at Blanche, who was breathing heavily and had a hand to her heart. "Are you sure you're all right?"

"Yes, Master Donal." She nodded. "The witch never laid a hand on me. Miss Lucy never gave her the chance to aim her pistol at either of us."

Horace approached his wife with a concerned face.

"Which reminds me," Lucy said, falling to her knees to retrieve the weapon from under the sofa. "I kicked it away so she couldn't grab it."

"Well done, Miss Lucy!" Ox looked like he wanted to pick her up and kiss her. She grinned, wondering what Donal would think of that.

"Ox, take your mother back to the cottage, will you?" Donal ordered, and Lucy hoped he might be the least bit jealous. In truth, he had no reason to be, nor did she believe he really was. He knew that her heart was his and always would be.

"I'm sorry for all the excitement I've caused," Lucy said, her apology to the Gentrys heartfelt, for putting them all at risk. "Hopefully, it is now over, and we can all get back to a normal routine." Even as she spoke the words, she knew her life would never be the same again. The baroness may have been subdued, but she still had to contend with the Duke of Wooton.

He was not a threat to her life, of course.

But he certainly could threaten her happiness.

Blanche distracted her from her thoughts by giving her a hug. "We'll miss ye greatly, lass. Now ye'll go off and be the new baroness. The rightful one. I hope ye'll not forget us, for we'll never forget ye. Wouldn't have missed a moment of the time spent with ye. But I will admit I am quite spent now. Are ye certain ye don't need anything more from me tonight?"

Donal shook his head. "You have been a gem taking care of Lucy and the rest of us. We'll handle matters from here on out."

The woman took hold of her son's arm. "Well, I'll see ye in the morning then. Well done, Miss Lucy."

Lucy waited for all the Gentrys to lumber out before she turned to Donal. "What happens now?"

"We take our prisoner down to the kitchen. The magistrate will be happy to take her into his prison for the night. She needs to be more securely restrained and then questioned."

The woman emitted a menacing hiss.

Lucy tried not to respond, but she still looked incredibly dangerous with her glittering eyes and wicked smile that held deadly secrets.

There was such malice in the woman's gaze.

You have bested her.

Yes, she had and was not about to give this murderess the pleasure of seeing her back down.

She took a step closer.

"Yes, that's it, Luciana. Come to me. I don't bite," she purred, looking every bit the poisonous spider.

"Oh, but I am sure you do."

"Are you afraid of me, little mouse?"

"No." Lucy shook her head in denial, but she had been exactly that until a few weeks ago, a timid mouse scurrying about unnoticed by all until Donal had believed in her. "It is over, Andrea. I would have welcomed you into my home and cared for you as family. My mother would have done the same. But you wanted it all, and now you have nothing. That man with you at the old bridge in Tunbridge Wells, was he your husband? He seemed devoted to you, willing to die for you, and now even he is gone."

Andrea shrugged. "A marriage in name only. Alonso was weak. He did not do this for me, just for himself. We were attracted to the greed in each other, but I was always the more ambitious one. Come closer, Lucy. Let me kiss you, my dear cousin's daughter."

"I don't think so. I was curious to see the face of evil. Now that I have seen you, I have no intention of drawing near. Give my regards to my father. You'll see him in Exeter before I do, I expect."

"Your father." She threw her head back and laughed. "I'll never reach Exeter alive, surely you know this. He will see to it. You think I am a monster, but I am nothing compared to him. He is the Duke of Ice and rightly named. I don't need to raise a finger to destroy you. He will do it on his own, in his own cold, calculating time."

Lucy hoped she gave away nothing of her feelings, for Andrea was merely repeating her own concerns. Oh, she did not think he would beat her or deprive her of material comforts. But what of his love? Was he capable of feeling anything but ice? What might he demand of her once he officially recognized her as his daughter? And what of her love for Donal?

Even Donal was concerned about her father's plans for her.

She was in love with Donal.

What would the Duke of Ice do to him if he did not approve of their courtship?

❤

CHAPTER EIGHTEEN

DONAL REMAINED SURPRISINGLY subdued as he led Lucy upstairs. "This may be the last night I share a room with you, Lucy. We are almost at the end of this ordeal now. Fielding confessed all. Thank goodness for that. He passed not five minutes later."

"Oh."

"Now, there is only the baroness. There's nothing left for Wooton to do but a quick mop up in Dartmoor. He'll move fast to make other arrangements for you."

"Other arrangements?" She paused on the stairs. "Why should he not allow you to stay on and guard me whether I remain in Exeter, return to London, or go to Dartmoor? There must be a lot to do, even if it is mostly administrative now. You said he chose you because of the affection he sensed you held for me."

"That does not mean he will keep me on now that the danger has passed. Quite the opposite, if my usefulness is at an end, he will no longer want me anywhere near you."

She put a hand to her stomach as it began to roil. Was this not exactly her concern? And yet, Donal seemed not concerned about it at all.

She stared at him incredulously. "He would do this, and you still admire him? That is the most venal thing I have ever heard, to use you like this and then discard you?"

"I am not discarded. I will remain one of his top agents. Possibly be recommended for knighthood as Lorcan was. Do not be incensed. Wooton had to choose me to protect you. I would not have allowed him to select anyone else…which probably saved your life that first night in London because Fielding wanted the assignment."

"Donal!"

"Odd, the turns life takes. Nor will I allow anyone other than me to guard you in Exeter if I sense you are still in danger. You never have to worry about that." He kissed her on the nose. "Or perhaps you will be the one to guard me. You were brilliant tonight, Lucy. I'm so proud of you."

They continued upstairs to the bedchamber they shared. Lucy glanced at the pallet beside the hearth. He'd slept there every night except for the one time she'd needed him to hold her in his arms.

"Share the bed with me," she said in an aching whisper.

He sucked in a breath. "I almost crashed the bookshelves atop us with my lust for you. I dare not climb in with you. This is the worst possible night to ask it of me."

She was certain his logic was backward. It had to be tonight, or they might not have the chance again anytime soon. His brothers were taking Andrea…she refused to think of her as the baroness any longer. This was the title she stole from Lucy's mother. Andrea was to be taken to the magistrate's prison in Weymouth and would be guarded there by Donal's brothers tonight.

The new plan was for Donal's brothers to ride to Exeter with their prisoner first thing in the morning.

She and Donal would follow shortly afterward.

They were all in agreement about keeping her and Andrea apart. She understood their concern, for she'd seen the depth of hatred in the woman's eyes.

The plans were set.

She and Donal were now safe.

More important, they were in love. "Please, Donal. Share the bed with me. I will not force you to do anything you are not willing to do."

He threw his head back and laughed. "I believe that should be my line to you. You're the sweet, young miss. I am the wolf."

"I also have lots of questions you need to answer, and we do not need to be shouting back and forth to each other from across the room."

"Ah, I see. That is the only reason you want me in your bed? To converse?"

"Of course not. I would love to be wolfishly ravaged by you. And I will tell you now, if it is a choice between princely riches or you, I will choose you every time. I do not need to attend grand balls or take tea with the elite of society. I do not want to be surrounded by people who care nothing about me but will fawn over me because they want the connection to Wooton. Nor do I wish to spend my days rattling around a big, lavish manor house, having servants wait on me hand and foot. What I've lacked all my life is love. Whether it is family love or romantic love, I've never had any of it until I met you. How can you even question that my choice will always be you?"

She began to nibble her lip.

He sighed. "I've upset you."

"No, it isn't that."

"Then what?"

"I do not doubt my feelings for you. But…why are you suddenly backing away? Do you truly love me, Donal? Do you think I will change and become a darling of the *ton*? The notion is laughable. I assure you, I won't. But it frightens me to death to think that you might change."

He studied her, obviously surprised. "How would I? I'm a thickheaded Brayden and quite set in my ways."

"That's it exactly. You are a Brayden. Honorable. Protective. That trait is so deeply ingrained in you. My fear is that you'll wake up tomorrow and realize it wasn't love you were feeling at all but a need to guard me. I wish you had read *The Book of Love*. You would understand the difference between what is real and what you only think is real."

"That book," he said with a grunt.

"Yes, *that book*. I am taking it to Exeter with us and not letting go of it."

"Stop thinking it is magical, Lucy. It isn't."

"You're wrong." She shook her head. "It brought you to me."

He sighed. "Turn around. Let me untie your lacings. But I am not sharing that bed with you because we both know what will happen if I do. That privilege is for your husband."

"Which you will be if you truly love me."

"I do love you."

"But you are still not going to share my bed? Fine. Be a martyr if you wish, and spend another night on that hard floor. It will not change my feelings for you other than to question just how smart you really are."

He chuckled and came around to face her. "Why will you not let me be honorable?"

"Because there is nothing honorable in telling me that you love me, ravishing me against the bookshelves, and then refusing to do the same in here with me. I am yours. There is no other man for me. If you have no doubts and I have no doubts, then what are we talking about?"

She slipped out of her gown and draped it neatly over a chair. "The matter is simple. No one gets to keep us apart. Neither of us is going to get much sleep anyway. And I haven't even started asking my questions, which I shall now have to shout across the room to you because you are afraid to climb into my bed."

"I am not afraid. It is only for your protection."

She removed her shoes and stockings.

He followed the slow slide of her stockings down her legs.

Then she began to untie the bowstring of her shift.

He placed his hands over hers and swallowed hard. "What are you doing?"

"Taking off all my clothes."

"Bollocks, you are going to send me to an early grave. Don't do this to me."

"Why not? You have already seen me naked." She tipped her head up and gazed at him. "Turn away if you wish."

His smoldering eyes remained fixed on her for the longest time. "You are remarkably irritating for a bookish bluestocking."

"I am still going to take off all my clothes." She glanced at his hands still perched on hers. "What's it to be?"

The silence between them stretched interminably, then his lips twitched upward at the corners in the barest hint of a smile. "Let me help you with that bowstring."

CHAPTER NINETEEN

D ONAL KNEW HE should have kept his mouth shut and not told Lucy he loved her. But she touched his heart, and he could not allow her to enter London society as vulnerable as she had been when they'd first met.

How was she to deal with Wooton, the Duke of Ice, if she had no confidence in herself?

Yes, the man was her father.

But he would manipulate the hell out of Lucy. He was a master of that fine art, and Lucy was a lamb just waiting to be eaten alive.

Donal was not going to allow this to happen.

No one had ever loved this beautiful girl until he came along.

He was going to make sure she understood just how precious she was to him. He loved her completely, utterly, and without question.

Which is why he was in this predicament, trying to convince himself that lying naked in bed with Lucy was harmless, not at all the stupidest decision he had ever made. He groaned as he rolled atop her and propped on his elbows so as not to crush her with his weight. "Will you marry me, Lucy?"

She cast him an impertinent grin. "You cannot help yourself, can you? You have to do the honorable thing. Are you asking me to marry you because you are certain you love me? Or because it is the only way to ease your noble conscience now that you are about to claim my maidenhead?"

"Bollocks, I am going to throttle you. Did you not just point out that we love each other and there is no point in holding back?"

She nodded. "I did."

"Then I am no longer holding back. Will you marry me?" He kissed her lightly on the lips. "I love you...and your exquisitely perfect body. Don't leave me in agony any longer."

"I feel the same about you. I promise, I do. Besides, I think I know more about the meaning of love than you, especially enduring love, because I've poured over *The Book of Love* so often, the pages are worn down."

"You still haven't answered my question."

She put her arms around his neck and drew him closer. "There is no one else for me. I will not change, no matter how many titles or riches are thrown at me. My heart is yours completely and forever. Yes, Donal. I will marry you."

"Thank you, love." He proceeded to finish what he had started in the library, once more caught up in this overwhelming desire to claim Lucy.

Not merely desire.

Unquenchable thirst.

Savage need.

Her breasts were glorious.

Her body luscious.

Her smile captivating.

He caught the bud of one lush mound and began to taste and tease it with an insatiable hunger. She tasted like honey, soft and silky, deliciously sweet. She responded with breathy moans and clutched his head in a death grip as she arched up to meet his mouth.

He took his time with the one beautiful breast, then moved to the other and took the soft, pink bud between his lips. He flicked his tongue over it, laving and suckling, reveling in Lucy's response.

She cried out and clutched his shoulders. "Donal, my body is exploding."

"It isn't yet, love. But it will be soon." He knew she was aroused and her breasts sensitive, her skin tingling. But he had only just started, and she wasn't *exploding* yet.

He moved lower, kissed his way down her wriggling body, and closed his mouth over her core to taste all of this woman he loved.

Kittenish purrs spilled from her lips with mounting urgency.

He stroked intimately between her legs and suckled her there, teased her with his tongue until he felt she was close.

She gripped the sheets.

She tugged on his hair.

He knew she was close.

And still he kept on, unable to get enough of her, for she was silk and sweetness.

"*Donal*. Oh, heavens."

He felt her shudder as she now experienced her first release.

It filled him with pride, filled him with wonder that someone as perfect as Lucy existed just for him.

He moved back over her and wrapped her in his arms.

For once, she had no words.

She gazed at him wide-eyed, bewildered over this new experience. "Are you all right, Lucy?"

She held onto him with all her might. "I never knew love could be like this. I am still floating. Hold me close, for I fear I shall fly away like a feather on the wind."

He rolled onto his back and drew her up against him, burying his hands in her silky curls. He wanted to lie with her like this every night of their lives, breathe in the honey scent of her body as they drifted off to sleep in each other's arms.

"Donal?"

"Yes, Lucy."

"It has not escaped my notice that despite all the naughty things you did to me, I am still a maiden. Is there not something more you should be doing?"

He could not help the smile escaping his lips. "Funny thing about that. True love changes a man. I could not bring myself to take you outside of marriage. I thought it would not matter to me, but it does. With you, it does. When you give yourself to me, I want it to be as my wife."

"What if Wooton will not allow us to marry?"

"I'm not worried about it. If you want me, then he cannot stop me. He'd have to kill me first."

She gasped.

He stroked her hair. "Don't worry, he won't. Despite what you think, he considers me too valuable to maim."

"Don't jest about this. I have no idea what sort of man my father is, and you've already told me he can be ruthless. As for me, my heart is yours no matter when you decide to plow my virgin field."

He arched an eyebrow. "Your virgin field?"

"I read it in a book."

"Blessed saints, why am I not surprised?" He let out a rumble of laughter and drew her tightly into the circle of his arms. "I love you."

She nestled against his chest, her long hair tumbling over his arm as he lightly stroked her body. "I love you, too. You cannot stop me from saying it back to you. I love you so much."

He held her in silence, caught up in the moment and the moonlight spilling in through the open drapes. It felt good not to have to hide their existence any longer.

Lucy looked ethereal in the silver glow.

Even her eyes sparkled as she tipped her head up to look at him. "Will you tell me now what Fielding said? I suppose he confirmed it was Andrea who hired him."

He drew her hand to his lips and kissed it. "It was her husband who approached him. At his urging, Fielding put together an elite team of assassins. But we know Andrea was involved from the start because we saw her kill Mel."

Concern played upon Lucy's face. "What do you know of her husband? She so much as said he was the man on the bridge with her that day. Is it so?"

"Yes."

"Do you know his name?"

"Fielding knew him as Alonso de Poitiers. He took on the de Poitiers name instead of his wife taking on his family's surname. Wooton will know who he is exactly, although we might figure it out sooner by digging into his background. He must be listed somewhere in my grandfather's books."

"Too bad those men in London cannot talk. You shot the first two. They were the ones whose bodies were found in the carriage. What a ghastly end for them."

"They knew the risks involved. Besides, they were already dead by the time it burned and would have felt no pain." He thought it was important to point out to Lucy because she had a soft heart, and he knew she would never forget the violence of that night.

Time might dim the memory, but it would always be there in the shadows of her recollection. "A third was severely burned when he hurled that fiery torch into the carriage. That flame is called Greek fire and cannot be doused by ordinary means. Extremely dangerous, as the fellow found out."

"What of the fourth man?"

"Fielding claims Edgeware picked him up when he circled back to see what had happened to the others. Turns out, he was the burned man's brother. The pair of them were Hessian mercenaries, just arrived in England. They were looking for any work they could find. Unfortunately, that is the plight of most soldiers since the Napoleonic Wars ended. They were among the many discharged from service and left with no income to support themselves."

Lucy frowned. "And what of the others you shot tonight?"

"The last of the Hessian assassins. Fielding and the little army he gathered are now all dead or imprisoned."

"Assuming Fielding is to be believed. Do you really think it is over?"

"Yes, love. Andrea's presence here reveals she had run out of options and was planning a last, desperate assault. With her Alonso dead, who does she have left to do her bidding? He was the one who made the contacts and doled out the payments. Wooton will make certain every last farthing is confiscated from her. She'll be left penniless and rotting in prison because she was never the rightful baroness and has no privilege of peerage to protect her."

He'd been holding her in his arms all the while, lightly caressing her as they spoke. He wished their discussion could be about light, frivolous topics as they lay with their heads upon the pillows and revealed their innermost thoughts.

"Did Fielding make mention of my mother before he died?"

"No, love. He was told nothing about the past, nor did he care to know. But we did ask him as part of his questioning."

"How can we be certain Fielding did not lie about that?"

He kissed the top of her head. "He gave us a deathbed confession. Oddly enough, it was in the way he admitted his betrayal that convinced me he was telling the truth. The disdain in his voice when he spoke of those Hessians and his admiration when speaking of agents of the Crown, as though he considered himself still one of us."

"How sad to end an otherwise noble career like his."

"He devoted his entire life to his work, never married. Never had an existence outside of his duties to the Crown. My brothers and I sat in silence for a long moment after he took his last breath. The work we do on behalf of the Crown can suck the soul out of a man. This is why Shayne left. He felt it had taken over his life. Not that his duties in Taunton turned out to be much easier, but it provided a bedrock for him. A town in which he established roots and built friendships. Now he has Willow in his life, too."

"And Lorcan has Cammy. I never saw him crack a smile except when he was around her."

"Finding love is what saves men like us."

"Then you really ought to read that book. It says there can never be a true and lasting love without trust."

"I know."

"You do? How do you know this?"

"It is no different in my work as an agent. Trust in one's partner, in one's team, is vital. The slightest doubt or hesitation could have disastrous consequences. Same for marriage. Lack of trust is like a worm that eats you up from inside."

"Yes, that is it exactly. This is why I will marry no one but you. I need you more than ever if I am to assume the responsibilities of baroness. And what of Wooton? If he is really my father, then what better man to stand up to him than you? Not that I want you to fight my battles for me, but it will help to have you on my side. Indeed, it would be irresponsible of you not to be there to protect me."

He laughed when she reached up and began to kiss his face, her attempts to convince him not quite at an end. "Because I need a big, strong man like you to—"

"Ha! You proved tonight that you are more than capable of protecting yourself. However, I find that I cannot live without you. I am going to marry you before the week is out. I'll obtain the common license as soon as we reach Exeter."

Her eyes lit up like starlight, but in the next moment, she inhaled lightly. "Donal, I am not of age yet. I still need…oh, Lessing is not my father. Wooton will deny you. What are we to do if he denies you his blessing?"

"Lucy, you miraculously survived getting shot in the chest because of a necklace you never take off. You believe in a magical book of love you think made me fall in love with you. I assure you, I was in love with you before Cammy ever handed me the book."

He paused to kiss her and then continued. "I am convinced you've had angels watching over you all of your life. And after the strength you showed tonight, Wooton doesn't stand a chance. He will deny you nothing." He tucked the covers around her. "Get some sleep, love. We'll have a busy day ahead of us tomorrow."

His words must have soothed her, for she curled in a little ball against him and nestled against his heat. After a moment, she looked up at him with her big, round eyes and smiled impertinently. "I don't think I can sleep. What you did to me…what you made me feel…"

"Was it nice?"

"No, it was quite naughty."

He arched an eyebrow. "But in a nice way?"

"Yes, Donal. In a very nice way. And now I am wide awake."

He shifted their positions so that she was once more on her back under him. "Well then," he said, propping on his elbows to absorb most of his weight. "Let's see what I can do to tire you out."

CHAPTER TWENTY

L ucy was nudged out of a deep slumber in the middle of the night by Donal shaking her awake. "What is it?"

"I don't know…maybe trouble. I heard riders outside." He had already rolled to his feet, drawn on his trousers and boots, and was now checking his pistol. "Get dressed," he said, handing the weapon to her, "but stay here. If you hear shots, run for the secret door in my grandfather's bedchamber. You are to do nothing but hide. Do not shoot unless you are cornered, understand?"

"I do." She wasn't trained to shoot under any circumstances, much less trained to keep her aim steady and fell an attacker while she was being shot at herself. "Be careful."

"I always am. Love you, Lucy." He grabbed his rifle and hurried downstairs.

Lucy scrambled to put herself together, all the while straining to hear what was going on below. A moment later, she heard Donal's footsteps coming down the hall. "What happened?"

Her heart gave a hitch when she caught sight of his expression.

"Andrea's dead."

"What?" Lucy gasped. "How?"

Had his brothers…no, they would not kill anyone in cold blood.

"She must have had a poison tonic or powder hidden on her.

It wasn't in her ring. We searched all her jewelry for secret compartments. Perhaps she had it sewn into her gown. I suppose it does not matter now."

"So, you think she killed herself?"

"Yes. A woman like that, used to luxury and giving commands, would prefer death to facing Wooton's wrath or spending the rest of her life rotting in prison."

"And it is not pretend? You know, an elixir to mimic the appearance of death?"

"As in Shakespeare's Romeo and Juliet? No, love. It is real."

"I see. Perhaps she loved her Alonso more than she let on and could not go on without him."

He laughed incredulously. "That woman loved no one but herself. Her husband was just another expendable toady. She got what she deserved, this viper who destroyed everyone close to her. Do not soften toward her."

"I wasn't. It just feels…I don't know…as though I have just been through the strangest dream."

"I know, love. Speaking of dreams, Lorcan and Shayne are going to grab a few hours of sleep, then we will all ride to Exeter. There's no reason for any of us to remain behind now."

She nodded numbly. "All that's left is dealing with my father."

Donal closed the door to their bedchamber and gently took the pistol out of her hands. "Nothing we can do about him tonight."

His words did little to comfort her.

Nor did she feel comforted when he climbed back into bed with her and draped his arm around her.

She tossed and turned until it was time to pack up and leave.

Donal frowned as he watched her go through the motions. "Lucy, love. The danger is over, I promise you."

"Not completely. Oh, I expect the physical danger is over, but what about my father?"

"This is what has you worried? That he will object to my

marrying you?"

She nodded.

"Well, I doubt he'll be happy about it. But he'll agree to it in the end."

"I wish I could believe you."

They spoke no more about it as they prepared to leave, taking a moment to bid the Gentrys farewell.

The ride to Exeter was a difficult one for Lucy because the weather was raw, and they'd been engulfed in a light mist for much of the day. She was bundled well enough, but between the rain and blustery wind and her worries about meeting the Duke of Wooton, she felt exhausted by midday.

However, she endured because it was important to her not to slow Donal and his brothers down in any way.

She distracted herself by watching thunderclouds billow and shift as they were buffeted by strong winds. The further north they rode, the worse the weather turned, and now the sky was ominously black.

"This does not look good," Donal said. "We'd better stop at the Thistle Inn for the night."

His brothers immediately agreed.

"We're still half a day's ride from Exeter and wouldn't have made it tonight anyway," Shayne muttered.

Lorcan grinned. "You'll like the place, Lucy. Best food anywhere in England."

They arrived shortly before sundown, and Donal obtained two rooms, one for his brothers to share and the other for them.

Lucy held her breath when the innkeeper turned his hawkish gaze on her. Donal had signed her in as his wife. The innkeeper, obviously familiar with the Brayden brothers, inspected her. Would he accept Donal's lie or toss them all out?

The man merely scratched his head, congratulated all three brothers on their recent marriages, and had one of his maids show them up to their rooms.

Lucy did not expect their guest quarters to be much of anything. Indeed, she only needed a bed that did not have fleas in it.

But as the maid opened their door, Donal leaned close and whispered, "You're going to like it here."

Their room was not very large but surprisingly charming. She noted the blue floral wallpaper and silk drapes and the furniture of good quality cherrywood. The counterpane was of plain, white linen, but there were decorative pillows to match the wallpaper arrayed at its head. The room seemed to belong in an elegant country manor. "Well, love? What do you think?"

She turned to Donal with a smile of delight. "Much better than riding to Exeter in a rainstorm."

The window had been left open to air the room, and the scent of lavender blew in on the damp breeze. She crossed to peer out of the window and saw beds of purple blossoms in the inn's garden. "Oh, the rain's beginning to fall."

Donal came to her side and closed it tight. "It'll be a deluge tonight."

She looked around the rest of the room.

A basin and ewer stood atop a bureau in the far corner. The ewer was filled with fresh water. There were also clean drying cloths and soap provided for them.

Donal winked at her when she cast him another smile. "Glad it meets with your approval."

He marched to the door and held it open to give the maid a hint to leave. She was slow to make her way out, tossing him a starry-eyed gaze. "We'll come down for supper shortly. Ask the proprietor to have a private dining room readied for us."

She bobbed a curtsy and scurried off, giggling.

He shook his head and shut the door.

"You know you are handsome. She couldn't take her eyes off you."

He shrugged. "I only care about your eyes turning to starlight when you look at me. Go ahead and wash up, love. I'll do the same as soon as you are done. Then we can eat."

"You and your brothers must be hungry enough to gnaw the

furniture. We haven't stopped for a bite since leaving Weymouth."

"Famished," he said with a laugh and settled in one of the wooden chairs, casually rocking back in it as he watched her pour water into the basin. "Our Aunt Miranda referred to us as wildebeests when we were younger. Mostly that name was applied to our eight London cousins. But when we visited, we were eleven boys, cousins all fairly close in age and unmanageable whenever we got together. We played rough and ate like animals. For meals, she would toss a side of beef onto the table for us. It would be nothing but bones within minutes. Someone usually needed their hand tended afterward because they did not move fast enough and got speared with a fork."

Lucy adored how he spoke of his large family, especially loved the way his eyes lit up with mirth when relating tales of his boyhood. There was so much richness in his life, the summers spent in Weymouth with their grandfather and the occasional holidays celebrated in London with their large, extended family.

She let Donal go on, fascinated by his stories.

He was not one to talk much, but he was opening up to her now, and it filled her heart with joy. She nodded and smiled in encouragement, eager to learn all she could about him and the valiant man he had become.

She could not imagine what the Yuletide holidays would have been like, all the boys so close in age, thrown together in a house full of valuable furnishings. She expected his clever Aunt Miranda tossed them into an empty room to roughhouse from sunrise to sundown and only brought them out at mealtimes.

Her upbringing had been so different. Bearable whenever Eliza had been around to keep her company. Unbearable as Eliza grew older and was invited by her friends to all the best homes because she was cute as a button and lively.

That left Lucy alone with parents who ignored her.

She shook out of the thought.

This would no longer be her life.

Donal came up behind her as she finished drying her hands and face. "Did I say something to upset you, Lucy?" He wrapped his arms around her. "You suddenly turned quiet."

"No, not at all." She skittered to the chair he had just vacated and watched him take his turn washing up. "It's just that I have no memories of joyful times to share with you. I was nothing to the Lessings, and I have no idea what Wooton will think of me. I cannot imagine having any sentimental father and daughter moments with that man."

"I don't want you to worry about it. I won't leave your side for a moment. Nor will my brothers ever be far off. They know how I feel about you and will always look after you if ever I cannot."

They went downstairs to meet Donal's brothers and enjoy a hearty repast in one of the inn's private dining rooms. Within moments, the servers set out before them a haddock pie, Cornish pasties, and mounds of stovies. The stovies were a simple concoction of potatoes, onions, and bacon, but one would think these men had just found a pot of gold the way they pounced on those potatoes and devoured them.

Of course, they made certain to serve her first, behaving like gentlemen and not wildebeests until her plate was full. Then they released the tension obviously built up inside them over the weeks since the London attack and behaved like brothers. That they felt comfortable enough around her to act with their natural boisterousness was a great compliment to her.

It meant they were accepting her into their family.

Afterward, Donal led her upstairs while his brothers advised the innkeeper of their plans to leave for Exeter shortly after sunrise.

The simple act of walking to their guest-chamber felt monumental to Lucy, as though she and Donal were truly a married couple. But there had been no ceremony and might never be one if Wooton had other plans for her.

She did not speak of it to Donal because he was already concerned about what would happen tomorrow.

Instead, she undressed down to her shift and settled on the soft, feather mattress. "There is no saving my reputation. You may as well sleep comfortably in this bed beside me."

He groaned, rubbed the back of his neck, and then nodded.

She fell asleep in his arms, wishing she were better versed in the art of seduction because it seemed a terrible waste to lie in bed with this man she loved and do nothing but sleep.

But sometime in the middle of the night, she grew cold, and he must have felt her shiver. He drew her up against him and kissed her shoulder to calm her.

She turned to face him.

A soft groan tore from the depths of his soul.

He kissed her throat. Her lips. The swell of her breast.

He slid her under him so that he was settled over her, the solid weight of him warm and comforting. His hands were rough, workman's hands, but exquisitely gentle as he slipped the shift off her and worked his magic on her body. "You're so beautiful, Lucy. You are my treasure."

Afterward, he wrapped his arms around her and held her close at her urging because she was afraid she would float away.

He knew just how to touch her and make her shatter.

She found herself waking in his arms the next morning.

He growled softly and stretched his beautifully muscled body before rolling out of bed. "Did you sleep well, love?"

She nodded. "For the most part."

"I disturbed you, I know. I couldn't keep my hands off you."

"I didn't mind." She wanted as much of this wonderful man as he would give her. Who knew what would happen before this day was out?

She took extra care in preparing herself for meeting this Duke of Ice, who claimed to be her father. She had only Donal's grandmother's altered gowns with her, but they were passably elegant. She donned the prettiest one, the pale brown with a hint of rose, which was not really practical for riding. But they did not have far to go, and the weather was sunny and mild today. She was determined to face the duke with all the social grace and confidence she could muster.

Donal had gone downstairs to prepare for their departure, which gave her a few moments of privacy. He returned carrying a breakfast tray. "Dining room's crowded, and I wanted us to get an early start. I brought up a pot of tea and ginger cakes. That ought to hold us to Exeter."

He set it down. "Here, let me help you with the laces. You look beautiful, Lucy."

His kindness was going to have her in tears. When had she ever been treated with such consideration? His every gesture was thoughtful, and he did not even think of it as something special.

This is the sort of man he was.

Strong. Smart. Never a man to be crossed.

But when he loved, it was with all his being.

He kissed her lightly on the neck and then led her to the small table where he'd set the breakfast tray. He began to pour tea into the two cups he'd brought up with the pot. "Donal, you are making me feel like a princess. I can attend to this."

He laughed. "I thought my brothers were idiots when I caught them doting over their wives, but I understand now why they could not help themselves. I think we must all be born with a little piece missing in our hearts, a piece held by someone else…someone special and precious. When we find the person who holds that missing piece, everything suddenly falls into place. Our heart is no longer aimlessly searching."

She stared up at him in wonder. "Have you been reading *The Book of Love?*"

"No. I've told you already, I don't need a book to tell me what my heart needs. I knew what I was missing the first time I set eyes on you. I was always coming back for you, Lucy. I just had to convince myself I was ready to settle down. A man's brain can be a thick-headed thing at times. I knew it had to be you and still worked feverishly to delay the inevitable." He shook his head, gulped down a slice of the cake, and washed it down with his tea.

He then rose and quickly gathered their belongings. "My brothers ought to be finished with their breakfast by now. They were already downstairs and eating when I entered the dining room."

"Oh, then I won't delay us."

"No problem, love. Take your time. Are you all right?"

She nodded, knowing she must seem unusually fluttery this morning. "Yes, although I am a bit overwhelmed at the prospect of meeting my father."

Lucy was more than a bit overwhelmed when they reached Exeter at midday and stopped before the most imposing house in town, its red stone magnificence rivaling the finest castles in the surrounding Devonshire countryside.

Shayne and Lorcan had split from them to head to the magistrate's office and notify their cousin, Rafe Quinton, they had arrived. She suspected they would join them here shortly, bringing along their magistrate cousin to make certain Wooton did not disrupt the peace in this lively market town.

"Ready, Lucy?" Donal asked, helping her dismount.

She nodded.

In truth, she was fearless when beside him.

His strength, not only physical strength but his strength of character, imbued her with courage of her own.

But coming face to face with the man who had abandoned her was a jolt. She thought she had prepared herself to meet this Duke of Ice, but she hadn't.

Words failed her.

Her legs could hardly hold her up as she stood in his opulent parlor, facing this tall man whose hair was silver and eyes looked tired, but he otherwise looked quite vital and trim.

She had his eyes.

His mouth.

The realization knocked the breath from her.

She felt the flutter of butterflies in her stomach.

They stood a long moment simply staring at each other until he broke the silence. "It is good to see you, Luciana."

She ought to have said something equally polite and trivial, but she could not. "Why did you abandon me?"

He motioned for her to be seated and then nodded for Donal to leave them.

She grabbed Donal's hand. "No, he stays."

In truth, she knew Donal was not going to leave unless she asked him. But if anyone was going to be obstinate and contradict the duke's commands, it was better for her to be the one. He could not dismiss her from service to the Crown since she did not work for him. Nor could he do much to hurt her worse than he already had. "He stays," she repeated, meeting the duke's icy gaze.

He bowed his head and cast her a smile. "I can see you are my daughter. Impatient with social niceties and just want to get directly to the facts. I expect you are stubborn. Willful."

"Strong in heart," she added. "Why did you leave me with the Lessings all these years?"

"Sit down, Luciana. You too, Brayden." He rang for refreshments. "Do you have any bags that need to be brought in?"

She laughed at the notion. "No. If you will recall, I've been running for my life. There wasn't time to spend an idle day shopping. Even if I did have more than the clothes on my back, why would I have them brought here?"

"Because you are staying with me from now on. I would have thought Brayden made that clear to you."

"We didn't speak about it. But I'll tell you now—if I stay, then he stays."

The duke arched an eyebrow. "I see you've taken your duties to heart," he said with a noticeable chill to his voice as he turned to Donal. "Perhaps a little too much so."

"You knew how I felt about Lucy. Was this not precisely why you gave me this assignment?" He proceeded to give an account of what had happened to them on that first night in London and their last night in Weymouth. He briefly mentioned Fielding's confession and their discovery of her connection to Baroness de Poitiers. He'd written to the duke about the de Poitiers connection earlier, so Fielding's confession was the only new information provided to the duke. "Lucy now needs to know the truth from you. Why was she left with the Lessings? How did the baroness learn of her existence? What became of Lucy's mother?"

Wooton paused while his butler rolled in a cart filled with all manner of expensive delights, including a pineapple and oranges displayed among more traditional fare consisting of Devonshire splits and cucumber sandwiches. "You have your choice of teas from China or India," he said with a casual pride. "My preference is for Indian tea. A friend of mine brought these aromatic leaves back for me. A gift from one of the powerful maharajahs. You will not find this tea anywhere else in England since we have yet to establish trade routes there."

Of course, this was designed to impress her. Overwhelm her. Prove he was as powerful as a prince.

She ignored the pineapple, chose the tea from China, and nibbled on a slice of common Devonshire cream cake instead.

Wooton grinned. "I think I am going to like you, Luciana."

"Why shouldn't you? I am your daughter, am I not? Or was that a lie you told Baroness de Poitiers to rile her? And rile her, you did. She came after me most viciously. I suppose you are pleased she and her husband died? Saves you the bother of taking them into your custody."

Lucy began to fret her lip, afraid she had said too much.

But Donal showed not the slightest trace of concern.

Her father had a piercing gaze, and it was trained on her. "You ask a lot of questions."

"Is it not time I had some answers? Not only about the de Poitiers family, but specifically about my mother and you." She showed him the necklace she had not taken off in all the years since she'd received it as a gift. "And about this emblem. Did you give it to me? How did you get it? It is a de Poitiers symbol from an old smuggling consortium."

"Brayden reported all you'd figured out while in hiding. Clever girl." He glanced at Donal.

"Tell her, Your Grace. You've left Lucy in the dark long enough. You did the same when you assigned me to protect her. I was told nothing about who these villains were. Your daughter almost died because you hid the truth from all of us."

Wooton emitted a low, menacing growl. "I ought to discharge you, Brayden."

"And leave someone else to guard Lucy? Not a chance. I gave her my oath I would protect her, and I have no intention of breaking it now. I am going to see this through to the end. Nor will you carry out your threat because you know it would endanger her life. We both have to put aside our pride and think of her safety first. So, what else must I know?"

Lucy set down her cake plate. "Nor will I agree to anything until I know of your intentions for me. But before we get to that discussion, we need to have this one. What happened to my mother, and why was I placed with the Lessings? Donal and I figured out the timeline and know you could be my father. We also know you did not get back to England before my mother passed."

She took a deep breath. "Was she truly murdered by Andrea? Or did my birth kill her?"

Donal inhaled sharply. "Lucy, you cannot think you are responsible. A newborn babe is brought innocent into the world. Women die in childbirth, it happens often enough. It is an act of God, not to be blamed on the innocent newborn."

Of course, this was the sort of man Donal was. Kind. Honorable. She cast him a starry-eyed gaze because she was so infatuated with him. "You would think so because this is your noble nature. But I know nothing of my father's nature since I have never met him before today." She turned pointedly toward the duke. "Is this how you feel? That I am blameless? Or did you hate me so much you could not bear to be around me, and so you gave me away?"

She was surprised when the vigor suddenly drained from the duke.

He sank back in his chair and closed his eyes a moment. "Dearest child, you had nothing to do with my precious Olivia's death. It was all Andrea's doing. Thank the Good Lord she could not get her talons into you."

He reached out and took her hand, then emitted an anguished groan.

Lucy was not sure what compelled her to keep her hand in his, for this man had never been a father to her, and yet, in this moment, she felt the depth of his anguish. "Your Grace, am I really your daughter?"

"Yes, Luciana. You are. Can you doubt it now that we are face to face? You are my child. My treasure."

She gasped and turned to Donal.

He'd used the same words when describing her.

He grinned. "Don't be surprised, Lucy. This is what you are. I am not the only one who feels this way about you."

"When did you learn I was your daughter?" she asked, keeping hold of the duke's hand since he did not seem to have any desire to release it anyway.

He opened his eyes and stared at her. "I always knew, Lucy...may I call you that? You seem to bristle every time I refer to you as Luciana."

She nodded, momentarily unable to speak as his admission struck her like a punch to the gut. "Always knew? And you never came for me?"

She let go of his hand and struggled not to cry.

Donal put his arm around her to lend comfort. "Your Grace, why would you leave her to the Lessings?"

"It was never my intention, but everything slipped away from me in those early years. I came home to a dukedom in a mess, and everyone I loved dead. Father. Brother. Most of all, Olivia. It was as though the heart had been ripped from my chest when I learned she had died. Then to hear from her cousin Andrea that you had also died."

He buried his head in his hands. "You have no idea what this did to me. At the same time, every damn government minister was pounding on my door, begging me to take over the running of the Home Office and properly train its agents."

After a moment, he looked up at her. "Amid all this, Olivia's maid came to me with a wild story, claiming Olivia had been poisoned, and you were still alive."

"Did you not believe her? Is this why you never took me in?"

He shook his head in denial. "Oh, at first, I was doubtful. Then I paid a call on Andrea, saw that secret glint of triumph in her eyes, and immediately knew Olivia's maid had told me the truth. The woman was devoted to Olivia and would have swallowed the poison herself if she realized what was happening."

"You knew Andrea had poisoned her, and yet you did nothing about it for all these years?"

"How could I?" He shook his head and sighed. "People think I am a cold-hearted beast. Perhaps I am in many ways, but I still abide by the rule of law. Spotting a glint in someone's eyes is not reason enough to kill them. Also, Andrea claimed she was not with Olivia at the time, and no witnesses could place her there either. How could I prove it was she who had done this foul deed? Or even if any of what Olivia's maid had said was true. She might have gone mad and fabricated the story of her death."

"But I was real, and you never came for me."

"I had not the head nor the heart to add you to my pile of worries at the time. Also, I was concerned for your safety. If someone truly had killed Olivia, I knew they would come after you next. Her maid had already placed you with the Lessings. I contacted them and made arrangements for their continued care of you. The arrangement was only meant to last several months. But the months turned into years. Once I was ready, I realized it was too late to pull you from the only home you had ever known. You thought Eliza Lessing was your sister. I saw the two of you in the park one day when you were children. You looked so happy playing together."

His eyes misted as he continued. "Even then, I was not equipped to raise a daughter on my own. I had a dukedom to manage and a monarchy to protect. I threw myself into my duties and trained the finest agents of the Crown. Lucy, you are my true daughter. This was never in doubt for me. Your mother and I were secretly married before I returned to my military duties. Record of our marriage is with the bishop of Exeter Cathedral. It is valid. Her father's consent was not required."

Lucy leaned forward, now gripping the edge of her chair as she listened to the mystery of her past unfold. She ached to know more about her mother. Ached that Wooton had chosen to miss her childhood.

As he continued, she inhaled his words.

Tried not to cry over them.

"I had set up everything for Olivia before I shipped out of England. Ample funds so she would never lack for anything if her family ever turned her out. They were a bad lot. Ruthless. Avaricious. Olivia was the gem among them."

He laughed wanly. "That is what I called her, too. My treasure. I fell in love with her at first sight. It was the same for her. I was not permitted to court her because her father wanted an elevated title for her. Nothing less than a duke would do. It did not matter that I was wealthy in my own right and a duke's spare. But a second son was not good enough for him. Nor did he care about the fortune I'd gained from waging several successful military campaigns. When I heard the news that both my father and brother had died, I sailed home eager to see my bride and properly claim her now that I was to be the Duke of Wooton. I truly cared for my father and brother, and their deaths affected me deeply. I knew my Olivia would console me."

"But she'd died after delivering me," Lucy said in a whisper.

"Poisoned after safely delivering you," he corrected with a frown. "My heart fell to pieces, not only because I'd lost her…Andrea then told me the child had died, too."

"Andrea," Lucy repeated softly.

He cast her a mirthless smile. "Did you know she was actually my intended? My father and de Poitiers meant for us to marry. But I had taken no more than two steps into the de Poitiers parlor when I saw the two cousins standing together, Andrea with her haughty expression and Olivia with her angel smile. Obviously, that meeting did not go well."

His expression softened the littlest bit. "Olivia and I met in secret after that. I married her shortly before I left England. I had no idea she was with child, although we'd both hoped she would conceive."

"What did her father say when she told him?"

He shook his head. "She never told anyone but Andrea. Her father was not a good man, and she was afraid of what he might do upon learning she had disobeyed his wishes."

Lucy's heart sank. "So, she confided in Andrea instead?"

"Yes. Unfortunately, her trust was misplaced. Andrea arranged for Olivia to leave Dartmoor and secretly give birth to you at an abbey close to the Scottish border. From what I have pieced together, she told de Poitiers that she and Olivia had been invited to visit a dear school friend for the summer. He never suspected. Your mother carried small and was not showing even though she was months along."

"Then what happened?" She wanted to despise this man, but he'd loved her mother with all his heart, and her death had utterly crushed him.

Donal now took her hand and openly held it.

The duke noticed but did not comment. "Andrea fled to the Continent soon after I returned. Eventually, she married some dimwit, a low-level English diplomat who served in Greece. Alonso Goring is his name, although he took on the surname of de Poitiers because he is an ambitious toady and wanted to please the old baron."

"So, Andrea was out of your reach?"

"No one is out of my reach, not anywhere in the world."

"Oh, I see."

Her father cast her a wry smile. "But as I've said, despite what you think of me, I do not go around killing people on mere suspicion. The mother abbess thought Olivia's maid had concocted the story. She did not believe it was possible for Andrea to have poisoned your mother. As for you, she had also been duped into thinking you had died. She called you a lovely little thing with a mop of golden-brown hair and a lovely smile. But you were so frail, and Olivia was too weak to feed you."

Lucy closed her eyes as he continued recounting the past.

"For whatever reason, Olivia's maid led them all to believe you were at death's door. Perhaps she was worried about what Andrea might do to you, so she thought pretending you were failing in health might gain her the time she needed to steal you away. Lots of women came to this abbey to have their babes. Those who survived would be given away afterward. No one looked twice when someone walked out with a child in hand. This is how Olivia's maid walked out with you. No one noticed. Everyone simply accepted it as fact when she tearfully announced later that you had died."

He sighed and continued. "You were never meant to be given away, of course. But with my sweet Olivia lost and me not yet back in England, Olivia's maid had to protect you. She had the secret stash of funds I had given Olivia, so she used some of it to pay the Lessings. She knew I would return soon to claim you and dared not send you back to the de Poitiers family, for fear Andrea would get her hands on you. De Poitiers was never going to remarry or father more children, so you were all that stood between her and the title of baroness."

He shook his head and continued. "Can you ever forgive me, Lucy? I thought I was doing you a service to have you raised in a respectable family. They had a daughter close to you in age. Also, being in charge of the Home Office, especially the delicate and dangerous operations I was undertaking, would have required extensive security to protect my family. It was safer to leave you as you were. I questioned my decision often afterward. Over the years, I would look for you in the park with Eliza."

She opened her eyes and stared at him. "You saw me?"

He nodded. "Many times. You were a quiet child, but there were times when I heard you laughing. A sweet, infectious laugh that sounded so much like your mother's. You seemed happy. All seemed to be going smoothly. Andrea was still out of the country, and I was never certain of her guilt. When she and her husband threatened your life and mine a few weeks ago, I knew for certain Olivia's maid had been right about everything."

"But how did Andrea know about me? Who gave away the secret?"

His expression softened as he gazed at her. "You did, Lucy. Or perhaps I ought to blame myself for giving you that necklace. While de Poitiers died several years back, Andrea did not return to England until her husband's diplomatic posting ended. Perhaps they thought it wiser to avoid me at all costs, to stay out of England for as long as possible. But she was now baroness, and duty required her return. All her years of waiting were about to pay off. Then she saw you at Lord Trilling's ball, the one he hosts every year."

She nodded. "It was a crush. I remember it well."

"She bumped into you and noticed your necklace, then noticed you, and immediately saw the resemblance to your mother. You have the look of her, although you have my eyes. My mouth. But you have your mother's expressions and her softness. Andrea saw you enter his library and sneak into a corner to read one of his books. You were wearing a hideous gown, she claimed. Some bilious yellow thing, with ridiculous frills and bows."

Lucy gasped and spared a scowl for Donal.

He had told her the same thing.

He was biting the inside of his cheek and looking everywhere but at her.

But it truly wasn't important.

"It was sometime during that night she got a better look at your necklace and had no doubt about who you were. That crescent moon and lion rampant design gave you away. She knew you were the child she'd been told was dead."

"She confessed all this? When?"

"The same night you were attacked. I'd met her earlier in the day, and that's when she shot me. Some villains are so full of themselves, they cannot help but talk while they hold a weapon on you. This is what she did, told me all and then shot me."

"But you survived."

"And had to act fast. Brayden, here, is my best man. I sent him for you and not a moment too soon."

"Thank goodness you did." She glanced with love at Donal. "But all these secrets have destroyed us as a family. All this time lost between us. How can we ever recapture those moments?"

"We cannot, but perhaps we'll be able to make new moments for us, Lucy. You are my daughter. My *legitimate* daughter. I want you to know this. I could not in good conscience take your mother outside the bonds of marriage. She meant too much to me."

Her head began to spin.

Donal had said the same about her.

Would Donal become more like this Duke of Ice over the years?

She glanced at him in panic but saw only the love he held for her. Perhaps her father might have been as loving had her mother survived. They could have been a happy family together. She might have had siblings.

She gazed at her father and saw a deep sorrow in his eyes. He was allowing her to see into his heart, to glimpse the man he hid from the rest of the world. "I've made a mountain of mistakes, Lucy. Giving you that necklace is not the least of them. But I wanted you to have something of your mother. She had given it to me when I shipped out after we were married. It was all I ever had of her. When you turned sixteen, I knew I had to give it to you because it was more important that you keep this memory."

She fingered the necklace she still wore despite the damaged lion and crescent moon. "I'm glad you did."

He nodded. "As I said, I've made plenty of mistakes. But loving you has never been one of them."

He reached out and took her hand again. "Child, can you ever forgive me?"

"That depends."

"Tell me, Lucy. I shall devote my life to becoming the proper father you deserve. Obviously, I will need your help and guidance since I've been incompetent at it all these years. Tell me what I should do. Whatever you need, it shall be yours."

"Truly?"

He nodded.

She turned to Donal. "Will you let me marry this man?"

CHAPTER TWENTY-ONE

London, England
Duke of Wooton's townhouse
One week later

L UCY LOOKED UP from the gossip rag she was reading and quickly stuffed it in the drawer of the desk, slamming it shut as several visitors strolled in. "Good afternoon, Mr. Brayden," she said, unable to contain her smile as Donal walked into her father's elegantly appointed library, along with his brother Lorcan and Lorcan's wife, Cammy. "Did you want the library? I shall leave you to it."

He approached her with a heart-melting smile of his own and planted his hands on either side of her armchair. "No, Miss Lessing. I want you."

Her eyes widened as she sought to contain her happiness. "You want me? For what possible reason?"

"I mean to say, I am taking you into my custody," he teased, for this is how their adventure had started, and neither of them was about to forget that moment. "For the purpose of matrimony, if you'll still have me now that you are a duke's daughter and soon to be acknowledged as a baroness in your own right."

She gazed at him with love in her eyes. "In your custody? Will I be taken to the church bound in manacles?"

He winked at her. "Only if you are into that sort of thing."

"Then it really is a thing? I read it in a book and—"

He leaned forward and kissed her. "I missed you."

"We've only been apart for an hour."

"As I said, interminably long. Will you marry me today? I have the special license. Betrothal contract is signed. Minister has arrived. Guests are all here. All I am lacking is the bride."

She threw her arms around him. "Then I dare not keep them waiting. Your Aunt Miranda helped my father make arrangements for the wedding breakfast, although it ought to be called the wedding supper since the ceremony is taking place so late in the day. But I have seen you Braydens eat, and I know I am taking my life into my hands if I delay that meal."

Cammy laughed. "I think this is the secret to a happy marriage. Keep the larder well stocked. Willow and Shayne have arrived. I think this accounts for all the Braydens. All the Farthingales are here, too."

"Including your Aunt Sophie and Uncle John?" Lucy asked. Cammy's family had accepted her as one of their own, even though she wasn't a Farthingale. Which suddenly reminded her. "Cammy, I have your book. Donal refuses to read it, so I suppose it ought to go back to you."

Cammy frowned at Donal. "Why haven't you read it?"

He shrugged. "Lucy has. Isn't that enough?"

Lorcan groaned. "The answer to that question is no. Even I know that."

"Hold onto it for another few days, Lucy," Cammy said. "Traditionally, it is not to be handed back until after the wedding ceremony anyway. We can decide who gets it next later. Do you have anyone in mind?"

Lucy shook her head. "No. Should it not be an acquaintance of yours? Or of Lorcan or Donal's? Their cousin, Rafe Quinton, seemed awfully nice."

Donal and Lorcan broke into hearty gales of laughter.

"Rafe will kill us," Lorcan said, crossing to the decanter set out on a side table and pouring him and Donal each a glass of port. "Great idea. Yes, it must be Rafe."

Donal accepted his glass, holding up the dark ruby liquid contained in the beautiful crystal in a mock toast. "Agreed," he said, grinning from ear to ear. "But I am not delivering that book to him. You can take it to Exeter, Lor."

Lorcan shook his head. "I'm not taking it to Exeter. He'll bite my head off. We'll find some trustworthy dupe to take it. Some unsuspecting innocent. But who?"

The duke's head butler appeared at the door, interrupting their chortles. "Lady Lucy, your friend, Lady Augusta Nesbitt, has arrived. You asked me to bring her straight to you."

"Oh, thank you, Greeves." She turned to Donal. "She is actually Eliza's best friend. Since Eliza could not make the journey, I asked Auggie to stand in my sister's place. I would love for all of you to meet her. She's the nicest person, the only one outside of Eliza who was ever genuinely kind to me. Her father is the Marquess of Chelsford."

Donal shrugged. "Why not? We have a few minutes before the ceremony starts, right Lor?"

Auggie paused in the doorway when she realized Lucy was not alone. "Oh, dear. I did not mean to interrupt."

"Not at all," Lucy said, coming to her side and taking her hand to introduce her to Donal, Lorcan, and Cammy.

"A pleasure to meet you," Auggie said, smiling at all of them and giving Lucy a quick hug. "Thank you for inviting me to your wedding. The timing is perfect. I just came back from visiting Eliza."

"How is she doing? Is she happy? I miss her."

"Motherhood agrees with her. And Monkton is over the moon with joy." She dug into her reticule and withdrew a letter. "This note is from her to you. Well, I don't wish to delay you any further. I hope you can spare a few minutes for me after the ceremony. Otherwise, I won't be able to see you for quite some time."

Lucy felt some disappointment. "Oh?"

"My great aunt, Priscilla, is not doing too well, and I promised I would visit her next. She has always been a favorite of mine and is getting on in years. I'll be leaving town the day after tomorrow."

"I'm sure your visit will cheer her up," Cammy said. "Where does she live?"

"In Exeter."

Donal and Lorcan choked on their port, the pair of them spraying the carpet, which was, thankfully, similar in color to their drinks.

Lucy could have sworn some of it dribbled through Donal's nose. He was still sputtering and coughing as he said, "I don't believe it. Exeter? You're going to Exeter?"

Lucy gaped at Cammy, and the two of them began to laugh.

Auggie looked utterly baffled. "Am I missing something?"

"No, actually, I think you might have found something." Lucy cleared her throat. "What a startling coincidence. You see, Donal has a book he'd like delivered to his cousin, who happens to live in Exeter. In fact, he's the magistrate there. Would you mind terribly…"

CHAPTER TWENTY-TWO

LUCY GRINNED AS Donal carried her over the threshold into their bedchamber later that night. They did not remain in the Duke of Wooton's grand home but had taken a room at one of London's finest hotels. However, the duke had seen fit to have every amenity provided for them, including fruit, cheese, scones, champagne, cider, and other treats, so they did not have to leave their marriage bed for several days. "How do you feel, Mrs. Brayden?"

"Very happy, Mr. Brayden."

He kicked the door shut behind them and carried her in. But instead of depositing her on the mattress, he sat and took her onto his lap. "So am I, Lucy."

She curled her arms around his neck. "I want to pinch myself. I cannot believe we are truly husband and wife."

"Forever, love." He kissed her lightly on the lips.

"I was so afraid Wooton…er, my father…would not allow it. He surprised me by how easily he gave in. Then again, he'd denied me so much throughout my childhood, perhaps he did not wish to deprive me of anything more. He also had to know you are the best man in all of England."

Donal laughed. "I have you fooled, haven't I?"

But he turned serious a moment later. "He hopes to restore relations with you, probably desperate to fill that emptiness in his heart. He would trade all his wealth and power to hear you one day refer to him as Papa instead of Wooton or Your Grace. You'll know when it feels right. He's smart enough not to force it. And what did you do with the necklace, love? I notice you are not wearing it."

She shook her head. "I put it away. There is too much death surrounding it. I think it is a symbol of tragedy and unfulfilled love. Yes, it also saved my life. But I cannot bring myself to wear it any longer. I won't ever part with it, but perhaps we can pick out something new, something that represents *us*. Not anything expensive, maybe matching handkerchiefs embroidered with a P for you and an A for me."

He frowned. "Why those initials?"

"Because you are a…" She kissed his cheek. "Professional." Then pointed to herself. "And I am your Assignment."

He emitted a groaning laugh. "H is a better initial for you because you were always in my heart. In truth, you are my heart. And now you are my wife."

"Not entirely. Is there not something we ought to be doing other than talking?"

"Right, love. Let me unlace you and tend to that oversight now." He cast her a deliciously wicked grin and wasted little time in relieving both of them of their clothes.

Lucy watched him as he shrugged out of the last of his garments and now stood before her naked. Well, he had a fine body, bronzed from the sun during their time at Weymouth. She would often watch him as they whiled away the hours in the hidden cove, the sun shining on his chest and shoulders as he stretched out on the sand or swam in the gentle waves.

She sighed in disappointment when he doused the lamp before climbing into bed with her. "Oh, but I wanted to see you."

"This is not what love is about. It is about feeling, not merely seeing. Set all your senses free, not merely sight but touch, taste, scent, hearing." He settled his body over hers, propping on his elbows so there was just enough of his weight pressing on her to arouse her.

"I love you, sweetheart." His voice was a soft rumble. "Ready to explore these new sensations?"

She nodded.

His scent was familiar, a mix of hot spice and maleness that she always found incredibly exciting.

She ran her hands along the granite muscles of his arms. His skin was warm, and when she put her lips to it, she found he tasted a little salty.

"Close your eyes, love. Feel how the two of us fit together," he said and began to kiss his way along her body, his lips capturing hers as he began their intimate dance. Without the light to distract her, she responded to his every lick, his every touch, and to the tension in his tightly coiled body.

His hand slid intimately between her legs, stroking her until she was greedy for him and aching to take him in. She did not know how it would feel, but she was wild for him and did not hesitate to raise her hips to meet him as he entered her.

Their joining meant more to her than merely the uniting of their bodies, and she hardly felt the pinch as he broke through her maidenhead to finally make her truly his.

This man filled her heart.

He soothed her soul.

She reveled in the promise of their future, responded as he moved inside her body with barely leashed control, and shattered when he spilled himself inside her, making them one in every sense.

He kissed her to take her soft cries into his mouth.

He held her close so that the scent of their entwined bodies, her honey and his spice, filled the air around them.

When he rolled onto his back afterward and drew her atop him, she felt an exquisite contentment.

A belonging.

Yes, this is what it was.

She belonged to Donal.

He was her anchor, the safe harbor she needed to free herself to become the person she was meant to be.

The marvel of it was, he belonged to her as well.

"How do you feel, love?" he asked as she lay nestled in his arms, her heart still beating in a rampant rhythm that he must have heard as she was pressed against his chest.

"Happy," she said, too overwhelmed to say more.

"That's it? What happened to the talkative little bluestocking who couldn't wait to tell me everything she was thinking or feeling?"

She laughed. "She's still me. Oh, Donal, I truly am happy. I never thought anyone could love me, much less anyone as perfect as you. I fell in love with you the moment I met you. I looked up from the book I was reading in the Earl of Monkton's library, and there you were, handsome as sin. I never considered that you could ever love me back. Although sometimes, you looked at me as though I meant more to you than just an assignment. I used to dream that you desired me. No one had ever looked at me that way before. I was sure I was wrong." Tears moistened her cheeks. "I had resigned myself to living out my years alone and unloved."

"Never, sweetheart. It was the same for me the moment you looked up from your book and stared at me with your big, green eyes. My heart knew at once. This is the one for me."

"Oh, I'm crying. I don't mean to cry. But you have no idea how much you mean to me. All the time we were on the run, I was already in love with you. I did not think my feelings could grow deeper, but every day they did. You always made me feel protected, cherished. Important. But I knew it would all end one day, and my heart ached so badly. I dreaded the moment."

"I should have said something to you sooner. I'm sorry, love."

"You couldn't. I was your assignment, and you could not let personal feelings interfere with your duties." She glanced up at him and laughed. "I rambled on a bit longer than you expected. Do you mind?"

"No, sweetheart. This is why I love you."

She laughed and shook her head. "Because I will always give you the long-winded truth?"

"Since we are being honest with each other, I have a confession to make."

She searched his eyes but saw only merriment in them. "What is this terrible truth you must confess?"

He kissed her on the nose. "I've read *The Book of Love*."

She gasped. "When? Why didn't you tell me? I'm so glad you did. But why give in when you were so adamant about not reading it?"

"Because it was important to you." He stroked her hair with a light, affectionate touch. "I think this is what marriage is about, loving someone so much that you would do anything for them because it will make them happy. I had to read it for you, Lucy. How could I not? You are my love. My sweetheart...my greatest treasure."

"As you are mine." She sighed contentedly against his chest, falling asleep to the greatest happiness she had ever known.

Also by Meara Platt

FARTHINGALE SERIES
My Fair Lily
The Duke I'm Going To Marry
Rules For Reforming A Rake
A Midsummer's Kiss
The Viscount's Rose
Earl Of Hearts
If You Wished For Me
Never Dare A Duke
Capturing The Heart Of A Cameron
Tempting Taffy

BOOK OF LOVE SERIES
The Look of Love
The Touch of Love
The Taste of Love
The Song of Love
The Scent of Love
The Kiss of Love
The Chance of Love
The Gift of Love
The Heart of Love
The Hope of Love (novella)
The Promise of Love
The Wonder of Love
The Journey of Love
The Dream of Love (novella)

DARK GARDENS SERIES

Garden of Shadows
Garden of Light
Garden of Dragons
Garden of Destiny
Garden of Angels

LYON'S DEN SERIES
The Lyon's Surprise
Kiss of the Lyon
Lyon in the Rough

THE BRAYDENS
A Match Made In Duty
Earl of Westcliff
Fortune's Dragon
Earl of Kinross
Earl of Alnwick
Pearls of Fire*
(*also in Pirates of Britannia series)
Aislin
Gennalyn
A Rescued Heart

DeWOLFE PACK ANGELS SERIES
Nobody's Angel
Kiss An Angel
Bhrodi's Angel

About the Author

Meara Platt is an award winning, USA TODAY bestselling author and an Amazon UK All-Star. Her favorite place in all the world is England's Lake District, which may not come as a surprise since many of her stories are set in that idyllic landscape, including her paranormal romance Dark Gardens series. Learn more about the Dark Gardens and Meara's lighthearted and humorous Regency romances in her Farthingale series and Book of Love series, or her warmhearted Regency romances in her Braydens series by visiting her website at www.mearaplatt.com.